A BETTER ANGEL

✳

Farrar, Straus and Giroux

NEW YORK

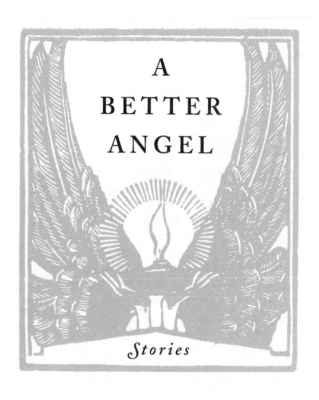

A
BETTER
ANGEL

Stories

CHRIS ADRIAN

FARRAR, STRAUS AND GIROUX
18 West 18th Street, New York 10011

These stories previously appeared, some in slightly different form,
in *Esquire*, *McSweeney's*, *The New Yorker*, *Ploughshares*, *Story*,
Tin House, and *Zoetrope*.

Library of Congress Cataloging-in-Publication Data
Adrian, Chris, 1970–
    A better angel : stories / Chris Adrian. — 1st ed.
        p.   cm.
    ISBN-13: 978-0-374-28990-4 (hardcover : alk. paper)
    ISBN-10: 0-374-28990-5 (hardcover : alk. paper)
    I. Title.

PS3551.D75B47 2008
813'.54—dc22
                                                    2008007875

Designed by Gretchen Achilles

www.fsgbooks.com

1   3   5   7   9   10   8   6   4   2

For MR

CONTENTS

✳

A BETTER ANGEL

✳

HIGH SPEEDS

That November I'm nine and stealing: candy from the super-market; toys from the dime store; books from the bookstore. And not *Curious George and the Bad Touch* or *Tales of a Fourth Grade Fuck-Up*, though I am in fourth grade, and fucked-up. I'm too smart for those books, too smart for the fourth grade, but Mama won't let them skip me. I'm too smart for Miami Springs, and too smart for my own good.

In November of 1979 I'm four feet ten inches tall, and Papa has been dead for nine months. My little brother is crazy, and I want sometimes to take over the world. I am nine but not nine. I am ancient in blood and heart and bones. Sometimes I feel as wise as a pharaoh. I am in class, listening to Miss Ouida Montoya read to us.

> *Wild Nights!—Wild Nights!*
> *Were I with thee*
> *Wild Nights should be*
> *Our luxury!*

She goes on, finishing as passionately as she began. She's panting when she stops. "Can anyone tell me who wrote that one?" she asks into the silence. She's not our real teacher, just a substitute who came to us after Ms. Orton's incident with the bus.

"No one?" This is the first time she's done the poetry thing. Yesterday we mostly made paper-plate turkeys and paper-cup Pilgrims for the upcoming Thanksgiving feast, held annually in the cafeteria, at which we will sing Thanksgiving hymns in between courses of turkeyburger, canned corn, and pumpkin pudding. The day before, she extended our Spanish lesson, reading to us all day from a Spanish translation of *The Mouse and the Motorcycle*. "Well?" she asks.

"Ask Con," says Maria Josiah, a girl from Hialeah with an ax-shaped head.

There are snickers all around the room. Buddy Washington, behind me, kicks my chair. "Freaky boy," he whispers.

"Well, Con?" says Ouida Montoya.

"Well what?" I ask, in a sharp, little-bastardly voice.

"Can you tell me who wrote this poem?"

"Isn't this a little advanced for us?"

She looks at me, then takes off her glasses. "You know, Con, I got up this morning in a very good mood. I was thinking, I'm going to make a difference today. I'm going to go into class and I am going to make a difference there. I'm going to use this little spell of substitute time to make some small change in your lives. Some small change, a tiny little change." She snaps her fingers very softly, so I can barely hear it. "And what better way to make a little change than with a little poetry?" She smiles at me, a sweet, honest smile, aiming her teeth right at me.

"But poetry makes nothing happen," I say. She puts her glasses back on and lifts her head up, like she just smelled something interesting or nice.

"Who wrote our poem?" Our poem, I think, but I know right off she doesn't mean it that way.

"My life closed twice," I say, "before its close. It yet remains to see."

She smiles wider—impossibly wide, so I think her top lip is going to flip over her nose, and she uncrosses her legs, then crosses them again. In the quiet I can hear the sound of nylon scraping against nylon.

"If immortality unveil," she says.

"A third event to me," I reply.

"So huge."

"So hopeless to conceive."

"As these that twice befell. Parting is all we know of Heaven."

"And all we need," I say, "of Hell."

Maria Josiah bursts into laughter. "Con said the H word!" She covers her own mouth, as if she was the one that said Hell. The rest of the class just looks at me like, "Weirdo!" and looks at Ouida Montoya like they're afraid of what she might do next.

"Miss Emily Dickinson," she says. "That's who wrote these poems. Everyone please repeat after me. Emily Dickinson!"

"Emily Dickinson!" they say, sounding a little fearful.

"Very good," she says. "Shall we hear another?" She waits until someone raises a hand. "Yes, Maria?"

"Can't we just finish our turkeys?"

"Possibly. Let's take a vote."

Turkeys win twenty-four to zero, with me abstaining. So we get out the turkey halves we had previously cut from paper plates and spend the rest of the period stapling them together and coloring them. They are supposed to serve as place markers at the feast, but I write on mine, *Happy Birthday, you sorry ass little fucker.*

What's in a birthday? Get over it, asshole. Your bellyaching is grating on my anus. Birthdays make nothing happen. They survive in the valley of their own making.

I am very intent on this, making every letter in a different color and all that shit, so when Ouida Montoya comes over I don't even notice she's there until it occurs to me that the flea-spray smell in my head is her perfume. I put my hand over the turkey but she moves it away so she can read the last lines.

"Everything is so hard," she says, leaning down to put the hyphen in *sorry-ass* with her red substitute teacher's pen.

At recess I'm on top of a jungle gym that everyone avoids when I'm on it. I'm looking out at all the children playing, and I'm thinking, You! Maria Josiah! Death to you! A razor across your eye, Maria!

Buddy Washington, a shovel hard on your head, so hard that raspberry jelly flies out of your nose!

And Molly LaRouche, your head in a vise!

Sammy Fie, coat you in honey and feed you to the bees!

Rosetta Pablo, feed you to a dog with dull teeth!

I run all down the class list. This is how I pass my recess. When they're about all dead I hang upside down and close my eyes until I hear somebody come up next to me. It's Yatha McIlvoy, who happens to be the only person I habitually spare.

"Happy birthday," she says. "I made you something." She hands me a Pilgrim. *Birthday Pilgrim for Con*, it says.

"How'd you know it was my birthday?"

"Ms. Orton said. Last week. Remember?" Ouida Montoya is coming over. She's in the sun. From where I'm hanging it looks like she's coming in like an enemy plane. She puts her hand on Yatha's shoulder.

"Could I talk to Con a moment, Yatha?"

"Sure," she says and walks off backwards. After a few feet she waves at me, turns, and runs away.

"May I join you?"

"No," I say and pull myself up. I'm sitting on top again when she gets there.

"You aren't happy," she says.

"I'm fine."

"I'm sorry I forgot your birthday yesterday," she says.

"I don't care."

"This says different." It's the turkey card, which I'd torn into eight pieces and thrown away. She's taped it back together.

"Not to you," I say. "I don't care about you, lady. My mama forgot."

"Ah," she says. "Poor Con."

"Hey," I say. "Fuck you." I wait for her to go away, or drag me to see the principal, Sister Gertrude, like Ms. Orton always does. But she just sits there, her long silk skirt hanging down between the bars.

"I said fuck you," I say. "Nobody asked you to play Good Samaritan to the lonesome birthday boy."

She leans back, putting her arms behind her, and puts her head back as far as she can get it and still be looking at me. "You're an angry little fucker, aren't you?" I just look back. I do not love her then, but when she talks to me like I'm real, when she's the first person in this bore-me-to-death place to talk to me like I'm real, then something happens, and I feel it. A little lurch, like something has just moved inside me. She says, "I meant it earlier.

This morning was halcyon. I looked at the sunlight on my wood floor, and I said out loud, 'Ouida Montoya, today you will help somebody.' And I never talk out loud when nobody else is there. *Never*. So let me help." She reaches out and touches my shoulder. "Won't you tell me what's the matter with you?"

"My mama forgot my birthday," I say. "It's no big deal."

"It's more than that," she says. "I read your file in the office." She brings her face close to mine, close enough for a kiss. Wild Nights, I'm thinking suddenly, and I get a little dizzy. Christ, lady, I think. It's life, is all it is. I fall back away from her, and swing down backwards through the bars to drop to the ground.

"See you in class," I say, walking away and not looking up.

"Let's go for a ride, later!" she calls after me.

"Whatever," I mutter. I want to mangle something, so I crush Yatha's pilgrim, and then I feel bad and smooth him out, but he still looks pretty fucked-up.

At home yesterday there was the note on the television:

Con and Caleb
    Gone shopping for guitar picks etc. with Milo. Back early
evening about. Five dollars in the secret place for dinner.
Love,
    You-Know-Who

I felt something sharp in the appendix zone when I read it. I don't care about birthdays. I haven't cared about them since I was three but still there was that sharp pain like somebody got me with a voodoo, and a little voice, somewhere in my middle ear, whispering, "She forgot."

I went into the room I share with Caleb. He was napping on the bottom bunk. I took out the *Boy's Life* I stole for him from the school library and put it on his chest. He'd been a Cub Scout when he went crazy, insisting that he was from Mars and that they lit fires like *this* on Mars, and that they ran their soap-box derbies in *this* manner, and it was all superior to how they did it in the Cub Scouts Chapter Earth. I am not glad he's crazy but I'm glad they threw him out. I would rather he was a brown-pantied little fascist Brownie than a Cub Scout but better neither than either.

I sat down by the bed, watching him sleep. His face was puffy, his eyes were rolling around behind his lids. I emptied my book bag on the floor. I had stopped by the bookstore, too, and bought *Thuvia, Maid of Mars*, and the October issue of *Scientific American*. Frieda, who owns the place, sells me the last month's issue for half price at the beginning of the new month. She's a lesbian. I know about lesbians because I have stolen, from Frieda's Little Professor Bookstore, *The Joy of Lesbian Sex*, *The Joy of Sex*, *The Joy of Gay Sex*, and *More Joy of Sex*. They lurk under my mattress. I've looked in these books and seen all the gory fucking, every brand. I know what it's all about, generally and specifically.

Also I got myself *The Seven Storey Mountain* but didn't pay for that. Generally I follow a policy of buy one, steal one from the Little Professor. I'm reading Thomas Merton to become a better person.

And I stopped at the dime store and got two giant chocolate bars and two squirt guns—presents for me and for Caleb on my birthday. These fell out on the floor with the Merton and the magazines. I put the chocolate and the gun on his chest, too, then sat with my back against the side of the bed and read aloud until Caleb started to stir.

9

"Con," he said, sitting up.

"Nice nap?"

"Too short. But I dreamed." He picked up the gun and the magazine, hugging the magazine to his chest. It really broke his heart when they threw him out. "Thank you."

"No problem," I said. "Happy birthday."

"It's not mine. It's yours."

"You know that. I know that. Somebody doesn't know that."

"She knows."

"She forgot. So it's hamburgers for us tonight."

"Hamburgers," he said. "That's okay."

"You hungry?"

"Okay." He shot me with the empty gun.

"Wash your face," I said. "It's all wrinkled." He got out of bed and ran to the bathroom, gun in one hand, *Boy's Life* in the other.

I went and watched him, standing in his bare feet in the tub, bending down to put his face in the water. He doesn't care for the sink. This face-under-the-tap business is how they wash up on Mars, how they do it, he says, at home. In the past nine months I've read *Stranger in a Strange Land*, *Podkayne of Mars*, *The Martian Chronicles*, and all of Burroughs's series except *Thuvia*, which for some reason is hard to obtain. All this to better understand my little brother. When Mama told us that Papa's plane had gone down in the Everglades, Caleb had looked thoughtful for a moment and then said, "Who?"

"Your papa," said Mama.

"And who are you?" he asked, turning to me. I didn't say anything. Caleb passed out, falling right onto the carpet. Mama and I watched him, like it was a trick we'd paid to see him do. Then we both freaked out. When he woke up he did not speak for two weeks, but only peered at us like we and everything else around him were totally unfamiliar. When he began speaking it was clear we would have to get to know him all over again. He insisted that his name was Belac, and that he came from Barsoom. Papa used to read to us from Burroughs on our weekends with him, when he couldn't sleep. First we got all the Tarzan books and then one through three of the Mars books. Dr. Mouw, Caleb's shrink, and occasionally my own shrink, says we must live in his fantasy in order to draw him out of it.

Dr. Mouw dresses in dark suits and has dark, sad eyes and a pixie-cut hairdo, and I like her, usually, but only an idiot would become a psychiatrist. I wanted briefly to be a psychiatrist. Now I think I would like to become either a cat burglar or a Trappist monk, or else just a plain old evil genius, the kind that takes over the world.

"Ready," said Caleb.

"Put on your shoes." He put them on and looked at the laces. "Yes, you can," I said, before he could say that he couldn't tie them.

"We don't have these on Barsoom," he said crossly. But he tied the shoes. Mama ties them for him. Dr. Mouw and I agree that that is going too far.

I got the five dollars out of the lettuce crisper and we headed down De Soto to the McDonald's. Caleb had filled his squirt gun in the tub and was shooting all the palm trees.

"Hi!" he said. "Hi! Hi! Bowbee do impapa!"

"Speak English, dammit," I said.

"Die, enemies of Helium!" he said, then sucked thoughtfully on the gun. "Those trees," he said. "What do you call them?"

"You know damn well what they're called."

"Those trees look like the kalai-zee."

"I'm sure I want to know what those are."

11

"A race of scaly giants," he said. "With bushy green hair. You know when they've been eating children because the crumbs of skin stick around their mouths."

"Where do you get this morbid shit?"

"Just telling it like it is," he said, Papa's line whenever he recounted the gross things he saw working as a doctor when he was very young, before he met Mama, before he learned to fly, and before he became a drug smuggler.

"Fuck it's hot," I said. Caleb shot me in the hair. "You're lucky I didn't bring mine," I said.

"I'm cooling you off. It's hotter on Mars, anyway. When it is very hot we sit in the shade of the bolinga tree, under the feathery bolinga leaves, and drink iced hoopa."

Caleb is smart, like me, probably a little smarter, but he pours all his smarts into his delusion. In nine months it's gotten pretty detailed, yet it's still almost all stuff he got from Papa in one form or another. It boils down to about three-fifths Burroughs, one-fifth Dr. Seuss, and one-fifth shit he makes up all by himself. He could be in the second grade at St. Theresa's, getting all the normal socialization shit Mama insists on for me, but instead he's in an "indeterminate grade" at Dr. Mouw's Virginia Key Academy along with assorted little Napoléons and Jesus Christs and a scattering of ADD freak-outs.

"Happy birthday," said Caleb.

"Yeah."

"You're angry."

"No."

"On Barsoom we have a ritual of forgotten birthdays. When someone forgets, the offended shoots the offender with a harmless kama gun. Then we have a party." He handed me his gun, butt first.

"Knock off the Mars shit a minute," I said.

"Sometimes we use a zona gun, which is needlessly harmful," he said and put the gun back in his pocket and took my hand. I squeezed it.

At McDonald's Caleb spent five minutes trying to order a Happy Meal, except he was calling it a Biba Fa, and the guy behind the counter didn't have a clue what he was talking about.

"One of the ones in the box," I said. I didn't want to say Happy Meal because I would prefer not to buy into fucking McDonald's newspeak. Sometimes Frieda tells me to watch my language, and she doesn't mean don't say fuck, she means don't say Whopper or Barbie's Dream House or Happy Meal.

"We've got all kinds of boxes, if you want boxes," said the man. "All the big sandwiches come in boxes." Usually I have to fight like hell to order anything but a Happy Meal, because they start shoving them at you as soon as you open your mouth.

"Biba Fa!" says Caleb, for the tenth time. "Are you deaf?"

"You know," I said. "A children's meal."

"Oh," the man said. "A Happy Meal. Why didn't you say so?" We just looked at him. I didn't want a fucking Happy Meal, but the guy brought two and I just wanted to sit down. So I paid him and we sat by the window, looking out on NW Thirty-sixth Street, at all the airline buildings, which depressed me because they have to do with planes and flight and Papa going down in the swamp. I gave Caleb my top and then unwrapped my hamburger and looked at it.

"Hey," Caleb said. "This is called the Ela Ecksta formation." He spun the two tops toward each other.

"Eat," I told him. He put down the tops and started tracing his finger on the back of the box. "I'm going to eat your food if you don't start eating it right now." He picked up his hamburger, then smelled it and took a little bite. I bit into mine and thought it tasted like disappointment. And then I thought, You little baby, it's just a birthday, and it means nothing. And then I thought, Happy birthday to me. And then I thought, Fuck!

Mama came in after midnight to say sorry. Caleb was asleep, worn out from watching TV all evening, which is something we can't do when Mama's home, but I think it's a good idea for him to see Nicholas on *Eight Is Enough* and perhaps want to be like him.

I was staring at our ceiling, at the fake glue-on constellations that Papa gave me last birthday. I was doing powers of three, which usually makes me sleepy. When she came in and started singing I lost count. She stood right by our bed. I looked over and saw her head, a dim shape underneath the false stars.

She was singing some dumb-ass song to the tune of "Happy Birthday," about how she was sorry and she loved me and I lived in a zoo, and she hoped I would forgive her because she felt like a shoe. She had got herself a pretty severe vodka voice and I could see Milo swaying in the doorway. She reached out and touched my hair.

"Three," I said. "Nine. Twenty-seven. Eighty-one."

"I'm sorry," she said.

"Two hundred and forty-three. Seven hundred and twenty-nine."

"I didn't mean to. I thought it was tomorrow. I thought the seventh was tomorrow."

"Two thousand one hundred eighty-seven. Six thousand five hundred sixty-one."

"I'm so sorry. I know how mad you are."

"Nineteen thousand six hundred eighty-three. I'm not mad."

"Sure you are. You've got every right to be."

"Am not."

"I'm so sorry."

"It's fine. Birthdays don't matter."

"Sure they matter."

"Not to me."

"Come on out and we'll have a little party."

"No thanks."

"Come on. I'll sing you another song."

"I'll just go to sleep now."

"Please, come out for me. I got you a present."

So I got down and held her arm as we walked through the door, so she wouldn't tip over. Milo reached to take her in the hall, but I pulled her right past him into the living room, because I didn't want it to be like I was *giving* her to him. Papa's been dead for nine months but they were divorced for a year before that.

She and Milo appear to be a pretty sure thing. He is not a bad sort—tall and handsome with a big heart and red hair and green eyes, a real Ashkenazi gem, as he describes himself. I do not mind him usually, but sometimes he annoys me.

"Mazel tov, Markie!" he said to me in the living room, pouring himself a drink. He annoys me when he calls me Markie and when he pulls the Jewish-uncle shit. The uncle shit is bad enough alone but it's worse when he rubs my shoulders and offers me piggyback rides like I'm three, or just hangs around being so friendly I want to poke out his eyes.

I sat down and looked at them both. "Get the present, Milo," said Mama, collapsing across from me. Milo got a bag out of the kitchen and gave it to me. "This is temporary," Mama said. "Real present comes later." Inside the bag were black beans and a can of rice and some frozen chicken.

"It's for your birthday feast!" she said, but it was obviously the sort of thing a pair of drunks could pick up at the all-night Cuban market. I nearly threw the chicken at her because she was smiling so sweetly, like this was the chicken of love or something, but I didn't, because at least she had tried.

"Feliz navidad!" said Milo.

"I'm really tired," I said.

"Poor baby," said Mama, standing up and wobbling over to put both her hands on my face. "You go to sleep and dream of your birthday feast, your big birthday party."

"I'd rather not have a party."

"You dream of a party," she said. Milo winked at me, and he was lucky I didn't happen to be carrying an awl. I went to my room and got in bed and closed my eyes, but I could hear their voices, and the ice in their drinks was making this terrible fucking racket, so I got down again and shut the door, which Caleb doesn't like, because on Mars terrible things happen in the dark.

After school Ouida Montoya pulls up alongside me while I'm walking down a lonely stretch of De Soto. "Time for your ride," she says.

"No thanks," I say.

"You sure?" she asks. All day she read poetry. There was no more voting after recess, we just had to take it. We got more Dickinson, and Yeats and Keats and Shelley and Mistress Shovel-face Bradstreet. And she never let up on me. "Who's this one, Con? How about this one?"

"Would you please leave me alone," I say, very calm indeed.

"I will not," she says. "I know you! We have something in common. Something so special, and so horrible."

I throw my books against her Volvo, not harming it at all but making a loud noise. She stops the car.

"Come on, lady!" I shout. "Just don't fuck with me, okay? Just fly yourself right out of my life!" She opens her door. I step up close to her—her face is about even with mine when she's sitting—and scream, "Fuck the fuck!" I don't even know what that means. All I want is for her to leave me alone.

But now she's mad. She grabs me by the front of my white uniform shirt and pulls me right over her lap, throwing me down on the passenger side, so my head is where your feet ought to be. Then she takes off, and I feel the bumps when she runs over my books.

"What are you doing! What the fuck are you doing?"

"Just be quiet," she says, pinching the bridge of her nose with one hand and steering with the other. "I'm very angry. I'm very angry and you need to let me calm down." She squints, and pinches so hard I can see the tendons flexing in her wrist. She drives faster and faster, barreling down De Soto, past my house, past the McDonald's and out onto NW Thirty-sixth.

"Stop!" I'm shouting as I scoot around and sit up, but she gives me a look that shuts my mouth.

It's only about four minutes before she takes her hand away and starts to slow the car.

"There," she says. "You made me very angry, Con. Please don't make me angry like that."

"You kidnapped me."

"So much has gone wrong lately, I've got to do something right. I've got to help someone somehow, or else I'll go all to pieces."

"I'm going to tell."

"Nothing's working like it did. Usually if I'm feeling down, all I have to do is drive at high speeds and it's like everything gets left behind."

"You're fired, lady. You are so fucking fired." But I say it sweet, like "you are so fucking nice," or "you are so fucking beautiful." And she is beautiful. Her face is still flushed, and her hair is charged up and curly around her head like her anger made it that way.

"So I'm thinking just give somebody a hand and God will lift you up, too. There is also love in the world, and I want to be that." She turns her head to look at me. "Do you understand?"

"Sure, but you should take me home."

"I saw your card, your awful card that said how much you hate and hate and I thought, Ouida Montoya, there is also love in the world and it is needed right here in this very moment. In this little boy."

"I'm not really a boy," I say. "I don't count as a boy, except that it's a serious offense to kidnap me."

"You said you understood, but you don't understand."

"I have to go home. I have to take care of my little brother. You take me home right now."

"Soon," she says. "Fasten your seatbelt. My brother died at high speeds, and that's only the half-worst part of my awful year." She stomps on the accelerator and her Volvo, which heretofore had been gliding smoothly down NW Thirty-sixth and then I-95, flies madly across the Julia Tuttle Causeway, across the bay. Where is all the traffic? That's what I want to know. Where are all the people to whom I might scream for help?

"Ai yai yee!" she calls, gnashing her big white teeth. "Isn't it beautiful?"

Well, it is, with the sun on the water and Miami Beach rushing toward us. She fiddles with the console on her armrest and all the windows go down. She yodels again, or yiddles, whatever it is, that sound like some rebel parrot would make. She puts her hand on my leg and squeezes.

"Do you feel it?" she asks.

"Oh, yes," I answer, though I don't know what she's talking about and I'm starting to be afraid.

"It's all our troubles, losing their breath behind us. We're too fast for them. Do you really feel it? Are your troubles falling behind? Are your birthday troubles back there?"

"Yes," I say, though all I feel now is her hand on my leg. I am thinking of *More Joy of Sex*, of all the penetration lovingly rendered in charcoal. And for once I care, it's more than gory pictures like in *Dissecting Your Feline*, not just knowledge but experience, a hand on my leg. She doesn't mean it like that. I can tell that when she brings her hand up and tweaks my nose, but even when she takes her hand away to wave it in the wind outside the window, the feeling stays.

"I'll tell on you so bad you'll never work in this state again," I say.

"You won't tell," she says, not looking at me. "I read your card and you're just like me." She's right, or I wish she was, or maybe I don't know about anything. She turns on the radio. It's "Lucy in the Sky with Diamonds" playing, and she accelerates again, to fantastic speeds, during the chorus.

I don't tell.

"You're late," says Mama, when I get home.

"Yeah. I was talking to the teacher. We have this sub."

"I see." She's in the kitchen—not her usual place. She turns away from the sink. "Yorkshire pudding," she says. "And roast beef!"

"Nice," I said. "Milo coming over?"

"No. I thought we ought to have a special dinner. A birthday dinner."

"What about the chicken?" She stares at me, wiping her hands back and forth across her jeans.

"I'm real sorry. I thought yesterday was the sixth."

"Like I said, no big deal."

"But this isn't your birthday feast, anyway. We'll have a real party, later."

"You're not serious."

"It'll be good for you."

"Like hell."

"Watch it!"

"I do not want a party."

"You'll like it. We'll have a cake and hats and candles and games—everything."

"And where will you rent the friends?"

"Relax. Just relax! It's going to be great."

"It's going to be a disaster." Caleb comes up behind me, reaching up to put his hands around my eyes, but all he gets is my mouth.

"Beth baloo?" he says.

"Arthur Treacher," I say.

"Niha," he says.

"Flip Wilson?"

"Niha. Try again."

"Con Markowiecz Clooney?"

"Close."

"Caleb Cartoris Clooney?" I say.

"Sia-fee," he says. "You're very hot."

"I give up."

"Not allowed."

"Well, it might be Belac of Helium, but I understand he perished fighting the synthetic men of the poles."

"Lies!" he says, giggling, and moving his hands away to tickle me.

"Look, Caleb," says Mama. "Roast beast!" She holds the bound meat up to us, bleeding between its strings, and high-steps it over to the oven with flourishes. I am thinking that it is a nice little moment, even as I am thinking that it is so fucking weird.

The next day I walk to school and past school. I don't want to go where Ouida Montoya is. So I play tourist for a while, taking the bus to Villa Vizcaya, Mr. Deering's pink abomination. When someone looks at me like I'm a truant and asks me questions, I fake a French accent and say I'm looking for my daddy, he's right over there in the bushes, and then I run away.

The grounds at Vizcaya are lovely, and it's mostly there, among the live oaks and banyans fronting a big chunk of the bay, that I spend the next three days. There are no calls from school. In fact, I'm having a pretty good time, though all I do all day is sit in a tree and watch the sky and think of Ouida Montoya driving fast, maybe flying, maybe skywriting in her Volvo.

After three days a letter comes for me in the mail. From a pen pal in Puerto Rico, I tell Mama, but it's not. It says:

*You didn't tell, I didn't tell. Go for a drive? De Soto and
De Leon, Thurs 430p. Okay?*
OM

So, Thursday at 4:15 I tell Mama I'm going to Frieda's and then to the library and she says fine but I must be back by 7:30. And down on the corner of De Soto and De Leon the silver Volvo is lurking. The silver Vulva, I think, and giggle inside like a silly eighth-grader.

"I wasn't sure you'd come," she says when I get in. I shrug.

"Thanks for not telling Sister Gertrude on me."

"Same same," she says. "So what do you want to do?"

"Like before," I say. At the beach the other day we sat on the hood of her car and looked at the water. "You can run away," she told me, "but I'll only catch you again." I didn't want to run away, because she had gathered me into her lap, and she had her arms around me, and she was telling me that she would break me open and that all my troubles would fall out of me and melt away in the sun.

She goes back to the beach but doesn't stop there. Instead she drives up Collins to Broad Causeway and heads to 95, where she opens up the Volvo and we do eighty-five toward Jacksonville. She puts a hand on my leg again and starts talking. "I've never got a ticket," she says. "My brother is watching over me."

"Did he linger?" I ask her.

"No. He got a sharp blow to the head and that was that. Volvos are the safest cars in the world, but he didn't have a Volvo." She is silent a moment before she asks, "What carries for you?" I don't understand and tell her so. "Car wrecks carry for me," she says, with a squeeze. "Crumpled metal, even little tin cans in the road. And shattered glass. And head injuries. These things bring back a feeling like I've eaten a stone. It's in my stomach, usually, but sometimes it's all through me like it's in my blood. Blood carries, too."

"Airplanes," I say. "And airplane-disaster movies. I don't like the swamp anymore, or alligators."

"Crushed vertebrae," she says. "Broken necks. Medical terms like 'C1' and 'C2.' And this word is awful: 'petechiae.' It almost hurts just to say it."

"Flight," I say. "Birds."

"Copper caskets. And flowers. Red roses and yellow roses and sunflowers."

"Even the scent of flowers," I say. She's got all the windows open again and she drives till the sun starts to go down. It begins to drizzle and the road gets slick, but I am not afraid of an accident.

Somewhere near Pembroke Pines I tell her that I have to get back by 7:30 or I'll be in trouble. She drives back, not to my house, but to the St. Theresa's parking lot. It's totally empty. We have not said so much, but for such a long time her hand was on my leg, squeezing, squeezing in time to the radio music. It's been very nice, I think. A nice date. But when I go to get out, she says, "Hold on. You want to learn how to drive?"

I am pretty tall for my age. I can reach the pedals and see over the steering wheel, though I must peer and lift myself up a little.

"You look like an old lady," she tells me. I drive back and forth across the parking lot three times, then around the light poles. Eventually I'm circling one at a leisurely pace. This is easy, I think.

"Faster," she says. "You've got to learn to drive fast or I've taught you nothing."

I speed up a little, and she reaches over and shoves down hard on my knee with her left hand. The Volvo lurches forward but I handle it and we go around and around, faster and faster like on the Round Up at the annual St. Theresa's fair held every May in this very parking lot. Irresistible forces are hurling Miss Ouida Montoya over to my side of the car. I'm thinking of the Coriolis force, of round hurricane eyes, and other round things: oranges, apples, eyeballs. I'm pressed hard up against the door and it seems to me that this circular force is drawing something out of my body.

"Faster," she says. So I speed up.

"Faster, faster," she says. "We need another master!" I look over at her face. She's smiling like crazy, like she's quite crazy. Her eyes look manic, like they might pop out of her head and dangle on springs. "You're doing fine!" she tells me. Beyond her the world is just a big pole until I hit the pole. We glance off it and spin, all the way around once, twice, and another half a time. I hit the brakes and the car shudders, then stops.

"I wrecked your car," I say, crying like a stupid baby.

"It's okay," she says, Her face is right in mine, close enough for a kiss. Past her I can see that one headlight has gone out, while the other illuminates the school like a prison searchlight.

"What do you want?" she asks. "What do you want?"

I moan and cry mundane little-boy sobs. I cannot name it but somehow I know what it is. She closes in on me, her arms sneaking around for a hug. She really is close enough for a kiss—so I do it. I strike like a serpent, and maybe five seconds into it I realize that her tongue is not playing with my tongue, it's seeking to evade my tongue, and she's pushing me away.

"What are you doing?" she wants to know.

"I was—taking something," I say.

"I didn't want that," she says, wiping her mouth.

"I know," I say.

"You better get out."

"Sure," I say. I knew better than to do it. I knew she was offering her sicko pseudo-motherlove but I took the other because it was close. I feel evil, but I feel better, too.

"You wrecked my car," she says, as if she has just noticed. I get out and walk away, not looking back, but when the horn starts honking in staccato bursts, I imagine she must be banging her head against it.

I walk home, wondering, Did Satan feel like this when he almost conquered Heaven? Is there a baby nearby whose head I might dash against a stone? Am I human? The palm trees loom like kalai-zee, chuckling deep in their bellies, each one full of child. I am broken open, I think, and something awful has hatched out.

At home I pause outside the door, listening. It's quiet on the other side. I go around and look in the dining-room window. There's Yatha McIlvoy, putting candles on a cake. Caleb is in Mama's lap, on the other side of the table. There are others, all Yatha's friends. I figure she must have talked them into it or Mama paid them off somehow. They're all girls.

I am thinking, World, life, I got you this time. I've had my kiss and nobody can take it away, nobody can take it back. At the door again I fumble with my key, make it loud in the lock so they'll think they're ready for me. Then I throw open the door and leap through, screaming like a banshee, shrieking, "Happy Birthday!"

THE SUM OF OUR PARTS

Beatrice needed a new liver. Her old one had succumbed to damage suffered in a fall one month earlier from the top of a seven-story parking garage. She lay in a coma while the hospital prepared for her imminent transplant, but she was not asleep. That part of her which was not her broken body stood by her bed in the surgical intensive care unit and watched as a nurse leaned over her to draw her blood. Beatrice's unusual condition gave her access to aspects of people that usually are utterly private. So she knew that the nurse, whose name was Judy, was thinking of her husband. It was eleven-thirty p.m., just about his bedtime, and Judy imagined him settling down to sleep. He would take off his shirt and his pants and fold the sheet down neatly so it covered him to just past his hips. He would turn on his side and put a hand under his cheek. Judy missed acutely the space between his shoulder blades, into which she was accustomed to settling her face as she waited for sleep to come.

Distracted, she missed the vein, and cursed softly when she noticed that no blood came into the tube. Beatrice's body lay unprotesting as Judy shifted the needle beneath her skin, questing after the already sorely abused vein. Beatrice did not feel it when Judy found the vein, and the borrowed blood (in the first hours of her stay, Beatrice had received a complete transfusion) slipped quietly into a red-topped tube. When that one was full, Judy proceeded to fill a gray-topped tube, a lavender-topped tube, and, finally, a tube with a rubber stopper the color of freshly laid robin's eggs.

Judy straightened up and stared at her patient as her hands went automatically about the business of attaching red-numbered labels to the tubes. Beatrice was a medium-sized woman with rich, curly red hair but otherwise unremarkable features. Beneath obscuring tubes and wires, her skin was pale and slightly greenish, and under her spare hospital nightie her once generous form was getting bony. In the same way, her hair was not so lovely as it had been on her admission, when it was bright and coppery. Now it was duller, though still pretty, and at the roots it had darkened to a muddy, bloody color. As she wrapped the tubes in a laboratory requisition form and tucked the little package into a plastic bag, Judy resolved to come back and give Beatrice's hair a full one hundred strokes of brushing. This seemed to Beatrice, who no longer cared about her hair, a waste of time.

The blood neatly and safely organized, and all her sharps-waste disposed of, Judy turned on her heel and walked out of the semiprivate recess that Beatrice occupied in the first bay of the SICU. Judy walked down the bay, nodding to the nurses and doctors whose eyes she caught. Beatrice followed her out. She was nodding to people, too. No one saw her.

Judy walked up to the front desk, where a perpetually idle nursing assistant named Frank was flipping through an old issue of *Reader's Digest* and looking bored.

"Here you go," she said, pushing the blood at him. "Take this up to the lab and tell them it's extra-stat."

"Sure thing," he said, closing his magazine. He took the blood from her and felt a familiar dislike. Mouse-face, he thought to himself. Others in the SICU agreed with him that Judy had mousy features: a small, forward-sloping face beset with a long, thin nose; prominent, well-cared-for front teeth. Whenever Judy was in a mood and taking it out on the other nursing staff, he would whisper to one of his friends, "Perhaps the rodent would like a piece of cheese." He had not gone so far as to leave a piece of cheddar in her locker, but he planned to do that one day.

The thought of her expression as she beheld the cheese sitting on top of her street shoes, and the thought that followed that one, of her bending down with alacrity and nibbling it up, amused him greatly. He laughed out loud on his way out of the bay, even as another nurse hurried up to him with a full gallon jug of urine to carry up to the lab. Beatrice, who did not find any of the mouse business amusing, and did not particularly care for Frank, followed him out of the SICU, walking just a few steps behind him and watching as he swung the jug of urine back and forth and hummed to himself.

Walking down the wide hospital hallway, Frank looked out the enormous windows on his right. Outside it was snowing, but he could just barely see that. What the windows showed him was mainly his own reflection. Looking at himself, he regretted not wearing a shirt beneath his scrubs, because he thought the cut of his sleeves made his arms look thin and weak.

He took the elevator labeled EE up to the sixth floor, not noticing that Beatrice had stepped in behind him. On the sixth floor he walked straight out of the elevator and down a hall that looked over a balcony into an atrium whose main feature was a shiny black grand piano. The atrium extended in a shaft up through every floor of the hospital. Sometimes people came in and played something cheery on the piano, but never during his shift. Beatrice had heard them during the day. Her favorite was a little Mennonite girl who sat primly under her paper hat and played hymns. Turning right, away from the hallway, Frank and Beatrice entered the pathology department.

Frank was always surprised by how nice it smelled there, not at all like a hospital, or even like a lab. There were no foul odors like what proceeded from people with failed kidneys, nor any sharp chemical smells to make your nose itch. Rather, the lab smelled like the perfume of the beautiful women who worked there. To Beatrice it smelled sweet also, mostly because there were people there whom she counted as friends, though none of them had ever met her. The lab was one of her favorite places to spend time.

Frank had a passing interest in one of Beatrice's friends, a blue-eyed hematology technologist with poor dental hygiene but very handsome hips. His name was Denis. He wasn't there when Frank dropped off the blood and urine. Two women and one man were intent on their computer screens, typing in various patient information, ordering tests, and entering results. They did not notice Frank in the window.

"Stat!" Frank shouted. They all jumped. Beatrice wanted to smack him.

"Thank you," said the man, a funny-looking, taciturn fellow with enormous ears. "You can leave it there."

"It's super-stat," said Frank, setting the urine in the window.

"All right," said the man.

"We need you to get right on it. This lady's getting her transplant started in the morning."

"Right," said one of the women, who was thin with long straight hair. Frank envied her her eyes, which were green and gold. She rolled her chair over to the window and snatched the blood from his hand.

"Thank you," she said, setting the tubes next to her computer terminal but doing nothing with them. Her name was Bonnie. She made a show of being focused on her screen, waiting for Frank to go away. Go away, she thought, exerting the full force of her will upon the odious nursing assistant. Beatrice tried to help her out and wished fervently that Frank would return to his hell of shrewish nurses.

"He's gone," said the man with the ears. His name was Luke.

"I can't stand the way that guy looks at me," said Bonnie, adroitly unwrapping the blood, unfolding the requisition, and entering the requested tests into the computer.

"Like a snake," said Olivia, the other woman.

"Damn!" said Bonnie. She'd noticed that the urine had no name on it. She stuck her head out the window and called down the hall, "Hey, Urine Boy!" If Frank heard, he made no response.

"What's wrong?" asked Luke.

"They didn't label the urine. What a pain in my ass."

"I'll call them," he said.

"Thanks," Bonnie said. She watched Luke as he got up and walked over to the phone, wondering why he always cut his hair so short instead of leaving it long to cover his silly ears. They really are very large, she thought, and wondered if that signified anything, in terms of personality. Men with large hands were said to possess large penises, red-haired people were said to be volatile, but she had never heard anything special said about people with large ears, except maybe that they heard a little better than most folks. Someone might have told her that, maybe her grandmother or her sixth-grade science teacher. To Beatrice, Luke's ears indicated oafishness, because her big-eared father had been a great oaf. But regardless of the ears, Beatrice found herself partial to Luke.

Luke hung up the phone and said, "They're sending it up." Behind him self-adhesive labels were printing out for Beatrice's specimens. Bonnie looked him up and down again, and thought about how she might have found him attractive in some other lifetime, one with different standards of beauty. For what seemed to her the hundredth time she imagined him shirtless and was disappointed. She got up from her chair and handed the specimens to Olivia. "Would you label these, please?" she asked.

"Sure," she said. "Hey, it's the jumping lady."

"Is it?" said Bonnie. "I didn't notice."

"I wonder how she's doing?" said Luke.

"Not too well," said Bonnie, "if she needs a new liver."

"But as well as can be expected," said Olivia. "I mean, considering." She was labeling intently.

"You really should wear gloves when you do that," said Luke.

"I know," said Olivia.

"One of the tubes might break in your hand. Then where would you be?"

"All bloody," said Bonnie. "I know. It happened to me once. Lucky I had gloves on."

"Would you like me to put on some gloves?" Olivia asked Luke.

"I don't care," he said. "It was just a suggestion."

"Jesus," said Olivia. Beatrice came through the window and stood next to her. You have nothing to fear from my blood, she said, but Olivia did not hear her. Olivia was, in fact, wishing she had put on a pair of gloves. She smoothed a label onto the round edges of a lavender-topped tube and suffered from the perversity of her imagination. She imagined the tube breaking in half as she held it, the jagged glass edge piercing her thumb to the bone, inoculating her with the jumping lady's blood and whatever diseases it carried. In the same way she sometimes imagined being a bystander in a bank robbery, standing behind a security guard when he got shot with such force that the bullet passed right through him and into her. Who could tell what she might get? Who could speculate on the sexual habits of that security guard, and whether or not they spelled death for her?

Olivia shook her head and walked the blood through the lab, back into the chemistry section, where Otto, the great big chemistry technologist, sat with his feet up on the Hitachi 747, a very accomplished machine that was capable of all sorts of magnificently complex chemical analyses of serum and plasma, as well as urine and cerebrospinal fluid, and even stool, provided it was of a sufficiently liquid consistency. Beatrice had followed right behind her, and now she watched as Olivia watched the sleeping Otto, admiring his strong jaw. Olivia was committed to a girl she'd met in her organic chemistry class, but she felt no guilt admiring Otto's jaw, or any other portion of his vast anatomy.

"Wake up," she said, putting the red- and the gray-topped tubes in a rack by Otto's foot. She wiggled the tip of his shoe with her hand.

"I'm not sleeping," he said. "Just resting my eyes."

"Sure," she said. "You're not allowed to be tired yet. We've got seven more hours."

Otto sat up, picked up the tubes, and began to transfer them to his centrifuge. "Oh," he said. "It's the jumper."

"Yeah." Olivia walked off toward the hematology section of the lab, then turned back. "I guess you can take some of this for the ammonia level," she said, offering him the lavender-topped tube. "But give it to Denis as soon as you're done."

"Sure," he said. "Thanks." The thought of having an excuse to go in search of Denis appealed to him. He felt the same way about Denis that Frank and Bonnie did.

As quickly as he could, he pulled off a small aliquot of Beatrice's blood and put it into a small plastic test tube. He was careless in his haste; a single gorgeous drop fell and landed on his ungloved index finger. Panic flared in him because he thought for a moment that he had a raw hangnail on that finger, but it was actually on the index finger of the other hand. Nevertheless he hurried to the sink and sprayed bleach from a squeeze bottle onto his finger. The smell reminded him of the bathroom he grew up with, which his mother had religiously disinfected, practically after every use. Beatrice stood next to him and said, You have nothing to fear from my blood.

When he was all cleaned up, Otto got the ammonia level and other analyses running in the 747 and hurried down to hematology. He found Denis hunched over a magazine full of details about the lives of musicians. Denis looked up when Otto rounded the minus-70 freezer.

"Hi," he said. Beatrice came in, sat on the freezer, and began to drum her legs silently against its side.

"Hi there," said Otto, gazing not at Denis's hips but at the upper portion of his biceps. Those muscles appealed to him not because they were particularly large (they were only about a third the size of his own) but because they were very shapely, and because he could imagine himself drifting off to sleep with his cheek resting against them.

"What's up?" Denis asked.

"Got some blood for you. They want a CBC and a diff and a sed rate."

"No problem." Denis held his hand out for the tube. Otto placed it in his palm, taking care despite himself not to let any part of his hand touch Denis, but his pinkie scraped Denis's wrist as he drew his hand away.

"It's the jumping lady," said Otto.

"Oh," said Denis. His placid expression belied his true reaction. He thought he could feel his heart rising in his chest, and he wanted to bring the blood to his forehead and hold it there, but of course he didn't. Otto was standing in front of him, looking down and smiling awkwardly.

"Looks like she's getting a transplant," he said.

"Another one?"

"Liver this time." The previous one had been a kidney.

"Where do they get all these organs?"

Otto shrugged. "Got to get to work," he said, walking away. The phone rang. Denis picked it up and listened for a few moments, then hung up and walked out into the hall. He could see Otto down past the other end, bending over his machine. "Hey, Otto!" he said. "The liver's on its way! They're sending up some donor blood for serology!"

"Okay!" Otto shouted back. Denis walked back to his lab, sat down, and began to work. He felt very strongly about the jumping lady. It was his conviction that he was in love with her, and had been ever since she had first arrived, ever since he had heard her story and handled her blood for the first time. It was not an attraction that made sense in any way that he could explain to himself, but every night he worked in the building where she lay, and every time he handled her blood, she became a little more irresistible. He closed his magazine and sighed. He leaned his head against the machine that was busy counting and sorting her blood cells by type, waiting for the information, which was precious to him because it concerned her.

Beatrice sat and watched him, feeling sad because if she was in love with anyone in the lab it was not Denis, and was probably nobody, but just might be Luke with his enormous ears. She could not bear to watch Denis mooning over her, so she left his lab through an open back door and headed up to the roof, where she waited in the blowing snow for the arrival of her new liver.

She looked out on the city from a familiar height. The hospital, like the parking garage, was seven stories tall. She could see the university campus spread out before her, neatly bisected by the river. When she tried to leave, she got only as far as that river. Some force held her bound to the hospital. She supposed it was her living body, and wished it would die. It was not for no reason at all that she had thrown herself off the garage. Not that she could recall the reason, in her present state. She only knew that she did not wish to go back, and that it all had to do with a crushing sadness under which she had labored for most of her life, and which she had never blamed on anybody.

She heard the helicopter before she saw it. It was incredibly loud. Covering her ears with her hands, she watched as it came out of the snowstorm and settled onto the helipad. She watched the flight nurses scramble out, one of them with a Styrofoam cooler held between his hands. Just as they had with the kidney, they would take it downstairs, where doctors would examine it and make it ready for her. After the nurses had disappeared inside the hospital, Beatrice turned and stepped off the roof.

It was never like the fall that had brought her here. It was slower, for one thing, and it did her no harm whatsoever. In fact, she fell so slowly that she had time for reflection on various subjects, and this time as she floated down, she watched the snowflakes passing her and thought about her very first boyfriend. His name was Boukman. They had been eight years old together. Her parents had disapproved of him because he was black. They would not let him swim in their pool. This was in Miami, where in the summer it was practically a medical necessity to swim every day.

So she swam in his family's pool, and exulted in his strangeness. Boukman claimed to have been born of a dog, and that he could fly. These were not his parents who applauded when he and she did synchronized back dives into the pool. His real mother's name was Queenie, and she was a Great Dane, just like Scooby-Doo. He was from Haiti. He said such things were common there. She believed him all through the summer, and looked forward to the flying lessons he promised her.

On the day of the first lesson, she gave him a lingering kiss on the mouth, and then they ran hand in hand along his flat roof. She balked at the edge and watched him go flying out alone. He went out and straight down to fall directly on his well-formed, closely shaven head. She looked down at the gruesome angle of his neck. Because she was a child, she did not realize right away that he was dead.

In later years she wondered if it had been her doubt that cost him his life. If she had jumped with him, would they have flown over all the low houses of their respectable neighborhood, and scraped their toes against the tops of the highest royal palms?

As she approached the ground, Beatrice realized that Boukman was not the great sadness of her life. It was not for him that she had made her leap, though she would always think of him as the beginning of a long arc of sadness, as the person who taught her that there's no such thing as a boy who can fly, and that nothing is born of a dog but puppies and blood.

Beatrice walked into the ER, following behind a pair of EMTs who were wheeling in a motorcycle accident victim. The few people in the waiting room looked up as the man was pushed past them. He was crying out, "Louise! Louise!" at the top of his lungs. Beatrice watched as they rushed him down the hall to the trauma center. Snow swirled in around her before the doors closed again, and the waiting people went back to staring absently at their entertainment magazines or the television. Walking unseen through the restricted area, Beatrice could hear people having their various emergencies behind the curtains that separated the exam beds. She did not pause to look at the shattered kneecaps or the scalp wounds, or the blue and gray asthmatics wheezing desperately. She walked as quickly as she could, trying to catch up with the flight nurses who were carrying her liver up to surgery.

She didn't catch them. Her fall had given them a long head start on her. But somewhere near the cardiovascular intensive care unit she happened upon Olivia, who was striding confidently down the hall carrying a phlebotomy basket and singing "Maria." Beatrice followed her clear across the hospital to the nurseries, where Olivia had been called to perform a blood draw on a brand-new baby. Olivia did not mind being called to do phlebotomy. In fact, she liked very much to escape the confines of the lab, but sometimes it disturbed her to have to cause an infant pain, even if it was for its own good. They entered the nursery and saw a large nurse rocking and feeding a baby. The flesh of the nurse's thighs spilled out from under the armrests of her rocking chair.

"There she is," she said, pointing to a warming bed in a far corner of the room. Beatrice took a moment to admire the cheery decorations: rabbits and ponies and kittens, and a fine triptych of three dogs under a candy bush. The first dog's eyes were big as saucers, the second's as big as dessert plates, and the third's as big as dinner plates. This last picture made Beatrice feel sad.

Next to the warming bed, Olivia was preparing the baby for her blood draw.

"Hello, darling," she said. "You're so beautiful!" She scrubbed vigorously at the baby's foot with an alcohol-soaked cotton ball. The baby found this a not-unpleasant sensation. Olivia, full of regret, unwrapped a lancet from its sterile foil package and drove it into the fleshiest part of the baby's heel.

"Sorry, darling," she said. The baby, who did not yet have a name but would one day be called Sylvia, did not immediately begin to scream. First a look of perfect incredulity passed over her small face. Only when that had been replaced with an expression of outrage did she begin to scream with such force and volume that Beatrice thought it would blow Olivia's hair back like a hot wind.

"Yes, yes," said Olivia. "Life is hard. Don't I know it?" This is only the beginning, Beatrice whispered behind her.

Olivia had caught the heel in the well between her thumb and forefinger, and now she began to squeeze with the full force of her hand. Sometimes Olivia thought she heard the heel bone making crunching noises under the pressure, but Bonnie had assured her that it was all in her head, and that it was quite impossible to crush a baby's heel because the bones were so fresh and green.

A dark red pearl of blood had formed from out of the wound, but Olivia wiped this away with a piece of gauze because it was too full of clotting factors to be useful for analysis. She continued squeezing, and caught the next drop in a tiny plastic tube, and the next drop, and then the next. She counted twenty-five of them before she had collected the requisite 250 microliters.

It took a very long time. The blood was slow to come. Olivia began to suffer because of the heat lamps that kept the chilly babies warm like so many hamburgers. There was a lamp in the roof of the warming bed, directly above Olivia's neck where she bent over the baby. She wished for an assistant to wipe away the sweat from her brow before it dripped down onto the baby. Beatrice would have been happy to help her, if she could have.

"Like the Sahara under there, isn't it?" said the fat nurse, who was watching Olivia sweat.

"I think I'm getting dehydrated," said Olivia, squeezing out the final drop. She capped her tube and put a festive adhesive bandage across the heel. The baby continued to scream, even though both Olivia and Beatrice stroked her arms and belly to try to calm her. Even after they were gone out the door she screamed. Beatrice lingered at the observation window and watched the beet-red baby writhe and scream while the cooing blob of a nurse burped her nursery mate. Beatrice put a hand on the window and said, It only gets worse and worse and worse.

When they got back to the lab, Beatrice and Olivia found the others clustered around a table, getting ready to draw each other's blood. Bonnie looked up at Olivia from where she sat with her bare arm spread out before her.

"How'd it go?" she asked.

"Tough. That baby had blood like glue, but I got it."

"Congratulations. Have you seen a blue-top floating around? Denis says he's missing one. He's all upset."

"I thought we got one on the jumper. I know I labeled one."

"Well, he didn't get it. I guess it's with Jesus now."

"Want to get drawn?" asked Otto.

"Sure," said Olivia. "Just let me get this back to Denis."

"Bring him back with you!" Bonnie called out after her. Beatrice stayed behind and watched as Luke stroked the crook of Bonnie's arm with his gloved hand, trying to get the vein to rise.

"Hurry up," Bonnie said. "This tourniquet is killing me."

"Sorry," he said. "I think I have it now." Beatrice stood next to him and observed closely as he slipped the needle into Bonnie's vein. His motion was certain and swift. Bonnie, looking away like she always did when she got her blood drawn, did not even notice the entry.

"We haven't got all night, you know," she said.

"Yeah," said Luke, biting his lip as he pushed a vacuum-filled test tube up into the plastic sheath that covered the bottom of the needle. Inside the sheath was the sharpened back end of the needle, and they could all hear a dull popping sound as it broke the vacuum in the tube. Beatrice watched, fascinated, as Bonnie's living blood beat into the tube. She imagined herself in Bonnie's place, imagined Luke's sure fingers caressing the crook of her arm. She stood closer to him and pretended that the growing erection that shamed and disturbed him was inspired by her. He pulled out the needle and pressed a pad of gauze against the wound.

"You big smoothie," said Bonnie. "I didn't even notice."

"That's the idea," said Luke. "Who wants to draw me?" He hoped it would be Bonnie, but she was absorbed by her own blood, holding the tube up to the fluorescent light from the ceiling and swirling the contents.

"Sit down, Luke," said Otto. "I'll take care of you."

Otto put on a pair of extra-large gloves and proceeded to draw Luke's blood. He used a new needle, but Luke almost wished Otto would use the same one he had used on Bonnie. That would be a certain type of closeness, he thought.

Olivia came up behind them with Denis just in time to observe the penetration. As she watched Otto execute a flawless phlebotomy procedure, she imagined him, with his swollen muscles and great strength, driving the needle straight through Luke's arm and out the other side.

"You're getting good at this, Otto," she said, patting him on the back. She left her arm resting on the back of his shoulder and felt the subtle workings in the great muscle as he switched tubes, then finished the draw.

"Thanks," he said. He drew her next, then Denis. It was something of a thrill to watch Denis roll up his sleeve and expose the vein that stood out in bold relief all the way down his arm. As he felt the vein under his thumb, he imagined his own heart beating in exact time with Denis's, then had a vision of their two bodies, especially their chests, pressed up against each other, and both of them marveling at the synchronicity of their hearts as they held each other.

When he was finished, Otto sat down and tried to roll up his sleeve, but he could only get it as far as his upper forearm. Beyond that, his arm was too thick for the cuff, so he was forced to remove his shirt. Beatrice stood by Denis as he performed the draw, and admired the pattern of black hair that spread from Otto's belly up his abdomen, over his chest, and under his arms. It looked soft and well cared for, as if he used expensive shampoo on it instead of soap.

Olivia admired it, too, fiercely, and pictured her face against it, and even went so far as to position herself next to Otto to see if she could catch a scent from under his elevated arm. Bonnie found herself appreciative of the flat lines of Otto's stomach, and the wide stretch of his chest, and especially the thick, winglike extension of the muscles along his sides. Luke watched Bonnie watching Otto, and envied him. Denis thought solely of his jumping lady.

He thought of her lying in the OR, perhaps already opened up, and prayed silently that her operation would come off without any complications. Beatrice muttered a prayer of her own to thwart Denis's: She prayed for a power outage or an incompetent anesthetist or that someone would drop the liver.

She waited a little longer in the lab, while Denis and Otto performed the analyses on all the blood, because she wanted to make sure her friends were healthy. It turned out that Luke's iron level could have been higher and that Bonnie's glucose was dreadfully low.

"Time for lunch!" Bonnie said when she learned this, and went to go find Denis to convince him to help her hunt down the traveling food cart. Luke watched her go, then picked up the phone, which had just begun to ring. He listened with a grave expression and said, "All right," then hung up. He folded his arms across his chest and said to Olivia, who was busy entering results into the computer, "Transplant's canceled. The jumping lady is dead."

Beatrice, upon hearing this, did not stay to see Olivia's reaction but made directly for the river. She was severely disappointed when she realized that she still could not pass over the bridge. She puzzled over this the whole way back to the hospital. She wondered, Will I be stuck here forever? She went looking for her body.

When she found it her questions were answered. It was still in the SICU, though now in a different room. Outside she saw a team of doctors arguing with each other. "What am I supposed to do with this liver?" one of them wanted to know.

Another doctor was interrogating Judy, who felt close to weeping with frustration. She repeated her story, that Beatrice had coded while she was brushing her hair.

"And who told you to go around brushing people on their hair?" a doctor asked her. He was from Iran. Judy had never liked him.

"For God's sake, I was trying to be nice!" said Judy. "And if you don't like that you can just go fuck yourself!" She turned and stormed away, damning the consequences of her outburst. As she ran out of the bay, Frank turned to a fellow nursing assistant and said, "The mouse roars." Beatrice went and looked at her body.

This was not the first time that her body had experienced a spontaneous and universal shutdown of organ systems, but every other time somebody had revived it. Her body looked the same to Beatrice as it ever did, but she knew from the conversation around her that she was certifiably brain dead. Now machines gave her a semblance of life, keeping her unruined organs alive for transplant to someone else.

Beatrice turned away from her body and wandered out of the bay. It would be a while before they took her off the machine and began to remove her organs. There were blood tests to run, and the organ harvesting team would need to be roused from their beds. She went and found her liver, still waiting for her in the OR. It was the sole occupant of the room. She went and looked at it where it lay in a volume of pale pink fluid that was not blood. But the whole thing reeked so strongly of blood that she thought she might faint.

Be happy, liver, she said to it, and went back up to the pathology lab because she wanted to spend her last hours at the hospital among friends.

Halfway back to the lab she heard music and followed it. It took her downstairs, through many different hallways, always sounding very close because the acoustics in this part of the hospital were strange. It was not unusual for a stray groan to come floating down the hall to disturb a candystriper on some innocuous mission.

The music led her to the third-floor balcony over the atrium, where she looked down and saw Bonnie playing on the big piano while Denis sat glumly beside her. Bonnie played sprightly in a high octave and sang:

Fingers are fun,
Toes are nice,
Brains are soft
And gray like mice
But blood is best.

Yes blood is the best,
Oh blood is the best,
Even your mama will tell you
That blood is the best because
Blood is the sum of our parts.

She stopped singing but continued to play softly. "My mother the nurse taught me that song. A crazy lady in housekeeping taught it to her. She—the housekeeper, not my mother—got fired for slurping clotted blood out of used specimen tubes. Said it tasted like oysters." Bonnie was trying to amuse Denis because he was so sad. When she went back to ask him to lunch, he was just putting down his phone. He stood frozen over his machines for a moment, then burst violently into tears. For a moment Bonnie was uncertain what to do, but then she ran to him and threw her arms around him, saying, "It's okay, Denis," which was the first thing she could think of.

Denis didn't particularly want to be held. He hated Bonnie briefly, because she was alive and his lady was dead, and if in that moment he could have traded one life for the other, he certainly would have. Bonnie held him, and he cried into her lab-coated shoulder for a few minutes, then stood back from her. "I don't know what's wrong with me," he said.

"It's been a long night," she said, though it hadn't, really. It had been almost relaxing, so far, because it was so slow. I'm holding him! she thought. What else matters?

"It's the jumping lady," he said. "She's dead."

"I didn't know!" Bonnie exclaimed. "I didn't know you knew her!"

"I didn't," he said. A fresh sob rose up from his belly and burst out of his mouth.

Bonnie looked over Denis's shoulder and saw Luke staring at them from the hall. He turned and walked away. "Let's get out of here for a minute," she said, taking him by the hand and leading him out the back door. He did not protest, even as she led him all the way to the piano, sat him down there, and began to play.

Above them, while Bonnie moved her fingers over the lowest section of the keyboard and started a new song, Beatrice stepped off the balcony and began to float down. She managed a perfect landing on the piano, and sat down cross-legged on it, staring intently into the faces of Bonnie and Denis, who were not looking at each other. Bonnie stopped playing.

"Are you feeling better?"

"Sure," said Denis. "Thanks. It's weird how it got to me like that." He did not plan ever to tell anyone that he had been in love with the jumping lady. He could not explain the attraction to himself; how would he ever explain it to someone else?

"I think it's a good thing," she said. "You'd make a good doctor."

"No thanks." A nearby elevator opened its doors and a security guard emerged from it. He approached them warily.

"You're not allowed to be playing that piano," he said.

"Yeah, right," said Bonnie. "Whatever." She launched into "Chopsticks."

"I'm going to have to ask you to stop that."

"If you want me to stop, you're going to have to shoot me," said Bonnie.

"Maybe we should be going," said Denis.

"I'm enjoying myself," said Bonnie. "Is it a crime to enjoy yourself in a hospital? Are people allowed only to suffer and die here?" She began to play "Für Elise." The guard peered at their nametags and made notes in a small black book.

"We're on our way," said Denis, pulling at Bonnie's arm.

"I'll have to file an incident report," the guard said.

"File away!" said Bonnie. She felt giddy. Perhaps it was the after-effect of having Denis in her arms, or of being next to him.

"I'll see you up in the lab," said Denis. He got up and walked away. She stopped playing and walked after him.

"Wait!" she said. "Let's go find the food cart." The guard walked away, thinking of all the patients wanting their sleep. Beatrice remained on top of the piano. She lay on her back and looked up all the way to the top of the atrium, seven stories up. She saw people walking by occasionally, along the balconies, carrying blood to the lab or moving a patient. She saw the beautiful Filipino woman who worked in the dietary department wheeling the third-shift food cart along the balcony and eating a candy bar.

She closed her eyes and imagined all her friends from the lab standing spread out on all the different levels and balconies while she herself floated above the piano. She imagined them calling out to one another: Olivia to Otto, Otto to Denis, Denis to her, she to Luke, Luke to Bonnie, and Bonnie to Denis.

When she returned to the lab, Beatrice found it in chaos. The respite they'd been enjoying was over, and things were very busy again. She sat in the window and watched Luke as he rushed around, looking hapless.

He felt lost in a rush of fluid. They were getting tests now not just for blood but for urine, and CSF, and all manner of effusions. Nursing assistants came and dumped specimens in great quantities at the window. There were even small pieces of people coming up now, discrete bits of organ or tumor to be processed and frozen for a pathologist to look at in the morning. Someone dropped off a whole human brain in a Tupperware container full of formaldehyde.

And there was much stool, most of it quite runny, packaged in blue plastic containers that looked to Luke a lot like the containers in which delis packaged their potato salad. In the hurry to get things done, he dropped one. He was acutely grateful that it didn't break open on the floor. Instead it bounced and rolled, coming to rest nestled against Olivia's shoe.

"Sorry," he said.

"That's okay." Olivia had another moment of perversity in which she imagined picking up the container and throwing its soupy contents all over Luke, and all over the walls and windows of the lab, all the while shouting, "Shit! Shit! Shit!"

"I'm getting very tired," she said.

"Tell me about it," he said. Much time had passed, though Luke barely noticed. It was almost five. He could go home at six.

They all could, but he wasn't particularly looking forward to it. He wondered if one day he and Bonnie might leave together and go to his apartment. Otto wandered up from the chemistry lab.

"Make it stop," he said. "I don't want to work anymore."

"I think it's slowing down," said Luke.

"Where's Bonnie?" Otto asked, sitting down at one of the empty terminals.

"In the back," said Olivia. "With Denis." It was a quality of her perpetually sweaty palms that they made a sucking sound when ground together and rapidly pulled apart. She made those sounds now, and winked. In fact, Bonnie was only helping Denis do differential cell counts. He had forgiven her for causing a scene, and she had been so bold as to make plans with him for later in the day.

"I'll be right back," said Luke. He walked out of the lab, down the hall, and into the men's bathroom. Beatrice followed right behind. She watched him at the urinal, craning her head around his side to get a glimpse of his penis. It was not very exciting, and she realized with a very mild sort of sadness that she did not really desire him physically. Rather, she dreamed of haunting him, of climbing unseen and unfelt into his single bed at night, of lying there on him and in him and by him while he gazed at the two-by-four-foot hole in his ceiling where the plaster had fallen down one night. He had woken with a start when it fell near the foot of the bed.

She leaned against the sink while he washed his face, then watched him stare into his own eyes in the mirror. Putting her face next to his, and staring where he stared, she could hear perfectly what he was thinking. It was, What's wrong with me?

When Luke and Beatrice left the bathroom, the phlebotomists were arriving. Luke continued back to the lab, but Beatrice stopped to watch them pass. Every morning she came up to watch the arrival. It was like a parade. They came down the hall in twos and threes, some with their arms around each other, some having recently left the same bed. Their names were Alan, Elaine, Wendy, Randy, Eric, Arthur, Phuong, Louisa, Amanda, Loric, Oliver, Nathan, and Elizabeth. Beatrice thought they were all very pretty, especially Oliver, who had a humongous head and beautiful pale skin that was always pink and vibrant-looking from the cold when he arrived. He looked to Beatrice like the sort of boy who drank great quantities of milk.

She liked to smell them, because each one wore a different cologne or perfume. Some days she spent her whole morning following them around as they slipped in and out of patients' rooms, drawing blood. But she would not do that today.

Today she waited patiently at the window and watched her friends as they finished up their work. She waited an hour before everyone was ready to go. It was customary for them all to go out to breakfast together. Otto suggested a pancake house. Everyone said that was a fine idea except Luke, who said he was too tired to eat and started off down the hall. Beatrice did not follow him right away. She paused to watch her other friends walk off together in the opposite direction. She sent a prayer after them.

Let it happen this way, she said, gathering up her hair and waving it at them as if that might make what she wanted for them so. Let it be that Olivia and Otto encounter in each other something lovely, and Denis and Bonnie inspire each other's joy, and let something nice happen to Luke.

She knelt in an attitude of supplication and willed joy on her friends. In her mind's eye she could see the future as she desired it to be: Denis and Bonnie kissing in the bitter cold inside her car while they waited for the engine to warm; Otto and Olivia rubbing their feet together as they watched a movie in his apartment, and falling asleep with their heads touching and their breath on each other's faces. But for Luke she could imagine nothing.

Beatrice hurried after him, catching up as he was walking down the hill toward the river and the bus stop. The hospital grounds were beautifully landscaped, complete with a small wood that extended to the river. Snow was everywhere on the ground and trees, and still falling thinly. It was very cold. Luke had moved from Louisiana. He thought, on his way down the wooded hill, of his parents' house, and of his old bedroom. An ambulance wailed by him, going to pick someone up. He began to cry, but stopped by the time he reached the bus stop.

There was a girl there, huddled in a big coat, reading by the light of the streetlamps. She gave him a sullen look and turned back to her magazine. Luke sat down as far from her as he could. Beatrice sat next to him and considered trying to hold his hand. Luke closed his eyes and thought, for no reason he could think of, of the hole in his ceiling. He had still not cleaned up the plaster. He heard laughter.

Opening his eyes, he saw a woman coming toward him. She was dressed in a black shirt and white pants, and looked to him as if she had been out dancing. Her makeup was smeared on her face. He noticed, when she came near, that she reeked of booze.

"Excuse me," she said. "Pardon me." She was no one he knew.

"Yes," he said. He looked at her hair. It was all messy, but he could tell that it had at some recent time been elaborately styled.

"Can you help me?" she asked.

"I don't know," he said. There was little concern in his voice.

"I'm really bleeding," she said. "I just got my period, and I'm sort of without supplies. You know? Do you have any?"

"I think you should ask her," he said, indicating the reading girl with his head. The girl raised her head and looked at them briefly, then ignored them.

"I did. No luck. Have you got some tissues? A hankie? Anything?"

"Sorry," said Luke. He wanted her to go away.

"It's really bad," she said.

"I can't help you."

"Well," she said, touching her white pants, "am I spotting? Can you at least tell me that? I can't bend over enough to see. I think I'd fall. I'm not myself right now." Luke met her eyes for a moment. They were blue. He looked down at her crotch.

The woman burst out laughing. "Made you look!" she said. Nearby a man was laughing, too. Luke saw him step out of a shadow. The woman went to him, saying, "Told you I could make him look!" She put her arm around him, and they began to stagger off. Luke looked at the girl with the magazine. She was smiling. He stood up and moved his hands from his jacket pockets to his pants pockets, looking away from her. His face was hot. There was something in his pocket. He took it out.

It was the blue-topped tube that Denis had been missing. Luke had sworn he did not know where it was when Denis asked him, but now he remembered picking it up when Olivia forgot it on a counter. The blood in the tube was dark but not clotted. He held it in his bare hand. It was warm, from being next to his leg. With his thumb he worked the stopper free, then began to run after the woman and her friend. When he was close enough, he splattered it liberally over their necks and backs. The woman touched her hand to the back of her neck and brought it forward to look at it. When she saw the blood, she screamed loud enough to startle winter birds away from the telephone wires where they perched and sang.

"There!" Luke shouted. "There!" The man came forward and punched him square in the face. Luke fell down on the snowy sidewalk, where the man kicked him once in the head, then walked away with his friend, trying to console her. The magazine girl got up to wait for her bus at the next stop.

Beatrice sat down next to Luke. He was staring, unblinking, up into the dawning sky. He felt strangely content lying there, and she was worried for him. She felt overcome by something. When she saw him falling back with blood spraying from his nose, love swelled in her like a sponge so she felt heavy for the first time since she'd awoken in the hospital. She reached out to him.

Though he could feel it when she stroked his forehead, he thought it was just a breeze. When she bent down and kissed him, he thought it was a twitch in his lip, possibly the result of brain damage from the kick to his head.

As she kissed him she had a vision of becoming his spirit wife. In time, she knew now, he would come to feel her and see her and know her. It would be as if she weren't even dead. The kiss itself, the contact, was thrilling. How could I have left this? she wondered, and she bent down to do it again.

But even as she kissed him, a sharp, clear note sounded in her head, and she knew with exquisite certainty that they had at last harvested her heart from her chest. It was on its way now to someone who needed it and wanted it. As her heart was taken, the veil obscuring her memory was lifted and she recalled with perfect clarity the motivation for her leap. As the last quantities of blood drained from her heart, she stood up and threw out her arms, as if in benediction to the whole winter landscape.

Finished! she cried, and ran off across the street and over the bridge. Halfway across she took off, went up and away, in search of a place without loneliness and desire; without misery and rage, without disappointment; without crushing, impenetrable sadness.

STAB

*

Someone was murdering the small animals of our neighborhood. We found them in the road outside our houses, and from far away they looked like the victims of careless drivers, but close up you saw that they were plump and round, not flat, and that their bodies were marred by clean-edged rectangular stab wounds. Sometimes they lay in drying pools of blood, and you knew the murder had occurred right there. Other times it was obvious they had been moved from the scene of the crime, and arranged in postures, like the two squirrels posed in a hug on Mrs. Chenoweth's doorstep.

Squirrels, then rabbits, then the cats, and dogs in late summer. By then I had known for a long time who was doing all the stabbing. I discovered the identity of the murderer on the first day of June, in the summer of 1979, two years and one month and fourteen days after my brother's death from cancer. I got up early that morning, a sunny one that broke a chain of rainy days, because my father was taking me to see Spider-Man, who was scheduled to make an appearance at the fourth annual Leukemia Society of America Summer Fair in Washington, D.C. I was eight years old and I thought Spider-Man was very important.

In the kitchen I ate a bowl of cereal while my father spread the paper out before me. "Look at that," he said. On the front page was an article detailing the separation of Siamese twin girls, Lisa and Elisa Johansen from Salt Lake City. They were joined at the thorax, like my brother and I had been, but they shared vital organs, whereas Colm and I never did. There was a word for the way we and they had been joined: thoracopagus. It was still the biggest word I knew.

"Isn't that amazing?" my father said. He was a surgeon, so these sorts of things interested him above all others. "See that? They're just six months old!" Colm and I were separated at one and a half years. I had no clear memories of either the operation or the attachment, though Colm always claimed he remembered our heads knocking together all the time, and that he dreamed of monkeys just before we went under from the anesthesia. The Johansen twins were joined side by side, but my brother and I were joined back to back. Our parents would hold up mirrors so we could look at each other—that was something I did remember: looking in my mother's silver-handled mirror, over my shoulder at my own face.

Early as it was, on our way out to the car we saw our new neighbor sitting on the front steps of her grandparents' house, reading a book in the morning sun.

"Hello, Molly," said my father.

"Good morning, Dr. Cole," she said. She was unfailingly polite with adults. At school she was already very popular, though she had only been there for two months, and she had a tendency to oppress the other children with her formidable vocabulary.

"Poor girl," said my father when we were in the car and on our way. He pitied her because both her parents had died in a car accident. She was in the car with them when they crashed, but she was thrown from the wreck through an open window—this was in Florida, where I supposed everyone always drove around with their windows down and never wore seat belts.

I turned in my seat so I was upside down. This had always been my habit; I did it so I could look out the window at the trees and telephone wires as we passed them. My mother would never stand for it, but she was flying a trip to San Francisco. She was a stewardess. Once my father and I flew with her while she was working and she brought me a glass of Coke with three cherries in it. She put down the drink and leaned over me to open up the window shade, which I had kept closed, from the beginning of the flight, out of fear. "Look," she said to me. "Look at all that!" I looked and saw sandy mountains that looked like crumpled brown paper bags. I imagined falling from that great height into my brother's arms.

"Spider-Man!" said my father, after we had pulled onto route 50, and had passed a sign that said, WASHINGTON, D.C., 29 MILES. "Aren't you excited?" He reached over and rubbed my head with his fist. If it had been just me and my mother, she would not have spoken at all, but my father spoke the whole way, talking about Spider-Man, talking about the mall, talking about the Farrah Fawcett look-alike who was also scheduled to appear, asking me every time if the prospect of seeing such things didn't make me excited, though he knew I would not answer him. I hadn't spoken a word or uttered a sound since my brother's funeral.

Spider-Man was a great disappointment. When my father brought me close to him for an autograph, I saw how his uniform was badly sewn, and glossy in a gross sort of way, and his voice, when he said, "Hey there, Spider-Fan," was pitched high like a little mouse's voice. I knew he was an utter fake, and I only wanted to get away from him. I ran away, across the mall, and my father did not catch me until I had made it all the way to the Smithsonian Castle. He didn't yell at me. It only made him sad when I acted so peculiarly. My mother sometimes lost her temper and would scream out that I was a twisted little fruitcake and why couldn't I ever make anything easy? She always apologized later, but never with the same ferocity, and so it seemed to me not to count, and I always hoped she would burst into my room later on in the night, to wake me by screaming how sorry she was, to slap herself, and maybe me, too, because she was so regretful.

"So much for Spider-Man," said my father. He took me to see the topiary buffalo, and for a while we sat in the grass, saying nothing, until he asked me if I wouldn't go back with him. I did, and though we had missed the Farrah Fawcett look-alike's rendition of "Feelings," he got to meet her, because he had connections with the Society. She said I was cute and gave me an autographed picture that I later gave to my father because I could tell he wanted it.

When we got home I went up to my room and tossed all my *Spider-Man* comic books and figurines into the deepest recesses of my closet. Then I took a book out onto the roof. I sat and read *Stuart Little* for the fifth time. Below me, in the yard next door, I could see Molly Pitcher playing, just as silent as I was. Every once in a while she would look up and catch me looking at her, and she would smile down at her plastic dolls. We had interacted like this before, me reading and her playing, but on this day, for some reason, she spoke to me. She held my gaze for a few moments, then laughed coyly and said, "Would you like to see my bodkin?" I shrugged, then climbed down and followed her when she went into the ravine behind our houses. I did not know what a bodkin was. I thought she was going to make me look inside her panties, like Judy Corcoran, who lived two doors down, had done about three weeks before, trying to make me swear not to tell about the boring thing I had seen.

But what Molly showed me, after we had gone down about thirty feet into the bushes and she had knelt near the arrow-shaped gravestone of our English sheepdog, Gulliver, and after she dug briefly in the dry dirt, was a dagger. It was about a foot long, and ornate, encrusted with what looked like real emeralds and rubies, with a great blue stone set in the pommel, and a rose etched on the upper part of the blade.

"Do you like it?" she asked me. "My father gave it to me. It used to belong to a medieval princess." I did like it. I reached out for it, but she drew it back to her chest and said, "No! You may not touch it." She ran off down the ravine, toward the river, and I didn't follow. I sat on Gulliver's stone and thought about all the little dead animals, and I knew—even a little mind could make the connection—that Molly Pitcher had been murdering them. But I didn't give much thought to it, besides a brief reflection on how sharp the blade must be to make such clean wounds. I went back to my house and went down to the basement to watch *The Bionic Woman*, my new favorite.

After Colm's death I got into the habit of staring, sometimes for hours at a time, at my image in the mirror. My parents thought it was just another one of my new autistic tendencies, and they both discouraged it, even going so far as to remove the mirror in my bedroom. What they didn't know was that the image I was looking at was not really my own; it was Colm's. When I looked in the mirror I saw the face we had shared. We were mirror twins.

People who knew our faces well enough could tell that together they made a perfectly symmetrical pair, the gold flecks in my left eye perfectly mirrored in Colm's right, a small flaw at the right edge of his lips mirrored by one at the left edge of mine. So when I looked into a mirror, even the small things that made my face my own made my face into his, and if I waited long enough he would begin to speak to me. He would tell me about heaven, about all sorts of little details, like that nobody ever had to go to the bathroom there. We had both considered that necessity to be a great inconvenience and a bore. He said he was watching me all the time.

There was a connection between us, he always said, even when he was alive, that the surgeons had not broken when we were separated. It was something unseen. We did not quite have two souls between us; it was more that we had one and a half. Sometimes he would hide from me, somewhere in our great big house, and insist that I find him using a special "twin sense." Usually I couldn't find him, but he always walked right to my hiding place when he was it. I could not hide from him anywhere in the house, or, I suspected, anywhere on earth.

After he died I found him, not just in mirrors, but in every reflecting surface. Ponds and puddles or the backs of spoons, anything would do. And always the last thing he said to me was, "When are you going to come and be with me again?"

Molly Pitcher appeared that night at my window. I was still awake when she came. At first I thought she was Colm. She stood in the open window, and it was not until a flash of heat lightning illuminated her that I saw who she was. When I saw the dagger flash in her hand I was certain she had come to kill me, but when she came over to my bed, she only said, "Do you want to come out with me?" Another flash of lightning lit up the room. The lightning was the reason I had been awake when she came. On hot summer nights Colm and I would stay up for hours, watching it flash over the river. Sometimes our parents would let us sleep on the porch, where the view was even better.

She sat down on my bed. "I like your room," she said, looking around. There was light from the hall, enough to make out the general lay of the room. Our father had built it up for Colm and me, making it look like a ship, complete with sea-blue carpeting and a raised wooden deck with railings and a ship's wheel. Above one bed was an authentic-looking sign that said CAPTAIN'S BUNK, while the other belonged to the first mate. While he lived we had switched beds every night, in the interests of absolute equality, unless one of us was feeling afraid, in which case we shared the same bed. The last time he slept in the room he had been in the captain's bed, and because the cycle could not go on any longer I had been in the first mate's bed ever since.

Molly pulled my sheets back and while I dressed she looked around the room for my shoes. When she found them she brought them to me and said, "Come on."

I followed her, out the window, over the roof, and down the blue spruce that grew close to the house near my room. She went down our road, to the golf course around which part of our community was built. The place where we lived had once been a Baptist girl's camp, but had in the century since its founding turned into a place where well-to-do white people lived in rustic pseudo-isolation. It was called Severna Forest. You couldn't live there if you were Jewish or Italian, and in the summer they made you lock up your dog in a communal kennel. The golf course had only nine holes. It was a very hilly course, bordered by ravines in some places, and in others by the Severn River. The part of it that Molly took me to was a wide piece of rough on the fourth hole, only about half a mile from our houses. Though the moon was down, I could see under the starlight that rabbits had gathered in the tall grass and the dandelions. I bent at my knees and picked one of the flowers. I was about to puff on it and scatter the seeds when Molly held my arm and said, "Don't, you'll frighten them."

For a little while we stood there, she with one hand on my arm, the other on her knife, and we watched the rabbits sitting placidly in the grass, and we waited for them to get used to us. "Aren't they lovely?" she said, letting go of my arm. She began to move, very slowly, toward the rabbit closest to where we stood. She moved as slow as the moon does across the sky; I couldn't tell she was getting any closer to the rabbit unless I looked away for a few minutes. When I looked back she was closer, and the rabbit had not moved. When she was about five feet away she turned and looked at me. It was too dark for me to see her face. I couldn't tell if she smiled. Then she leapt, knife first, at the little creature, and I saw her pierce its body. It thrashed once and was suddenly dead. I realized I was holding my breath, and still holding the dandelion in front of my lips. I blew into it and watched the seeds float toward her where she was stabbing the body again and again and again.

In school the next Monday, Molly Pitcher studiously ignored me. The whole morning long I stared at her, thinking she must give some sign that a special thing had taken place between us, but she never did. I didn't really care, one way or the other, if she never spoke to me again. I was used to people experimenting with me as a friend. Children, inspired briefly to kindness, would befriend and forget me like a puppy. I let them come and go.

I had given up on her by the time she finally spoke to me. After lunch, when we were all settling down again into our desks, in the silence after Mrs. Wallaby, our teacher, had offered up a post-luncheon prayer for the pope, who had just that day gone on a groundbreaking trip to his native Poland, Molly passed me a note. I opened it up, thinking, for some reason, that it might say, "I love you," because once a popular girl named Iris had passed me such a note, and when I blushed she and her friends had laughed cruelly. But Molly's note said simply, "You'd better not tell." I thought that was the most ridiculous thing I had ever read. I supposed she meant I had better not write a letter to the police. She did not really know me at all, I thought to myself. She couldn't know I wouldn't tell.

"What's that you've got there, Calvin?" Mrs. Wallaby asked. She strode over to me and squinted at me through her glasses. Before she arrived I slipped the piece of paper into my mouth and began to chew.

"What was that?" I swallowed. She brought her face so close to mine I could read the signature on her designer-frame glasses: *Oscar de la Renta*.

"What was that?" she asked again. Of course I said nothing. She heaved a great sigh and told me to go sit in "the Judas chair," which was actually just a desk set aside from the others, facing a corner. She was not a bad woman, but sometimes I brought out the worst in people. Once she saved me at recess from a crowd of girls who were pinching me, trying to make me cry out. She brought me inside and put cold cream from her purse on my welts, but then, after she spoke for a while about how I couldn't go on like this, I just couldn't, she gave me a long grave look and gave me a pinch herself. It was not so hard as what the girls were giving me, and it was under my shirt, where no one would see. She looked deep into my eyes as she did it, but I didn't cry out. I didn't even blink.

Molly came back a few nights later. At school, after the incident with the note, she continued to ignore me, except for flashing me an occasional cryptic smile. On the night of the first day of summer vacation, she came and got me again from my bed. She said nothing, aside from commands telling me to get dressed and follow her, until we passed the golf course and I started off to where the rabbits were. She grabbed my collar and pulled me back.

"No," she said. "It's time to move on." We spent the night hunting cats. It wasn't easy. We exhausted ourselves chasing them through the dark. Always they outran us or vanished up a tree.

"We need a plan," she said at last, and quickly came up with one. We went back closer to our houses and found a neighbor's cat by the name of Mr. Charlemagne who had run off before when we chased him, into a cat door that led into a garage. Molly positioned me in a bush by that door, then chased after Mr. Charlemagne, who up until that point had been eyeing us placidly. When she came at him he took off for his door, but I jumped in front of it. For some reason he jumped right up into my arms, looked up in my face, then turned to look at my companion. She had her knife out. He snuggled deeper into my arms, expecting, I think, that I would bring him inside to safety, but I threw him down hard on the ground. Molly fell on him and stabbed him through the throat.

*   *   *

Mr. Charlemagne's death did not go unnoticed. Not that the previous deaths had gone unnoticed, but the authorities of Severna Forest—the sheriff and the chairman of the Community Association and the president of the Country Club—dismissed the squirrel and rabbit deaths as the gruesome pranks of bored teenagers. When Mr. Charlemagne was discovered, draped along a straight-growing bough of a birch tree, a mildly urgent sense of alarm spread over the community. A crime had been committed. "Sick!" people muttered to each other while they bought vodka and Yoo-Hoo at the general store. Not one bit of suspicion fell on Molly or me. Everyone considered me strange and tragic, but utterly harmless. Molly Pitcher was equally tragic, but widely admired. With her blond hair and her big brown eyes, she was the picture of innocence, and she acted perfectly the part of an utterly good little girl. Sometimes I thought it was only because she stabbed that she could play the part of her sweet, decent self so well.

A few days passed before she came for me again, in the early evening after a lacrosse game. Every Saturday afternoon the Severna Forest pee-wee team had their practice. I was one of their best players, because I had absolutely no fear of the ball. I did not try to get away from it when it came flying toward me like a little cannon shot. Others still ducked, or knocked it away with their stick, instead of catching it. If it hit me, I didn't care. I scooped it up and ran with it, often all the way down the field because it rarely occurred to me to pass the ball. My cradling technique, made fine by hours of tutelage by the junior coach, a college boy named Sam Corkle, was the envy of every other player. I don't think I cared much for the game then (I didn't understand why it was so important for the ball to get from one side of the field to the other), though I kept playing, and many years later my father would be able to point me out in televised college games. But I liked to run, and to be exhausted, and I thought one day the ball might fly at me with such force it would burst my head like a rotten pumpkin.

That day I got hit in the eye with the ball. Sam Corkle hurled it at me with all his adult strength, thinking I was looking at him and paying attention. But I was daydreaming. When it struck my eye I saw a great white flash and saw a pale afterimage of Colm's face, which quickly faded. The blow knocked me down. I looked up at the sky and saw a passing plane, and wondered, like I always did when I saw a plane in flight, if my mother was on board, even though I knew she was at home today. Sam Corkle came up with the other coach and they asked me all sorts of questions, trying to see if I was disoriented and might have a concussion. Of course I didn't answer. Someone said I would throw up if I had a concussion, so they sat me on a bench and one of them watched me to see if that would happen. When it didn't, they let me back into the game. I went eagerly, though my eyeball was aching and starting to swell, hoping to get hit again and catch another glimpse of my brother.

"What happened to you?" my mother asked when Sam Corkle brought me home. She was sitting at the dining room table, where my father held a package of frozen hamburger to his own swollen black eye. He had gotten into a fight at a gas line when someone tried to cut in front of him. It was a bad week for gas. Stations were closing early all over town, having sold their daily allowance before noon. "You too, sport?" he said. He examined my eye and said I would be fine. My mother was relieved to hear I hadn't been beaten by bullies, and when Sam Corkle praised my fortitude in returning so eagerly to the game, she even smiled at me. While she held hamburger against my eye there was a knock at the door. Sam answered it, and I heard Molly Pitcher's voice ask very sweetly, "Can Calvin come out and play?" I jumped off my mother's lap and ran toward the door. She ran after me, and caught me, and said, "Take your hamburger with you." I stood at the door while she walked back to the dining room with Sam and I heard her ask my father, "When did your son get a little girlfriend?"

Molly had an empty mayonnaise jar in her hands. "We're going to catch fireflies," she said, not asking about my eye. I followed her through the dusk to the golf course, dropping my hamburger in a holly bush along the way. I ran around with her, grabbing after bugs, delighted that she had come for me in the daylight, and thinking that must mean something. She slapped my hands a few times because I kept grabbing at her flying blond hair as much as I did the fireflies.

I thought she was waiting for us to fill the jar so she could stick her hand in and crush them mercilessly, or bring them home and stick them with pins to a piece of cardboard, or distill their glowing parts into some powerful, fluorescent poison with which she could coat her knife. But when it was dark, when we had caught about thirty of them and they were thick in the jar, she took off the lid and went running down the hill, spilling a trail of bright motes that circled around her, then rose up and flew away down the hill to the river.

Soon there weren't any cats left for us. Not because we had killed them all, but because after the fourth one, a tabby named Vittles that lived with the Nottingham family at the bottom of the hill, was found stabbed twelve times on the front steps of the general store, people started keeping their cats inside at night. Our hunts were widely spaced, only about once every two weeks, but in between those nights Molly Pitcher would come to the door for me and take me out to play in the daylight. We did the normal things that children our age were supposed to do, during the day. We swam in the river and played with her dolls and watched television. By the time we had killed Vittles it was late in July, and after two nights of fruitless hunting for cats, she decided another change of prey would be in order. She took me through the woods, on an hour-long nighttime hike out to the kennels. I could hear the dogs barking through the darkness long before we got there. I thought they knew we were coming for them.

The kennels were lit by a single streetlamp, stuck in the middle of a clearing in the woods. There was a little service road that ran under the light, out to the main road that led to Generals Highway and Annapolis. I watched Molly Pitcher stalk back and forth in front of the runs. The dogs were all howling and barking at her. It was two a.m. There was nobody around, and nobody lived within a mile and a half of the place. The whole point of the kennel was that the dogs be separated from the houses between June and September, so their barking wouldn't disturb all the wealthy people who came to live in their cottages during the summer. It was a stupid rule.

Molly had stooped down in front of a poodle. I did not know it. It retreated to the back of its run and yipped at her.

"Nice puppy," she said to it, though it was full grown. She waved me over to her and, turning me around, took a piece of beef from the Holly Hobbie backpack she had strapped on me at the beginning of our excursion. Then she took out my lacrosse gloves and told me to put them on.

"Be ready to grab him," she said. She bent down and held the meat up in the meager light. "Come on," she said. "Come and get your treat, baby. It's okay." With one hand she held the meat and with the other tried to waft its aroma toward the dog, who continued to yip and snarl for a few moments, but then stepped up warily to sniff at the meat. She held on to one end while the poodle nibbled, and now with her free hand she scratched its head. She motioned for me to come up close beside her. It was the closest I had ever been to a poodle in my life. I tried to imagine the owner, probably a big fat rich lady with white hair, who wore diamonds around her throat while she slept in a giant canopy bed.

"Just about . . . now!" said Molly. I reached through the bars of the cage with my thick lacrosse hands and grabbed the dog by a foreleg. Immediately it started to pull away. "Don't let it get away!" she said, scrambling in the bag for her knife. When it tried to escape—at first just a gentle tug—and it gave me a "What are you doing?" look, I very nearly let it go. If she had not remonstrated me, I think I might have.

It was an awkward kill, because the bars were in the way, and it was a strong-willed little dog that wanted to live. It bit hard but ineffectively at my hands. It bit at the knife and cut its gums, and its teeth made a ringing sound against the metal. It snarled and yelped and squealed, and all around us the other dogs were all screaming. Molly was saying, "There! There! There!" in a low voice, almost a whisper. When she finally delivered a killing blow to the neck, a gob of hot blood flew out between the bars and hit me in the eye. It burned like the harsh shampoos my parents bought for me, but I didn't cry out.

On the way back I let her walk ahead of me. I watched the glint of her head under the moon as she ducked between bushes and hopped over rotting logs. I felt bad, not about the poodle, which I had hated instantly and absolutely as soon as I had laid eyes upon it, but about the owner, the fat lady who I thought must be named Mrs. Vanderbilt because that was the richest name I knew. I thought about her riding down to the kennels in her limousine with a china bowl full of steak tartare for her Precious, and the way her face would look when she saw the bloody cottonball on the floor of the cage and could not comprehend that this was the thing she loved. Molly got farther and farther ahead of me, calling back that I should stop being so slow and hurry up. As she got farther away all I could see was the moonlight on her head, and on the white bag, which she had taken, promising to clean my gloves.

When we had gone about a mile from the kennel I heard a train whistle sounding. It was still far away, but I knew the tracks were nearby. I went to them. In the far distance I could see the train light. I lay down in the middle of the tracks and waited. Molly Pitcher came looking for me—I could hear her calling out, calling me a stupid boy and saying it was late. She was tired. She wanted to go to bed. As the train got nearer, and I felt a deep, wonderful hum in the tracks that seemed to pass through my brain and stimulate whatever organ is responsible for generating happiness, I imagined my head flying from my body to land at her feet. Or maybe it would hit her and knock her down. She would, I imagined, give it a calm look, put it in the bag, and take it home, where she would keep it, along with my gloves, under her bed as a souvenir of our acquaintance. The train arrived and passed over me.

I suppose I was too small for it to take off my head. Or maybe it was a different sort of train that did that to Charlie Kelly, a fifteen-year-old who had died the previous summer after a reefer party in the woods when he lay down on the tracks to impress Sam Corkle's sister. The conductor never saw me. The train never slowed. It rushed over me with such a noise—it got louder and louder until I couldn't hear it anymore, until watching the flashes of moon between the boxcars, I heard my brother's voice say, "Soon."

All Severna Forest was horrified by the death of the dog, whose name turned out to be Arthur. A guard was posted at the kennel. For the first few days it was Sheriff Travis himself, but after a week he deputized a teenager he deemed trustworthy, but that boy snuck off with his girlfriend to get stoned and listen to loud music in her car. While they were thus occupied we struck again, after two nights of watching and waiting for just such an opportunity. This time it was a Jack Russell terrier named Dreamboat.

The kennel was closed after that and the dogs sent home to owners who kept them inside, especially at night. Sheriff Travis claimed to be within a hairsbreadth of catching the "pervert," but in fact he never came near Molly or me. She never seemed nervous about getting caught. Neither did she gloat about her success. She was silent about it, just like she was silent about why she went around stabbing things in the first place.

But she talked about her parents all summer. When I was not playing lacrosse, I was with her, sailing on the river in the Sunfish her grandparents had bought her in June, or soft-shell crabbing in the muddy flats off Beach Road, or riding around on our banana-seated bicycles. I envied her hers because it had long, multicolored tassels that dangled from the handlebars, and a miniature license plate on the back that said, "Hot Stuff." While we sat stuck on a calm day in the middle of the river I dangled my hand in the water and listened to her talk about her parents, about how her father was a professor of history at the same university where Sam Corkle would return to in a matter of weeks, and how he would tell her stories at night about ancient princesses, and tell her she herself was surely an ancient princess in a past life. Didn't she remember? Didn't she recognize this portrait of her antique prince? Didn't she recognize the dagger with which she had slain the beastly suitor who had tried to take her away to live in a black kingdom under the earth? Her mother, a cautious pediatrician, had protested when he gave her the bodkin, though her daughter was grave and responsible, and not likely to hurt herself or others by accident. "A girl needs to defend herself," her father said, but he was joking. The knife hung on her wall, along with an ancient tapestry and a number of museum prints of ancient princesses, and she was not supposed to touch it until she was older.

I listened and watched pale sea nettles drift by. Occasionally one would catch my hand with its tentacle and sting me. I wanted to tell her about my brother, about stories we had told each other, about our lighthouse game or our bridge game or our thunder-and-lightning game, or the fond wish we both had for a flying bed, of the sort featured in *Bedknobs and Broomsticks*, except that ours would be equipped with a matter transporter, à la *Star Trek*, so we could hover over our favorite restaurant and beam up many delicious pizzas. But I said nothing. Nothing could have made me talk, on that day, or any of the days that stretched back to Colm's funeral. Back then I didn't know why I would not speak. Different professionals had tried to get me to talk, with art therapy, play therapy, with pen and paper, and even, once, with anatomically correct puppets. I could not tell them what I did not know, and even if I had known, could not have said because the only communication I engaged in was my homework. I think now that the reason my throat closed up and my brain sealed up was because I knew, that day in the funeral parlor, that there was nothing I could ever say that would be equal to the occasion of my brother's death. I should have spoken a word that would bring him back, and yet I could not, and so I must say nothing forever.

Molly's birthday came in the first week of August. My mother took me shopping for a present. She spent much time in the Barbie section, agonizing over accessories, but I insisted silently on my own choice: a *Bionic Woman* combination beauty salon and diagnostic station, a deluxe playset where your Jaime Sommers doll (I had picked one of those out, also) could not just get her atomic battery recharged but her hair done, too. It was not the gift I really meant to give her, not the gift from my heart. I insisted on it because I knew Molly would show a complete lack of interest in it and I would be able to take it and play with it myself. Her real gift from me was a wide flat stone, taken from the Severn, with which she could sharpen her knife. I wrapped it in the Sunday funnies. When she opened it she smiled with genuine delight and said it was her favorite.

From her grandparents she got a Polaroid camera. Her grandfather, a man who had always believed in buying in bulk, bought her a whole carton of film and flashbulbs. In the evening after her birthday party, we sat on my roof and she sent flashes arcing over the ravine, tossing aside the pictures that popped out. They were of nothing, and she was not interested in them. I picked them up and pressed them to my nose because I liked the developing-film smell. After a while her grandfather shouted from their porch next door that we should stop wasting film, or else somebody might get her new camera taken away from her until she was a little more responsible. Of course she stopped immediately.

That night she came to my window, her pack on her shoulders. I had a feeling she would come and had gone to sleep fully dressed, right down to my shoes. To my surprise she took my shoes off, and my socks. While I sat with my feet hanging over the edge of the bed, she took a jar of Vaseline from her pack and, scooping out a plum-sized dollop, began to slather it over my foot and between my toes.

"We have a long walk tonight," she said matter-of-factly. I closed my eyes while she did my other foot, enjoying the feeling. When I put on my socks and shoes and walked on my anointed feet it was like walking on a pillow—or my father's fat belly when he would play with Colm and me and let us walk all over him in our bare feet, all the while yelling, "Oh, oh, the elephants are trampling me!"

We went far past the kennel, three miles from our homes. We walked right out of Severna Forest, past the squat, crumbling brick pillars that marked the entrance to the forest road. We walked past the small black community, right at the edge of the gates, where families lived whose mothers worked as maids in the houses of our neighbors. She led me into the fields of a farm whose acreage ran along Generals Highway.

"I want a horse," she said, standing still and eyeing the vast expanse of grass in front of us. In the distance I could see a house and a barn. I had seen it countless times from my parents' car, when my mother was driving and I had to sit right side up. I had always imagined it to be inhabited by bonneted women and bare-lipped but bearded men, like the ones in a coffee-table book on the Amish that sat in our living room and was never looked at by anyone but me. Molly started toward the barn. I followed her, looking at the dark house and wondering if some restless person was looking out his bedroom window, watching us coming.

No one challenged us, not even a dog or a cat. I wondered what she would do if a snarling dog came out of the darkness to get us. I did not think she would stab it. I had a theory, entirely unsubstantiated, that she was moving up the class chain, onward from birds to squirrels to cats to dogs and beyond, her destination the fat red heart of a human being, and I knew that once she had visited a particular animal class she would not return to it. According to my theory, she was storing the life force of everything she stabbed in the great blue stone in her dagger's hilt, and when she had accumulated enough of it, it would glow like the earth glowed in the space pictures that hung on the wall in our fourth-grade homeroom, above the caption "Nothing Is Impossible." And when it glowed like that I knew her parents would step from the stone and be with her again.

If the horse had a name, I never knew it. In the dim light of the stable I might have missed it, if it was carved on the stall somewhere. It was a tall appaloosa mare. Molly had brought sugar and apples. She fed it and whispered to it. It was the only horse there. The other stalls were empty, but looked lived-in. Molly was saying to the horse, "It's okay. It's all right. There's nothing to be afraid of." She smiled at it a truly sweet smile, and it looked at her with its enormous brown eyes, and I could see that it trusted her absolutely, the way I had read in stories that unicorns instinctively trusted princesses. In her right hand she held the knife, and her left was on the horse's muzzle. "Touch it," she said to me. "It's like velvet." I put my hand on the space just between its eyes. She was right. I closed my eyes and imagined I was touching my mother while she wore her velvet Christmas dress. When I opened them the horse was looking at me with its great eyes, and in them I could see my brother touching the horse, and behind him Molly striking with her dagger. It did not even try to pull away until the blade was buried deep in its throat. Then it rose up, pulling the blade out of her hand, and trying to strike us with its hooves, but they only fell on the wood of the stall. When it shook its head the knife flew out and landed at my feet. It was trying to scream, but because of the wound in its throat it could only make spraying, huffing noises.

I watched it jump and then stagger around the stall. I was still and calm until Molly took the first picture—I jumped at the flash. At thirty-second intervals another flash would catch in the horse's eyes. At last it knelt in a wide pool of its blood, and then it fell on its side and was dead. All the time it seemed very quiet, despite the whirring of the Polaroid, and the whooshing and sucking noises made by the wound, and the thumping. When the noise stopped I could suddenly hear crickets chirping, and Molly's frantic breathing.

Molly took me home and made me get in the tub with my pants rolled up. She washed the Vaseline from my feet, and the horse blood from my hair, and then she put me back in my bed, not an hour before the sun came up. I slept and dreamed of horses who bled eternally from their throats, whose eyes held perfect images of Colm, who spoke from their wounds in the voices of old women and said they could take me to him if I would only ride.

A real live police investigation inspired Molly to decide we must lie low for a while. While Anne Arundel County police cars cruised the night streets of Severna Forest we lay low, and even after they were long gone, we still did not go out. The summer ran out and school started again. Molly Pitcher mostly ignored me while we were at school, but she still came by occasionally in the afternoons, or on weekends. We sailed in her boat and once went apple picking with her grandparents, in an orchard all the way down in Leonardtown. Outside my bedroom window the leaves dropped from the trees in the ravine, so I got my clear winter view of the river, all the way down to the bay. In the distance I could see the lights of the Naval Academy radio towers, blinking strong and red in the cold. I would watch them and wait for her, my window wide open, but she did not come again until the first snow.

That was in December, just before Christmas break. That evening, down by the general store, all the children of Severna Forest had gathered under an old spruce, where a false Santa sat on a gold-leafed wooden throne and handed out presents. I knew he was a false Santa, but most of the children there didn't. It was actually Sheriff Travis, dressed like he was every year in a Santa suit, handing out presents bought and delivered to him by the parents of all the greedy little children. He sat in his chair, surrounded by bags of wrapped toys, and made a big fuss over whether or not this or that child had been good throughout the year. When he called my name I went up and dutifully received my present from his rough hands. It was a Fembot doll, the arch nemesis of the Bionic Woman doll, which had taken up residence in my room, after Molly rejected it. I was playing with it in my bed when she made her sudden and unexpected appearance at my window. I had to get up and open it.

"Go down and get your coat," she said. "It's cold out there." I did as she told me. My father had left for the hospital shortly after we got home from seeing Santa, and my mother was asleep in her room, exhausted from an all-night flight from Lima. Almost all the other Severna Forest adults were down at the clubhouse, having their Christmas party. Several of them were famous for getting drunk on the occasion, Sheriff Travis especially. He kept his Santa suit on all night, and people talked about his antics for weeks afterward. They were harmless antics, nothing crass or embarrassing. He sang songs and said sharp, witty things, something he seemed incapable of doing at any other time of the year, drunk or not.

Already there was about an inch of snow on the ground when we left. The storm picked up while we climbed a tree outside the clubhouse. We waited there while the party began to die down. I could see my parents' friends dancing, and Sheriff Travis standing on tables and gesticulating, or turning somersaults, or dancing with two ladies at once. Music and laughter drifted through the blowing snow every time someone opened the door to the hall. I got sleepy listening to the sounds of adult amusement, just like Colm and I always did when our parents had one of their dinner parties, something they did often back before he died. With our door open we could hear them laughing, and sometimes someone playing the piano, and I always fell into the most peaceful sleep listening to that noise.

I fell asleep in the tree, with my head on Molly's shoulder. We were wedged close together, so I was warm. It was snowing heavily when she jabbed me with her elbow and said, "Wake up, it's time to go." She climbed down the tree and hurried off. I jumped down, knocking snow from where it had accumulated on my back and shoulders, and I hurried after her. She was moving back toward our houses, toward the tee of the seventh hole. When I caught up with her I could see another vague shape stumbling through the snow, about thirty yards from us. We had to get closer before I could make out the distinctive silhouette of the Santa hat. Sheriff Travis was famous for refusing a ride home every year. He was very proud of the fact that, no matter how drunk he got, he always found his way home. He lived down by the river, in a modest cottage that I imagine must have been lonely, because his children were gone and his wife was dead. He was taking a short cut across the golf course. I knew he would cross through the woods beyond the green to Beach Road.

But we had caught up with him by then. He was singing "Adeste Fideles" in a loud voice and did not hear us come up behind him. Molly Pitcher, when we were about ten yards away, had taken out her dagger and handed me a short length of lead pipe. "Be ready," she said. When we were closer, she suddenly ran at him, looking slightly ridiculous trying to run through the deepening snow with her short legs. But there was nothing ridiculous about the blow she struck, just above his wide black belt, about where his left kidney must be. He fell to his knees, and she struck again, this time at his back, almost right in the middle, and then again at his neck as he fell forward. He screamed at the first blow, just like I thought he would, a great, raw scream like the one my father let go in the hospital room when Colm finally stopped breathing. She stabbed him one more time, in the right side of his back. In the dark, his blood was black on the snow. He lay on his face and was silent. I stood in the snow, clutching my pipe and wondering if I should hit him with it.

Molly grabbed my hand and dragged me after her. She ran as fast as she could, through the woods, then along Beach Road to a point just below our houses. "I got him," she was saying breathlessly, in a high voice. "I got *Santa*." Twice we had to crouch down behind tree trunks because of the approaching headlights of the last few stragglers headed home from the party. We tore up through the ravine, past Gulliver's headstone, and she gave me a push up the tree, saying only, "Put your coat back downstairs!" before running off to her own house. I did as she said. I would have, anyway. It grated that she thought I would be careless. I still had the pipe. I hid it deep in my closet, where the Spider-Man toys were still piled.

Back in bed, I looked out my window at the storm, which was still gaining strength. It would be almost a blizzard by morning. School would be canceled. I lay watching the snow that I knew was covering our child-sized footprints, covering Santa Travis's body. I thought of him dying, the coldness of the snow penetrating in stages through his skin and his muscle and his bone, a light veil falling over his sight like somebody was wrapping his head in layer after layer of sweet-smelling toilet paper, like Colm and I used to do when we played "I am the mummy's bride," or "the plastic surgeon just gave me a new face." I imagined Colm, waiting patiently by the door and suffering the snow to blow through to where he was suffering it to collect on him, or in him, waiting and waiting, peering at the slowly approaching figure.

Sheriff Travis did not die. A concerned citizen, worried because of the storm, had called his house. When he didn't answer, people went looking for him. They found him where we left him. He had not moved an inch, but he was alive. At the hospital my father took him to surgery to repair his lacerated kidney and fret over his hemisected spinal cord.

When he woke up he said he remembered everything. Despite the darkness of the night, and the snow, he gave fairly detailed descriptions of his two attackers. Two large black men had done it, he said, one holding him while the other stabbed him and called him "Honky Santa." Police visited the community just outside the Severna Forest gates, and two men were arrested when Travis identified them in a lineup. I saw them in the paper.

Molly was furious that Travis hadn't died. I had never seen her so angry as when she stood in my room, kicking my bed so hard that the wall shook and the "First Mate" sign fell down with a clunk.

"Why?" she said in a loud voice. "Why couldn't he have died? I needed him to *die*." I thought about her hungry blue stone while she kicked my bed some more, until my father came to the door and said, "Everything okay in here?"

"Yes sir," she said. "We were just playing kick the bed."

"Well, please don't."

"Yes sir," she said, blushing. I looked at the sunlight on the carpet and wanted my father to shut up and go away. Don't make her angry, I was thinking. I didn't want her to get him.

When he was gone, she said, "It's just not fair."

I thought it would be many more months before she returned for me at night. I thought we would lie low, but she came back soon, after only two weeks had passed, at the beginning of the second week of January. She had been gone, down to Florida with her grandparents over break, but she came for me the first night she was back. While she was in Florida, bitter cold had descended over the Atlantic coast from New York to Richmond. The river and even parts of the Chesapeake were frozen over.

When we went down the ravine to Beach Road, I thought for sure we were going to Travis's house, to finish him off. But when she got to the road she crossed it and stepped over the riverbank, onto the ice. She turned back to me. "Come on," she said and went sliding over the ice in her rubber boots. She went past the pier and the boat slips, out into the open water. Her voice came drifting back to me. "Don't be such a slowpoke." I hurried after the place where I thought her voice was coming from, but I never caught up with her—perhaps she was hiding from me. It was a clear but moonless night, and she was wearing a dark coat and a dark hat. I stopped after a while and wrapped my arms around myself. I was cold because my parents were both home and I did not dare go down for my coat. Instead I had worn two sweaters, but they weren't enough to keep me warm. I knelt on the ice and looked down at it, trying to catch Colm's image. I heard her boots sliding over the ice out in the dark, and I thought about a story people told about the ghost of a girl who drowned skating across the river to Westport, to see her boyfriend. On nights like this you were supposed to be able to see her, a gliding white figure. If you saw her face it meant you would die one day by water. I looked downriver, searching either for the ghost or Molly, but seeing only the lights of the bridges down past Annapolis. There was a flash, and for a moment I thought it was the winter equivalent of heat lightning until I heard the Polaroid whirring and realized she had just taken my picture.

She did it again, and again, from different sides. I suppose she was trying to upset me, or make me afraid. Maybe she thought I would run and slip on the ice. I just knelt there, and then I lay down on my back and looked up at the stars. My father had shown me the constellation of Gemini. It was the only one I ever looked for, but now I didn't see it. Molly came sliding up to me. She stood behind my head, and I could not see her, though I could see her panting breath.

I thought she would speak, then. In my mind I had heard her speak this speech—I had played it out many times: "I need you," she would say. "For my parents. They're stuck in here and I must let them out. You don't mind, do you?" Of course I didn't. I would have told her so, if I could have. I had been expecting her to say this ever since she had stabbed the horse, because I didn't know what animal she could turn to after that, besides me. That night Colm had said to me, "So very soon now!" But it was not so soon, and I waited.

She didn't say anything, though. She only knelt near me and put a hand on my belly. She wasn't smiling, just breathing hard.

The camera hung around her neck and the dagger was in her hand. She raised my sweaters and my pajama top so I could feel the cold against my skin and the goose bumps it raised. She put the tip of the dagger against my belly and when she looked at me I was so tempted to speak a word.

"Goodbye," she said, and slipped it in with as much gentleness as I suppose could possibly have been managed. I heard my brother's voice ring in my head. He, too, spoke one word: "Now!" For just a moment, when I felt it enter me, I wanted it, and I was full of joy, but not for long. A cresting scream rose in me and broke out of my mouth. It was the loudest sound I had ever heard, louder than Travis's scream, louder than my father's scream, louder than any of the dogs or cats or rabbits. It flew over the ice in every direction and assaulted people in their homes. I saw windows lighting up in the hills above the river as I scrambled to my feet, still screaming. Molly had fallen back, her face caught in a perfect expression of astonishment. I turned and ran from her, not looking back to see if she was chasing me, though I knew she was. I ran for my life, sliding on the ice, expecting at any moment to feel her bodkin in my back. I cried out again when I climbed over the seawall and ran across the road, because of the pain as I lifted myself. As I clambered up the ravine, I could hear her behind me. At the spruce that led to my bedroom she caught up with me, stabbing my dangling calf, so I fell. I kicked at her when she came again, getting her knee, but she didn't cry out. I held my hands out before me and she stabbed them. With a bloody fist I caught her in the jaw and knocked her down, and I got up the tree and into my room, too afraid to take the time to close the window. I rushed through my door and down the stairs into my parents' bedroom, where I slammed the door behind me and woke them with my hysterical screaming. My mother turned on the light. Despite my long silence the words came smoothly, up from my leaking belly, sliding like mercury through my throat and bursting in the bright air of their room.

"I want to live!" I told them, though my heart broke as I said it, because as my mother turned on her light, Colm's image appeared in the floor-length mirror that stood on the opposite side of the bed. He was bloody, like me, wounded, I knew, by my cowardice and betrayal. I saw him looking at me while my parents jumped out of bed and rushed to me, with their arms out, their faces white with horror at the sight of their bloody child. I cried great heaving, house-shaking sobs, not because I was bleeding from painful wounds, or because my parents were crying, or because I knew Molly was on her way back to the river, where she would turn her knife on herself and at last sacrifice a human life to her soul-eating dagger, which somehow I knew would happen, as it did. I didn't cry like that because I felt guilty over the animals and people, now that I knew just how much a knife hurt, though I did feel guilty. And I wasn't crying at my impending betrayal of Molly Pitcher, though I knew I would say I had no part in any of it. I cried because I saw Colm shake his head, then turn his back on me and walk away, receding into an image that became more and more my own until it was mine completely. I knew it would speak to me only with my own voice, and look at me with my own eyes, and I knew that I would never see my brother again.

THE VISION
OF PETER DAMIEN

❋

Peter had never been sick a day in his life. When all seven of his brothers lay in bed with the chicken pox (lined up by height and by severity of the rash, Tercin, shortest and most mildly afflicted, on one end and Thomas, tallest and oldest and most ill, on the other), Peter waited on them with their sisters, untouched even though Tercin spit on him every time he came near enough to hit. When Amy brought home the pearly botch and Kathryn and Louise and Anne got the oak gall on their knees, he was unaffected, and even when the whole family got the yellow flux he was the only one of them not jaundiced in his eyes and skin, though he'd snuck a second helping of Mr. Hollin's tainted bluefish. Lonely in his perfect health, Peter had rubbed his skin with hickory root, but his mother discovered the ruse. She beat him with the stick called Truth and exiled him to the barn for a week, because the only thing worse than telling a lie was to become one.

So when he woke that Lammas Eve, shivering despite the August heat and yet soaked with sweat, he did not understand what was happening to him. He wondered if Tercin had thrown a bucket of springwater on him, but his only younger brother was sound asleep on the other side of their room, uttering the sobbing sighs he always made when he dreamed, and anyway it would be more like Tercin to soak him with horse piss. He lay quite still for a few minutes, watching the moon rise in his window. The room he shared with his brother had been the last to be glassed, and the window was only fifteen days old. He knew it was a waning gibbous moon, though you couldn't tell it by its shape—the ripples in the glass twisted it into a shape as soft and irregular as a round of the soft cheese Mrs. Clark made from her goats' milk. The bubbles in the glass caught the light in such a way that they startled him—it was his own birthday glass and he had cleaned and admired it incessantly for the past two weeks, and yet now it was more beautiful than ever, and he felt all of a sudden a tremendous sympathy with those bubbles. He felt suspended in the thick transparent air, floaty and full of moonlight. So this is a fever, he said to himself, realizing the feeling his brothers and sisters had described, and he noticed a little ache in his bones that faded as quickly as it came. He turned over in his dampening bed and fell back asleep.

"I was sick last night," he told his mother at breakfast the next day, careful to keep even the smallest measure of pride from his voice. Though he had grown to almost twice her size she wouldn't hesitate to use the stick called Humility (and it was the second-largest of the seven that stood in a barrel on the back porch) on him if she thought his better parts would profit by it.

"A dream of sickness?"

"No, I had a fever and an aching in my bones. Now it's gone."

"A strange dream," she said. "Fevers don't come and go so quick. Lucky for us dreams of sickness never come true in the summer." Still, she looked over her family at the table, everyone, even picky Tercin, eating heartily of the oatmeal and honey and eggs, and not a runny nose or a dull eye among them, and she made a sign that Peter recognized as a ward against bad fortune. She scraped the edge of her finger down her nose. To anyone who didn't know her well it would have looked like she was merely scratching.

He almost believed her—after all, she was always right about everything, whether the coming weather or a mathematics problem or the right name for a tune—but he couldn't put away the memory of illness like he could put away the memory of a dream. "I have been sick," he declared to the radishes as he worked that morning in the salad garden. Yet after squatting for an hour along the rows of lettuce there wasn't a trace of the ache in his bones, and by the time he had to leave for school he had nearly forgotten the whole thing, distracted by his work and by the usual noises of the farm. His father was down at the forge, making nails; he could hear his mother and Elizabeth washing flax; he could hear Tercin quietly cursing where he sat near the house with Caryn and Genevieve, making rick vanes. Even Tercin's cursing seemed a part of the lovely day. There is nothing wrong, Peter thought to himself, because just the previous week Reverend Wallop had scolded them all for not properly appreciating the absence of affliction.

But later that morning in school he got the curious, suspended feeling back. Sara Cooper was reciting a poem in front of the class, and Peter had just noticed that Reuben Claflin had appeared at the window to watch. Reuben was Tercin's usual partner in truancy, but Peter's brother was nowhere to be seen. He thought Reuben's habit of daring the window—placing himself just out of Mrs. Clark's view—was stupid. "If you're going to skip, skip," he said. "There's relaxing to be done."

Reuben was ugly—it was something that the whole town agreed on. In fact, his ugliness was the standard by which the ugliness of other boys was measured, just as Tercin's was the true standard of naughtiness against which the others' behavior was measured and judged. "Why, that tinker was at least half as ugly as Reuben Claflin!" Peter's mother had said just the previous Saturday of a man who had come selling in town. And if a child did something egregiously bad, then any parent might tell him, "You are a veritable Tercin Damien today!" And that was how Peter knew the fever was back—he felt cold, not hot, and suddenly Reuben's face was the most beautiful thing he had ever seen. The pits and scars and the eyes set as close together as a vole's added up to something so lovely he thought the pain in his chest was on account of it.

He had the floating feeling again, but this time it was like something in him as essential as his soul was flying out to cleave to the hideous perfection of the boy in the window. Sara was just starting her recitation:

The day is cold, and dark, and dreary;
It rains, and the wind is never weary;
The vine still clings to the moldering wall,
But at every gust the dead leaves fall.
And the day is dark, dark, dark.

Peter stood up, knocking his desk over. He hadn't wanted to stand up, or knock over his desk, or throw his arms out in front of him, or speak, but he said a word—it sounded a little like "Reuben!" though he wasn't trying to say "Reuben." It was more of a moan, the way a tongueless idiot would pronounce the name. It occurred to him to be acutely embarrassed, and to be afraid—nothing like this had ever happened to his brothers or his sisters when they had a fever. Mrs. Clark was striding toward him, very purposefully but ever so slowly, and every face in the class was turned toward him, every eye curious and many of the lips already turned in hard mocking smiles. He was suddenly very aware of the breeze blowing slowly through the window. Mrs. Clark's feet were thunderous on the wooden floor of the classroom, but there was no other sound, until with a pop like a coal jumping in the fire a seam appeared across his vision, across the walls of the classroom and across the blackboard and across Sara's arms and chest and hands. No matter how he turned his head it was there, even transecting Reuben's still-beautiful face. Another endless moment and the seam burst, and the day unraveled into another day. Peter stood utterly still and calm as the vision beneath rushed over him. Then he was only his sight—he had no hands or feet or any body at all. The wind was gone, and the noise of Mrs. Clark walking and the other students laughing, and the pressure of the breeze. He beheld an empty blue sky, and then a woman falling through it.

He thought at first that she was a man, because she was dressed in a black jacket and pants, but then he saw the bones in her face and the length and richness of the hair that coiled around her head as she twisted in the air. She fell toward him, then caught him in her descent—though she never touched him, she tangled him up in her fall. He felt the lurch in his stomach, and the sting of the wind against his skin, and now he was close enough to see how frightened she was, and to understand that she was screaming, though he could not hear her. They spun together in the air—he caught a glimpse of a crowd standing in the middle of a stone causeway. They twisted again and he saw the two silver towers burning against the lovely blue sky.

Then he was in the classroom again, flat on his back on the floor. Mrs. Clark was kneeling next to him, her hand steadying a ruler stuck in his mouth. Sara was staring down at him, along with the rest of the class.

"Think of green fields!" Mrs. Clark said to him, speaking loud and slow. "Calm blue seas! Relaxing cloudless skies!" She explained to him—and to all the class, because not a sparrow dropped dead through her window or lightning struck the fields outside but a lesson of natural science was generated—that his brain had become overcome by the intense sincerity of Sara's delivery, and so he had a fit.

"No, ma'am," said Sara, putting her hand on his head. "I think it's more than just the poetry. He's burning up."

"It might be the orange glanders," his mother said. "Or the willow fever. Or the early early dropsy." For each malady she had a separate poultice, and so all afternoon Peter sat restless and bored under strict directions not to disturb the plasters on his back and chest and belly while the rest of the family kept busy with the Lammas preparations. He wanted to be heaping up the ricks or laying the bowers or cooking, anything to distract him from thoughts of the falling woman. He hadn't told his mother or anybody else about what he had seen. People see things when they get a fever—he knew that from the stories his brothers and sisters told. Caryn had dreamed that she saw their mother come into the room with a dripping bloody mallet, and as she held it over her in a way that was more blessing than threat, the drops became dark insects in the moonlight, and took wing to fly around the house. Horace had seen fiddling rabbits, and George a strange lady made all of fruits and vegetables. Peter wanted to tell them what he'd seen, because his vision was grander and stranger than any of theirs, but when he considered it he felt a drop in his stomach, like he was falling again, and he found himself sweating again, though the fever was long gone. "Nothing scary about a lady," he told himself, sitting in the kitchen while his mother chopped carrots, "even when she's falling through the sky."

"What's that?" his mother asked.

"I'm well," he said. "I'm perfectly well. Can I take off the plasters and go help with the chores?"

"Tomorrow," she said, but she relented two hours later, and he just had time before dinner to help Caryn finish her vanes. Then, except for the excitement and anticipation of Lammas, it should have been an ordinary evening. There wasn't a touch of fever on him, and when he held his hand out in front of him there wasn't even a tremble in it, but the lady stuck in his mind. When he closed his eyes he could see her, arrested in her fall: her legs up above her head and her face obscured by a dark curtain of hair. Caryn's blue dress, the same one she'd been wearing all week, was suddenly the color of that sky, and when Tercin stuck his sausages in his potatoes, trying to sculpt a goat with horns, all Peter saw were the two burning towers. He reached over with his fork and knocked the sausages down.

"What'd you do that for?" Tercin asked, and Peter only said one shouldn't play with one's food. But he thought he hid his discomfort well: he talked excitedly about the maze George was building for the coming feast, and though his mother had an appraising look about her whenever she caught his eye, and he caught his father frowning at him in the middle of the blessing, nobody mentioned his fit again, and his mother only put a single plaster on his chest before she said goodnight.

"You got the creaky doom," Tercin said, after their mother took away the light. "Everybody dies from that."

"Go to sleep," Peter said.

"I'll go to sleep," Tercin said. "But not like you. You will sleep the sleep of death. Nobody wakes up from that. Not until the last trump is blown. Goodnight, brother. Goodnight and goodbye!"

"I'm not even listening," Peter said. "None of your dumb talk matters."

"Yes, that's a sign. The deafness and then the spots and then the feeling in your skin like you're being flayed. Oh yes, I heard about another case down in Homer. A girl who took a month to die but she was suffering the whole time. Suffering!"

"Can't you just be good to me for once?" Peter asked, and then turned on his side and put his pillow over his head, not waiting for Tercin's answer. His brother was quiet after that. Afraid to close his eyes, Peter took a long time to fall asleep. He was afraid the woman would be there, painted on the back of his eyelids, suspended in the blue air. Yet when he slept he dreamed not of her but of Sara. He was salting corn for her at the feast, sprinkling grains from a cellar and asking her, "Is it enough, my love?" and always she said, "Just a little more, my darling!" And he would have been content to salt her corn all night long, but he was woken out of the dream by a gentle tickling on his face. Tercin was standing above him in the square of moonlight from the window, a brush in one hand and a pot of ink in the other.

"Aw shit," his brother said, throwing down the brush in Peter's bed, and slamming the ink pot down on the floor. He stormed out of the room. Peter washed his face in the bowl on their dresser. When he fell asleep again he dreamed of nothing at all, and when he woke the next morning he felt entirely well, no hint of fever and no ache in his bones, and even when he tried he could barely remember what the falling lady looked like. He was delighted to discover that he couldn't even remember if her hair had been brown or black.

His mother pronounced him well at the breakfast table, and no one tried to keep him from assisting with the final preparations for the Lammas feast. After lunch he helped George lay down the maze, placing the sheaves as his brother directed, pretending not to study it too much, because he would run the race with all the other children later that evening and didn't want to give the impression of cheating.

At the start of the feast, as Reverend Wallop blessed the corn and the meat, and during the marionette dance, a few people, Sara's mother and Mr. Hollin and some others, gave Peter wary stares. It's not a light thing, to have a fit, no matter Mrs. Clark's airy theories of the cause. Everybody knew it was bad luck to have one, or be around someone who had one, and Sara's mother had even suggested that they delay the Lammas feast by a week, so it wouldn't be spoiled by the bad omen. And he saw Tercin whispering here and there, spreading fantastic lies, no doubt—he had twelve more fits since he came home from school, one every two hours, yes, with every even set of chimes from the kitchen clock. But his mother turned away the appraising looks with her own glare, and his father came up behind Tercin as he was telling a tale and slapped him in the head so hard he fell off a bench. Then everyone laughed at him, and someone pointed out that it wouldn't be a proper Lammas if Tercin Damien didn't suffer for his mischief. Tercin spat and slouched off with a chicken leg in either hand, no doubt to find Reuben, who never missed a feast or a celebration, but always inhabited the darkness just beyond the reach of the bonfires.

Peter spared a thought for the fires, and how they had a thing or two in common with the burning towers in his dreams, but the vision seemed a hundred years away by then. And when Sara sought him out and lay down next to him, she took up all his attention.

"Peter," she said. "Do you know what I am thinking?"

"You wanted more sugar on your corn?"

"What? Who puts sugar on their corn?"

"You smelled something foul when you passed by Mr. Hollin's bottom?"

"No. You're awful at this game."

"Reverend Wallop says that only Satan knows the secret thoughts of girls."

"If you ever listened to the overblowing fool you'd know he says, 'Only the dark one knows the darkest thoughts of man.' It's phrase number seventy-two of the hundred he learned in Bible school. I'll give you one more try before you lose."

"And what's the consequence?"

"Something gruesome and surprising. Once more . . ."

"Well," he said, folding his arms over his chest. "Maybe it's that . . ." He didn't know what to guess, and he hated games, and he thought it was just bold enough to suggest that maybe she was enjoying herself. Before he could finish, George blew the Lammas horn, summoning boys and girls under the age of sixteen to run the bower. Sara was on her feet and halfway there before Peter was on his knees. "Maybe you are thinking that this is going to be a perfect evening," he said, and chased after her.

There was only a single torch burning at the center of the bower-maze, not light enough to make more than shadows of the children who were hurriedly picking their way toward the center. Whoever got there first would get a prize. Peter passed Sara when she got trapped in a blind end. "You should have stuck with me," he said, and she only frowned at him.

He noticed the brightness before anything else. Just when he was ready to break into a run—because he and Edgar Minton had both discovered the right path at the same time—he realized that he could see Edgar's face very clearly, down to the pattern of freckles that broke over his nose in a shape like the Big Dipper. It was like Edgar's face had turned into the sun, except it was ten o'clock at night and it had been full dark for two hours already. "Edgar," he said, "what's the matter with your face?"

"I know what's the matter with yours," Edgar said. "It's ass-ugly!" And he ran off toward the prize, while the patch of sunlight he abandoned spread over the bower and the field, and blue sky washed out the night.

"Oh no," Peter murmured, and turned when he heard a hard thump to his left. There was a lady there broken on the ground. Another fell on his right, a man this time—Peter collapsed, sure that he was felled by the rushing flight of something escaping from the man's body. He had never seen such a thing as a body twisted and ruptured like this, and he wondered if anyone ever had seen such a thing. "Help!" Peter said. "Help him!" But though he was not alone on this day, everyone else around was standing and staring at the burning towers. The maze had grown—it looked a mile across instead of a hundred yards—and the towers stood where the torch had, both shining in the bright sun but only one of them on fire. Here and there Peter saw other boys, Samuel Finch and Caleb Borley and John Sterling, arrested in the maze, hands shading their eyes as they watched the tower burn.

People were still raining out of the sky, but none fell so close to Peter as the first two had, and he couldn't tell from far away if any of them were his lady. He got up and ran toward one, leaping over the sheaves or just running right through them, violating the law of the maze, but before he ran a few yards, another would fall a little closer, and so he would turn to them, shouting, "Help them!" all the while. He didn't know how long he continued like that, running all over while everyone else was just standing and watching, until the noise came, something that broke in on the quiet burning, a roar and a scream that seemed the perfect sound to match the singular vision. Just as he was sure no one had ever seen such a thing as a body broken like that man's, or a tower such as this burning in the sky, certainly no one had ever heard a noise like this. A voice familiar to him cried, "Beware the angel!" When he turned he saw that it was Sara, standing not twenty feet from him, pointing away south, where something enormous was rushing through the sky. He supposed it might have been an angel—surely they were this fast and enormous. It passed over in an instant, and the noise and presence of it pressed him to the ground. With his chest pressed against the bloody grass he lifted his head and saw it collide with the unburnt tower—quietly, its huge noise disappeared into the fire it made. Then the only noise was Sara's screaming. The night came back in a snap, and only the torch and the bonfires were burning, illuminating a different chaos—twelve children caught in the maze, kneeling and weeping or screaming or trembling violently, their parents holding them or hopping and shouting at their sides. Someone was saying his name, not Sara but his mother, standing next to him. He became aware that her hand was on his shoulder and pushed it away. "That hurts," he said, because suddenly it did, there was a wild aching there.

You wrote that you are tired of being sick. Tired of your bones hurting and the mysterious bruises, and tired of Tercin. For someone so stupid his deprivations are clever, and he has a certain cruel genius. Sometimes I think he is not stupid after all, only distracted by laziness and spitefulness, and if he devoted but a quarter of the time he spends torturing you to studying, he would grow up to be President. But never mind him, dear friend, and never mind the fevers and the sores beneath your tongue. One day you will be free of him, and one day you will be free of this illness. Good or bad, brothers depart, and so must sickness. And I don't mean either that we will be free of it in death.

We missed you in church yesterday. Or I did, anyway . . . I do not think Wallop noticed your absence—for all that he prayed for us with increasing fervor all afternoon—Let this sickness be lifted, let it depart from them forever!—he hardly ever looked our way, as if it were catching at a glance, and as if it had made anybody sick yet who was older than nineteen years. I did miss you, though. All of us on two benches (Wallop said it was so the healing could find us all at once—does the hand of God need that help? I wanted to ask. We all knew it was quarantine). Eleanor sat between me and Sam Finch. We mortified her with our whispering, and she tried to quiet us with great vigorous shushes from out of the bottom of her belly, and made such a noise finally that Wallop turned to her and asked, "Ms. Crowley, can you tell me the meaning of this afflicting vision?"

Eleanor blushed so hard I could feel my own cheeks burning from the heat in her face. In her panic she looked at me and then at Sam, and then clear across the church at her mother, but the lady only stared into her lap. Then she looked back to Wallop and began to recite the Lord's Prayer in a tiny, frightened voice. He let her finish and said, "Indeed. Is there any other answer but prayer, in the face of such a question, and in the face of such an affliction?" I've never liked the man but never hated him till then, because I understood all of a sudden that my life (and yours, and Sam's and Edgar's and Aaron's and Lily's and Elizabeth's and Connor's and even Eleanor's—unless she is faking!) depends upon the answer to that question. Wallop would have us paternoster on it but I think the answer will require a more vigorous and dangerous pursuit. Yet he was right about that one thing. It

doesn't happen for nothing—we are not transported so fantastically
for no reason. The vision is a challenge and its meaning is a cure.

"An upsetment in the blood," said Dr. Herz, summoned all the way from Cleveland by Sara's father. For her he prescribed opium and antimony and cinchona, and though Arthur Carter was the only man in town who could pay him, he visited every sick child—by August 20, a week after the Lammas feast, there were sixteen of them lying about in various states of torpor. He came to Peter last, and over the objection of his mother, who had already formulated and initiated a plan of treatment. "Does he know lady's mantle?" she asked Peter, her captive audience, and anyone else who would listen. "Does he know motherwort or neem? And what's a nettle to him but a weed and a nuisance?" But her husband insisted.

"A grand and severe upsetment," the doctor continued, stoppering up the little glass vials he'd filled with specimens—every fluid or ichor he could coax from Peter he sampled and stored for analysis back in Cleveland. "That explains the visions. Heaps of blood in the brain block up the sinuses that usually drain away overheated thoughts—hence a vision of flame. Didn't you mention a burning tree, my boy?"

"A tower," Peter said, staring out the window at Tercin, seated on a rock and worrying a carrot with his nail.

"Ah—no doubt it'll be a tree in a few days, and then the other children will see a tree. It propagates, you see, like a ripple in a pond." He made a motion to illustrate the spreading effect, pushing out with his two hands and then sweeping them apart so it looked like he was trying to swim through the air. "Do you see?"

Peter said no, but his father nodded, and asked again, "How do we make it better?"

"That's simple enough," said Dr. Herz. "I'll have my elixir made up in a few days, and be back with it by Friday. Mr. Carter has kindly agreed to purchase enough to supply the whole town, though I suspect if we treat Peter the other cases will resolve on their own."

"God bless him," his mother said blankly.

"God bless us all," said Dr. Herz, "when we are subjected to trials, and sickness is always a trial. But what's a trial but a test, and how else do we become perfect except through examination, and what's perfection except the accumulation of mastered adversity?"

"We must wrap him in olibanum and meadowsweet flower," his mother said, and Peter stopped paying attention when she and the doctor started to bicker back and forth. He watched Tercin instead, who suddenly ate his carrot in three huge bites, then leaped up to roll and tumble in the grass, turning cartwheels and somersaults and running to jump off the woodpile and turn a forward flip. It was a display of perfect health and freedom meant to gall, but it only made Peter sigh, and wonder at his brother's malice. "It doesn't hurt," he'd tell him later. "You shouldn't bother with it 'cause I don't even notice."

Something popped in the room—there was a noise like a whip snapping, and then a rustle like heavy curtains in a strong wind, and a stab of pain in Peter's hip. He winced and drew up his legs. His mother opened her mouth and put a hand on his chest. She opened her mouth and spoke a question to him, and even though he couldn't hear a word of it he could tell what it was by the shape of her lips—"Is it the pain again?"

"I'm deaf!" he said, looking to his father, who was moving his lips rapidly and silently. "But I'm not—I can hear me!" And when he knocked on the windowsill he could hear that, too, but his parents and the doctor were all jabbering at him silently, his parents' faces twisted with worry and the doctor looking smugly calm. Peter thought he was saying, "Of course you are deaf! It's all part of the upsetment, my boy!'

Another snap, another twinge in his hip and a stab in his back, and then he was immersed in noise—his mother and his father and Dr. Herz were speaking, but in voices that were not their voices—from his mother came a man's voice that sounded like his father when you just woke him up after his Sunday nap, and his father spoke with a lady's voice, and Dr. Herz sounded like a little girl.

"There's a great deal of smoke billowing from the towers, Phil. We can see flame coming out from at least two sides of the building," said his mother.

"That looks like a second plane has just—we just saw another plane coming in from the side," said Dr. Herz.

"I don't believe this!" said his father. "The second tower has exploded from about twenty stories below in a gargantuan explosion." All of them were reaching now to steady Peter and calm him, because he was pressing himself against the wall and the window to get away from them.

"Be quiet!" he shouted at them. "Just hush up!" He felt a fever growing, and had the idea, with them pawing at him, and the fever coming on like it was reaching to gather him up, that he could get away from the vision before it came, if he only tried. So he launched himself off the wall, and rolled through them, out of the bed and onto the floor. And before his father could even turn around he was through the kitchen and out the door.

"What's your hurry, brother?" Tercin called to him as he passed. Peter didn't reply but tore away down the path and past the smithy and into the empty fields, sure that the vision was just at his heels. He hadn't thought such speed was in him—he'd been in bed for days, and just that morning the effort of cutting his breakfast ham had drained him. It seemed the faster he ran, the faster he could go. For just a moment it was thrilling, to sprint over the soft earth, to outdistance his illness and escape the vision. But it caught him before he was halfway across the field. The roar of the angel overtook him, and when he looked over his shoulder he saw its shadow rushing along the ground, though the sky above was empty even of birds and clouds. He found somewhere inside himself another burst of insufficient speed. When the shadow caught him it lifted him up, and then the field and the ringing forest were gone. Everything familiar to him was replaced by the blue sky and the shining towers, and he rushed toward them, part of the angel now, feeling angry and exultant and awesome and afraid.

Dr. Herz's potion tastes to me like a combination of rust and pine. Sam says gin and blood. Edgar Minton said pigshit and Sam asked him (all this by letter mind you) had he eaten pigshit, to know how it tastes? Edgar said he had smelled it and that's how he knew. And so they launched a five page argument over whether to smell a thing is always the same as to taste it, and declared at last that someone was going to have to eat pigshit to know for sure, and vowed that as soon as they were feeling better they would force Reuben Claflin to do it. So must Eloise have written to Abelard! I get pages and pages of this—the pile from these two alone is six inches thick on my shelf and yours is only one. Not to scold, though.

Father says the stuff is already helping. He tells me how much better I look, as if mere insistence could make it so. I feel the same, though the elixir helps me sleep, and isn't that a blessing? Still, my lady comes more frequently than ever—five or six times a day now. Do the visions come so frequently for you? Your lady is not my lady, you said last week, but you know I am starting to think they all share a quality, whether your falling lady or my lady in the window or Sam's burnt woman hurrying in front of the tide of ash. Maybe it was just elixir booze, but last time I thought I caught a glimpse in my lady's face of all the others. She was there at the window, same as always, staring out into the smoke, one hand on the glass, and same as always I marveled that any glass could be flawless and smooth, but her touch was my touch and I knew it to be true. Peter, how strange, but not how horrible, to be looking at her face, and to be inside her touch, and even to be looking out from her eyes as the angel rushed in. And then I saw it, a common feature not amenable to description. But this last time I also discovered a distinctive sadness in her, quite removed from the burning of the neighboring tower, and quite apart from what she read in the oncoming angel. She knew it was her death and felt . . . relief!

Well, it's a mystery and not just a chore and an affliction. Eleanor cries like a baby every time she has one, but I feel as elevated as debilitated by them. Such thoughts! Such feelings! It's almost worth the fevers and the pains. Dr. Herz says we shall all be well within a week, and looks to you to improve first as you fell ill first, yet he is also heartened by Sam's sudden absence of bruising. I told him his theory of propagation was more superstition than science. He said the evidence would bear him out.

Eleanor was here last night, borne on a litter like a queen by her brothers. They're all strong but hardly of a height, so she rolled and shrieked as they made their lopsided way up the street. She talked of nothing for an hour and then decided, out of nowhere, to slander you with blame. I smacked her frog-lips, and cut her with my ring. "A spasm," I said. I do get them sometimes.

Father has relented, and so I'll see you this Saturday. Be well, friend!

Peter dreamed of health the way he had used to dream of flight. To climb slowly over the treetops, moving his arms as if he were swimming through the air, seemed like the most usual thing in the world until he awoke. Then he realized what he had been doing, and scolded himself for failing to properly appreciate it, and for failing to make proper use of it—he never climbed high enough, or showed Tercin what he could do, or floated to Sara's window to take her out for a flight. So he awoke realizing he had been weeding in the salad garden again, pulling with his hands and his arms and his shoulders at a root that had wandered over from a beech, and when the bell had rung for school he had leaped up, dusted off his hands on his pants, and run full force down the path and through the woods that bordered on their farm. The school had been replaced by a half-scale model of the Colosseum, and that was what he wondered at in the dream. But when he woke it was the old usual strength in his hands and arms that he wondered at, which seemed as remote and miraculous as the gift of flight.

He was in his own bed—he only stayed in the window seat during the day—and saw by the moonlight on the floor that he was already late. This late in the summer it never fell across his door before two, and he had meant to leave by midnight. He listened for a moment for Tercin's snoring and for voices in the house, but it was so quiet he could hear the distant call of an owl in the woods. The effort of packing his bag had exhausted him earlier, and he had nearly been called out by Caryn when she saw him spiriting food out of the kitchen. "I'll bring you anything you like," she'd told him, and he'd said he got hungry in the very middle of the night.

He walked carefully, partly to keep from waking anyone, and partly because his balance was off, and partly because he was sure that a sudden movement might bring on a vision, and to have one now would be ruinous. All day he had husbanded his strength, and made his mother think he'd grown sicker, though in fact he felt better than he had all week. The kitchen door was the closest to his room. He nearly upset a candlestick with the edge of his bag. It teetered but didn't fall.

Outside he considered for the first time the distance to the woods, and the distance beyond that to a cave where Thomas had taken him once. It used to be a morning's walk, but now it seemed as far away as another country, far enough to make it a trip beneficial to all the others, if Dr. Herz was to be believed, and far enough to hide him from Mr. Hollin and his charitable intentions. Peter had heard them all talking in the kitchen two days before. They hushed their voices but he heard them plainly, as if the fever had sharpened his hearing, or some household wind was blowing their words directly to his ear. Dr. Herz spoke of a fulminating contagion, and argued passionately that the best thing for the other children in town would be a separation from the "index case."

"Then by all means take them away," his mother had said. Dr. Herz said politely that that wasn't what he meant.

"I know precisely what you mean, sir!" his mother had shouted then, and they were all very quiet. Peter knew they were listening for him to stir. When they continued they whispered even more quietly, but Peter was sure he could have heard them from a mile away. They argued, tense and polite, for another half hour, Dr. Herz describing in detail the homey comforts of his hospital in Cleveland, and Mr. Hollin assuring them again and again that every expense would be covered. Finally his mother threw them out—she told them goodnight over and over again, in response to every question they asked, until they just left. Peter opened his eyes enough to see them walking off down the path, hats in hand, each of them taking turns shaking his head. He heard the door open from the kitchen and was conscious for a long while of his mother staring at his back.

"Here I go," he said, after he had closed the door quietly behind him. It all went marvelously well for the first few hundred yards. He felt stronger with each step, as if walking were something that he only had to practice a little to master again, and he thought he would have enough strength left when he got there to sweep the floor of the cave to make himself a neat place to lie down in. But he wasn't halfway to the line of woods before he caught a hint of smoke in the air. Someone else is up late, he told himself, and has made a fire for tea. And believing that bore him up for a dozen more yards, until he couldn't ignore the alien quality of the smell. It wasn't just wood burning, and he noticed that his feet were feeling heavier and heavier.

Another few steps and he could not move his feet—though his legs were sturdy he felt stuck to the ground. His arms dropped down to his side and an apple he'd picked up off the kitchen table on his way out fell from his hand. Now the smoke obscured his vision, drifting across the smithy and obscuring the line of the woods. He felt a glow along his spine—something was forcing him to stand taller and straighter than he'd ever stood before in his life—and his eyes were lifted up. As if he were flying upward, the limits of his sight expanded: the school and Sara's window and the store and the church and even the curve of the night sky and Hamilton, where they left their lights on all night long. He cried out just before he felt the little sting in his leg, and then a moment later another at his cheek.

"It's just a kernel," Tercin said, stepping out from behind a tree, his slingshot dangling in his hand. "If I'd really wanted it to hurt I'd have used a stone." He drew on his brother again, standing just before him and aiming right at his face. Peter laughed because Tercin seemed so small. He was looking down at him from a thousand feet high, yet he could see perfectly the confusion and disappointment on his face, and hear him clearly even over the noise of wind and flames. The other tower was burning next to him. "Even with a kernel, I could put out your eye," Tercin said.

"Get away," Peter said. "The other angel is coming."

"Angels got no truck with me. I don't fear 'em. You're up late."

"Go away—it will strike you, too!" Peter said, though he wasn't sure why it would bother with something as small and crude as his brother. With his high sight he could see it coming, still very far but flying with such speed that he knew it was only moments away.

"Going for a trip!" Tercin shouted, finally understanding Peter's obvious purpose and slapping his pack. "Well, bon voyage and good riddance. Maybe we can talk about something else now at dinner, and somebody'll laugh again in that house. Even when we're not talking about you, we're talking about you!"

"It's coming," Peter said.

"There's other people in the world besides you, you know. Other troubles besides yours. But you'd never know it. In that house nobody'd know it. Well, go on, then. You want me to carry you?"

"Please," Peter said, feeling very small despite his height, and vulnerable despite his bulk, and sure that the violent touch of the angel would finally kill him, and surprised as much to find himself begging mercy from his brother as at how easily he threw off the weary despair of the long sickness to discover how very much he wanted to live. "Brother . . . please . . . do not let it strike me!" He thought Tercin must have heard it, because he turned and looked around him just before it arrived, and when he couldn't see it he turned back to his brother and looked in his face. Something he saw there must have overcome his natural animosity. He dropped his slingshot and turned and put his hands up and cried, "Get away!"

He was no impediment. The angel flew high above him and through him—gleaming, roaring, and big as a church, it struck Peter right in his heart and started a fire there. As it burned he made the biggest noise of his life, bigger than anything he thought was left in him after being ill so long, and though he couldn't walk, and Tercin had discovered his purpose, it was only then— imagining lights go on in his house and all through the town— that he felt he'd lost his chance of escape.

Very far below, Tercin was looking up at him, wonder and fear plain on his tiny little face. Peter wept at the pain of the fire. It loosened him. He shrugged, and pieces of his shoulders fell to the earth. Look out, he tried to say to Tercin, but he couldn't speak anything but sobs. People were falling from him, too. Leaping from out of his hair, dropping from his nose, squeezing like tears from the corners of his eyes—small as his brother they fell. He turned his head, shaking more from his hair, and saw that it was Sara standing next to him, just as tall and strong and ruined, but she had been struck first, and had been burning longer. Her bones were so hot he could see them shining through her skin. She spoke his name and then fell apart, her head riding a collapsing column of ashes and smoke to fall between her feet and shatter on the grass. The seizures took him then, and he didn't have to watch anymore.

The vision ceased for Tercin, too. While Peter twitched and moaned, Tercin lay prone with his hands over his head, and he didn't dare look up until Peter grew quiet. He looked around at the woods and the quiet night: there wasn't a burning youth or a falling body or a screaming angel in sight. He stood up and wiped his eyes and nose. "Look what you did now," he said to his brother, peacefully asleep now on the ground. "Now you gave it to me!" He kicked him hard in the ribs, and thought he could feel one break even through his boot. Still he kicked him again. "You nasty leper, now you gave it to me!" He turned and ran away into the woods, then came back a moment later for his slingshot. He kicked his brother once more and was gone again.

I saw you and I know that you saw me. I know you heard me when I spoke your name. I was about to say something else—something utterly important and wise. Now I forget it, of course, and I wonder sometimes if I spoke more than your name, if I actually gave voice to the feeling in me just before my burning bones gave out and I fell—I felt like I knew what it was about, that I understood the mystery beneath the affliction, and the reason that we are all suffering. A grand, high feeling—surely it would translate into unforgettable words. If I had spoken them I know you would remember them even if I didn't— but now nothing but silence from you for fourteen days. Are you pretending to be dead? My spies are everywhere, dear friend. Little Abby Crowley saw you reading yesterday afternoon in your window. You drew a picture of an owl and showed it to her through the glass, and yet you cannot write a few words to me.

Edgar is worse, perhaps you've heard. Maybe you have your own spies, or maybe your mother only tells you what she thinks it's good for you to hear. He has not been properly awake all week now, and he choked last night when his sister slipped the gruel between his lips. Now he has a fever. Dr. Herz spends three hours a day there patting his chest and back with a crystal glass. Artificial coughing, he says, because Edgar won't do it for himself. "He'll perk up," Dr. Herz says, "just you wait." I imagine him saying that over the corpse. Just give him a moment, he'd say, and prod him with some very special kind of stick.

I know what risk I run in telling you this. You will take it to heart in the wrong way, and say I was wrong when I said there was a strange and secret blessing in all this. It's only death, you'll say. Just another way to die, slower and more painful and more odd than most. Well, maybe for some.

Your brother is living with Reuben Claflin in a cave. Abby took a dime from Reuben to steal a pie and bring it to them. She gave the dime to me, as if that would undo the theft somehow. I enclose it because I didn't quite know what else to do with it, and surely Tercin owes you reparations for all the harm he's done. Abby is a clever little magpie. She described their situation and even did a sketch—it is all very cozy and domestic, and Reuben's hand is tender when he mops Tercin's brow. I wonder a little what he sees—I have had four visions since he fell ill and never found him once. Perhaps a debased spirit only perceives the horror, and hides itself from every decent friend in that world as in this one. In any case you should tell your mother he is thriving.

I am thriving too, Peter. Not that any ordinary person would notice it to look at me. The mirror me—the one that is all of this world and all surfaces—is spotted up and bruised and jaundiced and thin, and my hair, as Mother tells me, has lost its spirit. But beyond my body

I am a growing giantess, and every time I enter another vision I get a little closer to an end that I know is not death. You are a giant too—I see it no matter how you seek to hide from me. We stand over all the others the way the towers once stood over us, before we became them. Don't you understand the progression—from frail little person to soaring angel to monolith? What next, except the sky above it all, and a spirit that comprehends everything, and is apart from nothing? Never mind Reverend Wallop's good news, here is mine: Something wonderful is coming, dressed in a raiment of fire and destruction and grief. We will be elevated, and understand, and returning to health will be such a small thing we'll do it in a blink of the mind's eye. So never mind poor Edgar. His ailing decline teaches a false lesson, one to be ignored. Come out, my love—come out of your depths. Maybe Edgar Minton is going to die, but we are going to live.

A BETTER ANGEL

"I wouldn't do that if I were you," she told me the first time we met. Six years old, I was digging under a log, trying to turn it up to look for worms underneath. This was back when my father still had all his property and I could walk for the whole afternoon without leaving his orange groves. I spent a lot of time amusing myself that way, playing games I made up, inventing friends to play with since I really had none of my own, or looking for buried Indian or pirate treasure. My sisters were all much older than me and hated to have me underfoot, and so they'd draw me false maps, age them by beating them in the sand with a baseball bat and burning them around the edges, send me on a quest. I fell for this sort of thing for years.

She was sitting in a tree, gently pushing at an orange where it hung near her face, making it swing. My imaginary friends were not the kind you could see. I figured her for a smart-aleck picker's daughter, since it was the end of the season and the groves were full of Guatemalans. She wore a sleeveless yellow dress with a furry kitten face on the front—I remember that very clearly, and remember wondering later how, if she didn't exist, I could have made that up. Her skin was very dark. Her hair hung past her lap. She looked to be my age and like she could be in my grade. I ignored her.

As soon as I got the log up I disturbed a nest of yellow jackets, which flew out and attacked me, stinging me on my face and my neck and my hands. I could see her watching me while I slapped at them and yelled and cried. She said nothing but stood up in the branch, and spread her wings out behind her, which amazed and frightened me. I tried to run back home but could hardly breathe—I was having an allergic reaction. But I found a group of pickers having their lunch in the grass, and collapsed in front of them, swollen and wheezing.

She came to see me in the hospital. High on IV Benadryl, I told anyone who would listen that there was an angel in the room, and the doctors and nurses thought that was charming. Even back then I was a quick and subtle thinker when I was stoned, and when my father asked me about what I had said, I could tell by his tone of voice that it would be best to pretend not to know what he was talking about. But when we were alone, and she stood silently at the foot of my bed, looking strange not just on account of wings but because she was dressed now as a doctor, with a white coat and a stethoscope and her hair done up in a smart bun, I asked her why she hadn't warned me about the wasps. "I'm not that kind of angel," she said.

Though my father only ever knew a tenth of the trouble I've been in, I was still his least favorite child, and the last person he wanted taking care of him when he got very ill. But every one of my sisters was pregnant—one very much augmented and on purpose, and the other two accidents of fate. How they celebrated the coincidence, and then rued it when it forced them to bully me back to Florida from San Francisco. I was in clinic when they called, and it's a testament to their power-of-three invincibility that they were able to blow through the phone tree and the two different receptionists who routinely deny my existence when patients try to find me.

"Papa is sick," said Charlotte.

"He's been sick," I said, because this had been going on for a year, and though nobody gets better from metastatic small-cell lung cancer, he'd been holding his own for months and months.

"Papa is sicker," said Christine, and Carmen added, "Much sicker!" She is eldest and barely most pregnant.

"He's in the hospital," said Christine. "There's an infection."

"In his bladder," said Charlotte. There are two years between each of them but they've always seemed like triplets, all of them looking the same age with their furrowed brows and disapproving hatchet mouths, all as tall and light as I am short and dark, all with the same blue eyes that seem just the right color to stare a person down with. My eyes, like my father's, are nearly black, and Carmen says I can hide anything in them.

"A little cystitis," I said. "So what?"

"Dr. Klar says he's very ill," said Christine.

"She doesn't know if he'll come out of the hospital," said Charlotte.

"She always says that," I said. "She never knows. She's an alarmist. She's a worrier."

"You have to go!" they said all together.

"*You* have to go," I said. "You go if it matters so much."

"We're pregnant!" they said. And then the individual excuses: mild preeclampsia for Charlotte and Christine and a clotty calf for Carmen. They can't travel from New York, where they all live within waddling distance of each other.

"People travel when they're eight months pregnant," I said. "People do it all the time!" Though I knew that they don't, and now the angel was sitting on my desk and shaking her head at me.

"You're a doctor," they said all together, as if that should settle it, and I wanted to say I'm impaired, and a pediatrician to boot. I could have confessed it right then, to them and to the whole world: *I am an impaired physician*, and then started down the yellow brick road to rehab.

Instead I quietly hung up on them. The angel was still shaking her head at me. She was dressed to shock, with a plastic shopping bag on her head, in a filthy housedress, and with a dead cat wrapped around either foot.

"I barely know him!" I shouted at her, and she didn't respond. And I told her I had a patient waiting, which she already knew because there is nothing I know that she doesn't know, and nothing I've ever been able to hide from her.

"Put that lady and her evil children behind you," she said, not looking up as I swept by her. She did not like Mrs. Fontaine for the obvious reason but what she had against her two kids I could not figure, though she has always done that, pointed out the ones that will grow into car thieves or lottery-fixers or murderers, as if I am supposed to smother them with the great pillow of righteous prevention when they are six months old.

The Fontaines were waiting patiently in the exam room, Zebadiah splashing at the sink while his mother fed his sister and his aunt read *Highlights*. "Hey, everybody!" I said, and I locked the door. Zebadiah toddled over to check it, innocently part of our enterprise. "Baby," said Mrs. Fontaine, meaning me and not her son, "how have you been?"

"It's been a rough day," I said.

"Well, your friend has got just the thing for a rough day," she said, and, taking a little foil-covered package from her diaper bag, she laid it upon the counter near the sink, and that is all we said about it because one of our terms of business is a nearly silent sort of discretion. I put down my envelope and she took it, and when her package was in my pocket, then we talked about her babies. Her sister did a find-the-picture puzzle while we talked, interrupting us to ask, "Where is the boot?" and "Do you see a flute?" I said I didn't know, and she said I must not be very smart if I couldn't find the flute hidden in the tree.

"If you already knew where it was, then why were you asking?" Mrs. Fontaine said, and her sister lowered her lids to half-mast and said, "I was testing him." And then she laughed, like that was the funniest thing in the world. I examined Zebadiah and then his sister, Lily, who was just four months old, fat and happy, and singing wordlessly as I listened to her heart and fiddled with her hips. The angel paced in the confines of the room, the cats going squish and squash as she stepped, and Lily seemed to be watching her. "A fire from heaven should come down right now," she said. Though the medicine was only in my pocket, just having it near made it easy to ignore her.

"She's beautiful," I said to Mrs. Fontaine.

"She's all right," she said, ducking her head and smiling, and her sister reached out to take the baby and hold her a moment and proclaim that she was indeed a beautiful girl, and then she handed her to her mother, who handed her to me, and then without knowing why I handed her back to the sister. Sometimes it just happens like that, something entirely bearable, the baby smiling and laughing and going round and round, from hand to hand to hand, and her brother shouting, "I'm beautiful, too!" and lifting his arms to be picked up, and all five of us laughing while the angel scowled impotently. I wanted it to go on forever.

*   *   *

"Does everybody get an angel?" I asked her one day, about a month after I met her, when it finally occurred to me to wonder if every boy and girl had a guiding spirit invisible to me. I looked around my first-grade class, squinting to see them, the girls in jumpers standing next to the seated girls in jumpers, the boys in blue pants, looking so ordinary except for their immaculate posture and drooping folded wings.

"Only the ones who will be great, or do great things. And sometimes being great is enough. The great things go out, generated as easily as thought or love. Do you understand?" I cannot describe how gentle her voice could be in those days.

"No," I said. So when we got home she guided me to my father's library, ignoring my pleas not to enter there without his permission, and sat me down in front of the encyclopedia. I opened a book to random pages and she marked with her finger the men and women who had warranted an angel to guide them into their greatness. There were fewer than I expected, and as many who were greatly bad as greatly good. I flipped backwards through the A's, only familiar with one in ten of the names she touched, making the letters shine in a way I could see forever after. Attila I knew, having just heard of him in history, and taken part in a little skit where I dressed up in my mother's unused furs and shouted at the head of the class with five other boys and the girl whose long black hair had landed her the part of the Hun. "But he was bad," I said, and she said that not everybody listened to their angel.

I hate adult hospitals, and adult medicine, and adult patients. I could not wait to get away from them in medical school, from their aching lower backs and chronic depression and get-me-out-of-work–related injuries. I hated especially the little old ladies with their parchment faces and frail broken hearts, who'd die if you frowned at them. Even a half-dead preemie is more resilient. And I hated the smell of the place—children are not so smelly to begin with, and even as they get sick or die they do not give off that odor that fills up adult hospitals, and seems to blow out of the angel's wings when she shakes them in agitation. It always seemed to cling to me after a particularly egregious fuck-up in medical school, so for days afterward just by sniffing at my fingers I would be reminded of how I almost killed this or that poor old zombie with my bad math.

The angel seemed to like the place, but then she is pleased by death, or at least it seems to get her excited the way that doughnuts or handsomeness do for me. She was always making a show of sniffing at people and predicting the hour of their demise. It became the only thing I was good at, distinguishing the really sick ones from out of the confusing daily crowd of patients that was presented to me as a student, and then as a resident, though I never could remember how to save them. As we walked to see my father in his room, for the first time she had a spring in her step, and though she was dressed still as a bag lady, she'd replaced her cats with tissue boxes, and shined her wings, and put on an elegant, if very dirty, hat. It might have been the hospital or just the fact that I had come that made her happy. To her mind I had done the right thing, and so she had taken it easy on me all during the trip, and now she bounced along like a schoolgirl. I think she would only have been happier if I killed myself.

The nurses at the station did not look up when I walked past on the way down to the end of the hall, where my father had his room, or when I hurried by again, fleeing from him. "Here he is," the angel said when I walked in—she'd run ahead the last few feet and passed through the wall. And she gestured over him like he was a new car or a sexy motorcycle in a showroom. When I saw him last he was the same dour, black-eyed man I'd known unchanging all my life, my six-foot-four, imperious, responsible reflection, a man who I always knew should have had an angel of his own. Now he was laid out diapered in a dirty bed, as bald and toothless and somehow as grand as Aslan on his table. He looked up at me when I walked in and said, by way of greeting, "You!" and managed to invest the word with equal measures of disappointment, accusation, and surprise. I dropped my book and candy box and ran out.

I always feel at home in a bathroom. Some nights as a resident I would withdraw into one and leave the intern to flounder and drown, claiming later that I never got the frantic pages when in fact I had turned off the pager and was sitting on the toilet with my face in my hands or taking little hits of whatever I was really into that month. There was a bathroom near the elevator on my father's floor of the hospital, a nice one-person arrangement with a lock on the door.

A locked door or a feeling of really needing to be alone is no deterrent to the angel. She was there in just a few moments—I never know what delays her, when she can travel at the speed of guilt and sometimes seems to be everywhere at once. She berated me while I hid my face in my hands, her voice making the little room seem very full, all the *what do you think you're doing*'s and *you get back there*'s seeming to bounce off the white walls in discrete packages of sound. I am not this sort of doctor, I said to my hands. I am not any sort of doctor, and I don't know what to do about what's back there in that room. And she said that even if you are the sort of doctor who doesn't know anything about medicine, and even if you only passed your certifying exams because you paid a certain Dr. Gupta to bypass the pathetic security measures taken by the American Board of Pediatrics against cheats and impostors, even you can recognize a patient at the extremes of abandonment and grief, even you can do the smallest human thing to improve his lot.

In answer I gave her a little toot. Not Mrs. Fontaine but another supplier, someone who was a sort of girlfriend, though only snortable heroin had brought us together, had a little horn on her keychain she would bring out in the face of any sort of adversity—a flat tire or a broken foot or syphilis, syphilis being a two-toot trouble. "Toot them away!" she'd say, and laugh really quite innocently. She was beaten to death by a boyfriend more passionate but less gentle than me, and died one night at the General Hospital in the ER while I was on duty seeing children. I recognized her worked-over corpse when I went into the trauma room to fetch a warm blanket for a cold baby.

The angel changed with just the smallest hit. She'd barely warned me not to do it before she was stretching and shaking her wings, and there was the awful stench just for a moment, and then there was another odor, fresh grass and cookies and new snow on the sidewalk. And she put off her haggery with a few shakes of her head, her eyes bright now but not icy like my sisters', and with a few sweeps of her fingers—it's always as if she is primping for me—she undid all the tangles from her hair. Three times she shook her hips and the housedress became a lovely blue sari, and her pretty feet were naked.

"Take that!" I stuttered at her.

"Better have another," she said, and I did. Then she stood in front of me with her hands on my shoulders, steadying them while they shook. It wasn't the first time that I'd felt like I was flying backwards; the toilet was a vessel in the air propelled by weeping, and with her hands laid upon me she was steering me.

"Do I have to go back there?" I asked her, when I was feeling better.

"Not yet, my love," she said. "Not until you are good and ready."

When I was a child she was always good, but this is not to say she was never awful. Though many days she was so ordinary a tagalong that I hardly thought of her as an angel, every so often she would put on such majesty it made me cower. One day in fifth grade I was half-listening to Mrs. Khemlani's talk about cowboys and Indians. "History always moves west," she said, because that was one of the truisms she announced at the beginning of the semester, and she liked to point out how right she was about things at some point in every lesson. Books will always be burned, she said, and women are always second-class citizens, and history from the dawn of time has always swept in a westward circle around the globe.

I was only half-listening, daydreaming about Chinese ladies and their very small feet, about which we'd just been learning in social studies. I was fascinated by the pictures we'd seen, and had held on to the little cardboard shoe I'd made, though it was supposed to be drying on the windowsill with the others, so I could turn it over and over in my hand. The angel was standing or sitting around the class in her usual positions, done up today in the dress and skin of a Chinese girl—sometimes her form obliged my fancy, though I knew I could not control it, having already tried to make her take on the shape of a dog or an ear of corn by staring and concentrating at her until she said to stop it.

On little crippled feet she hobbled up to the front of the class when she heard Mrs. Khemlani talking about the grand sweep of history, a look on her face that I had learned to associate with anger at something stupid she'd just heard. I was used to getting lectures that no one else could hear, or having her place a hand on a book I was reading to say, "Listen, it was not so."

"Once the most important city in the world was Nanking," Mrs. Khemlani was saying. "Then it was Athens, and then it was Rome. Later it was Vienna, and after that it was Paris and then London and then Boston and then New York. But, look here, now it is becoming San Francisco, and where next after that? My husband says outer space because he is an engineer and has a very scientific mind, but I say west, and so back to the East!"

Cindy Hacklight, my neighbor across the aisle, asked what this had to do with cowboys or Indians, but Mrs. Khemlani's response was drowned out for me by the angel's voice.

"Not so!" she shouted, stamping her foot at the head of the class, standing behind Mrs. Khemlani and growing out of her child's form. It was the first time I'd ever seen her in the guise of an adult, and she made herself huge. Her head scraped the ceiling and her wings spread from one end of the class to the other. "Not west!" she said, and pictures started to flash in her wings, men whispering in dark rooms, and soldiers at war, and tanks rolling through villages like they did in old newsreels, and people just sitting quietly together. She had stopped saying words but her wings were certainly speaking to me, images blaring out of the white depths and, more than that, feelings radiating off them so I knew sadness and joy and rage and sourceless love together and in succession, the images and feelings a speech by which she communicated to me the true sweep of history. "It's toward you!" she said, unnecessarily, because she had given me to understand myself as riding an enormous tide—sitting at my desk, I could feel the relentless pressure of history under my feet, pushing me up through some mysterious medium toward a goal I could not describe except by its brightness, but I could see it in that moment very clearly. I leaped up from my desk, dropping my little torture-shoe, and threw up my hands above my head and gave my best up-with-people "Hooray!" I was eleven years old and thought I understood what she had in store for me, and felt sufficient to it in a way I can't comprehend now.

"Yes," said Mrs. Khemlani, who thought I was applauding her theory. "Hooray! Hooray for *history!*"

Better to be a garbageman than a doctor, when your father gets sick. If I were a tree surgeon or a schoolteacher or a truffle-snuffler, or even a plain old junkie, then sickness would just be sickness, just something to be borne and not something I was supposed to be able to defeat. For months my sisters had wheedled me into meddling consults with my father's doctors, and I had pretended to understand what they were saying to me, and offered ungrounded opinions to them and to my sisters and my father. Even if I hadn't cheated my way through medical school, the task of recalling the lost knowledge of pathology from second year would have been beyond me. I make my living praising the beauty of well children. I love babies and I love ketamine, and that's really why I became a pediatrician, not because I hate illness, or really ever wanted to make anybody better, or ever convinced myself that I could.

But nobody deducts the credit I deserve for being impaired and a fake. The doctors hear you are a doctor and enlist you in their hopeless task, and fork over the greater portion of the guilt packaged up in the hopeless task. The nurses hear you are a doctor and hate you immediately for judging their work and for interfering. And the angel, who has catalogued my every failing and should know better, berated me for failing to save my father's life as it became more and more obvious day by day that he was going to die. It was the least I could do, she told me, because even this miracle is nothing compared to what I was supposed to grow up to achieve. And if I could do this, then everything else would turn around. It was the first hope, besides death, she'd offered in a long time.

"He is not an enemy you can outwit," said Mrs. Scott, one of my father's Tuesday chemotherapy buddies. He got out of the hospital a week after I arrived home, and for another month I took him every week for his infusions. Lately he was too tired to talk, or else just sick of her. He fell asleep during every infusion, and left me alone to talk to her. He confided that he hated the way she whored after hope—every week something else was going to save her life—and I'd think he was faking it just to escape her if I didn't know firsthand the beautiful thick sleep that IV Benadryl can bring. Every session they began a conversation about whatever late discovery she had made in the pages of *Prevention* or *Ayurdevic Weekly* or *High Colonic Fancy*, and five minutes into it he would tell her he felt oblivion pressing on his face, and five minutes after that his chin was on his chest and he was snoring softer than he does in natural slumber. And because I could not put a shoe heel deep into her mouth to shut her up, I always suggested a game of checkers or cards or backgammon. Dr. Klar's infusion salon was packed with those sorts of diversions.

We played chess, a game that usually generated a lot of thoughtful silence—she'd put a finger to her temple and stare so hard at the board that I expected it to start vibrating in sympathy with the intensity of her gaze—but today she was distracted and a little agitated, maybe because she was getting steroids, or maybe because my angel was sitting so close to her, and despite her optimism she was getting sicker from week to week, and I swear that as they get closer to death people can start to feel the angel's ugly emanations.

"It's not a game of chess, you know," she continued when I said nothing. "I think I just fully understood that right now." I put my finger down.

"What's that?"

"You know," she said, putting her hand on her chest. Like my father, she had lung cancer. "Oncoloquatsi," she whispered. That was the name she had assigned to her disease, and she always whispered it, as if to speak his name too loud would be to summon strength to him.

"Oh, him," I said.

"I know it suggests a game, how you move and then he moves—you pick a chemo and he counters with a mutation, or you find the perfect herb to overcome him and he produces another measure of resistance, and the doctors play the game from organ to organ until your whole body is a board. They even doodle you up like one." She pulled down on the neck of her blouse to show a piece of skin below her collarbone—it was just a cross to mark a target for radiation. "But this is only a surface-seeming. Look deeper like I have and you will see the truth."

"I think I've got you," I said, moving my bishop illegally. She didn't even look down.

"How often have I heard that from him? But he never has gotten me, and it's not because of my disciplined mind. It's because

I have learned to resist him in the very marrow of my being. The very marrow, Doctor. It's not a lesson you would have learned in school, but I want you to learn it. I want your father to learn it. I have disciplined my soul against this enemy, and he must do it, too."

The angel sidled closer while Mrs. Scott was talking. She leaned over and took a sniff at the lady's turbaned head. "Three weeks," she said. And then she put her nose close to the thin, shining skin of my father's forehead—every day his skin seemed to get a little thinner, or stretch a little tighter, so I was sure that just the faintest rubbing pressure or the lightest scratch would reveal the dull-white bone underneath—and said the same thing.

"Shut up!" I told her.

"It's hard to hear," Mrs. Scott said. "I know it's not your common wisdom, but you don't have to be rude." Dr. Klar came in before I could answer or apologize.

"Hallo, everybody!" she called out. Thirty years in southeast Florida had not dulled her accent much. This appealed to my father, who liked that she was German, order and discipline having always added up in his life to success. Her immaculate white coat seemed the least perfect thing about her, but just being in sight of it I felt accused of slovenliness and failure. "Here is the grandma of your better nature," the angel said the first time she saw her.

My father woke at the sound of her voice, and smiled at her. "Charlotte?" he said. A week after I took him from the hospital, he started mistaking people and places, thinking a nurse or some solicitous church lady was one of my sisters, or thinking he was in his childhood home in Chicago, calling out for a dog who died sixty years ago. Me he never mistook for anyone else, though he often seemed surprised to see me. "Still here?" he said some mornings.

"It's Dr. Klar!" she said brightly. She said everything brightly, even things like *What's the use* or *If he's alive in a month it will be a miracle*. She was one of those oncologists who speak life out of one side of their mouth and death out of the other. For my father she had only good news; for me only bad. I hated her.

"Darling," my father said, closing his eyes again and still smiling. "When is the baby coming?"

"Soon," she said. "The baby is fine. Everything is fine!" She reached out to pat his shoulder but I caught her hand.

"The bad shoulder," I said. He had metastases all over, but his shoulder and his back bothered him the most. He nodded his head and fell back to sleep.

"How is the pain, then?"

"Worse. And we're out of Percocet. He's out of Percocet."

"Easy enough to fix," she said.

"An ounce of meditation is worth a pound of Percocet," said Mrs. Scott.

"In certain traditions!" Dr. Klar said, then she beckoned me out into the hall. "I think it's time to stop," she said.

"Stop what?"

"Stop hiding!" the angel shouted.

"Stop the chemo," said Dr. Klar. We had this conversation every week. "What are we doing? What good is coming of it? Why are you coming here every week, when he could be at home?"

"He doesn't want to stop. He wants to keep going."

"Just put out your hand to him and he will be healed," the angel said. "Just put out your hand to him, and you will undo all the pain you've caused me."

"Does he know what he wants?"

"He's always confused here. You keep it too cold. And the Benadryl before the infusion makes him sleepy."

"Carl," she said, putting her hand on my shoulder the same way she did with him, comfort for a dead person. "It really is getting to be time." And the angel said, "It has always been time!"

Things started to go wrong between the angel and me after Cindy Hacklight showed me her pooty in seventh grade. Cindy had made a sort of cottage industry of showing around her pooty to anyone—girl or boy—who would give her five dollars, a large sum back before high school inflation. You got the feeling that she didn't really care about the money, but sensed that what she had wasn't something to show for free. She didn't need to be paid, anyway. There were no poor children at our school.

"Go not that way," the angel said. She saved onerous fancy-speak like that for her most serious moments, for things she really meant, for things that really mattered. But I went with Cindy into the forest behind the gym, where she leaned against a narrow poplar and swore me, not to secrecy, but to respect for what she was about to show me. It was one promise I've managed to keep all my life, to keep reverence for her bald little pooty, then in seventh grade and ever after, even when I met it again one summer when we were both home from college. "Turn your face!" the angel shouted as Cindy lifted her skirt. And the angel was ugly for the first time ever, having put on the apricot face of our headmistress, Ms. Carnegie. I looked back and forth between them, startled by the contrast, how beautiful was the one and how ugly the other, until Cindy, keeping her skirt up with one hand put the other on my head and turned my face to her. "If you're going to respect it you've got to *look* at it," she said.

The angel berated me for days afterward—how mild it seems in recollection, compared to what she dished out in later years and decades. "How is a seducing pooty like a grand destiny?" she kept asking me, and then she would answer her own question, and eventually she trained me to give the right answer. "Exactly not at all," I said. Yet awakening lust wasn't the problem, though eventually the lust that awakened made me a monster and a fiend, and I would waste, and still waste, half my life in thrall to it, screwing whoever would hold still for me in high school and forever beyond, to the exclusion of work and food and sleep, but never of drugs. I think it was the first time that something so ordinary was as attractive to me as the extraordinary things the angel said I must dedicate myself to. When I lay with Cindy on the scented ground in my father's orange groves, what I experienced was a very ordinary comfort, and when she raised her skirt in the woods I understood that I could want—so badly—something the angel thought I shouldn't.

My father had a little bell that he rang when he wanted something. Mornings, I would hear it and rise from the single bed I'd slept in when I was five and go downstairs to see what he wanted. At first after he came home it was to be helped out into the yard to sit in the sun, and then it was coffee or breakfast when he could not get those for himself, and then it was just to be turned or for help retrieving a blanket that had migrated down past his hips, and then finally he would just ring it and ring it as constantly as a beggar Santa, not knowing what he wanted, in which case I gave him a pain pill (and took one myself, always supremely faithful to my rigorous policy of one for you and one for me), and this would settle him.

Janie Finn was our hospice nurse. I always hated hospice, and hospice people, nurses with smart heels and smother pillows, and the women in charge of the palliative care programs, who seemed universally to be dark-eyed and dark-haired and very tall. They dress like nineteenth-century Jesuits and cherish crushes on death. But Janie brought me liquid morphine and Ativan—and either of those would be enough for me to forgive anybody the mere crime of being. "Your jab and your hook," she said in the kitchen the day she met us. She had placed the bottles in my hand—I hadn't even had any yet and already I could feel a lovely warmth coming out of them, and they seemed to catch the afternoon light in a very special way. Janie set her feet and threw out two quick punches. "A one-two against the pain," she said. "One-two! Give it a try." With a bottle in either hand I gave it a try, and, yes, my fists seemed to have a certain heft to them. I threw a punch at the angel and she actually ducked away.

I made free with the drugs, and made a lot of trips back and forth to the pharmacy, and imagined the little man in the back filling the bottles from two big coolers of bright, pure drug, and dreamed of following him back to put my mouth to the spigots, because I was sure that if I could just take enough, then the angel would be permanently transformed, and if it happened also to be enough to kill me, then all right. I was sure that she would take me someplace bearable. How she hated those little bottles. If I'd had them when I was twelve, I might have made a normal life for myself with their daily medicine.

"Just put out your hand," the angel kept telling me. "Touch him and make him well." Though she hardly ever screeched at me in those last few days, it seemed like a worse torture than ever, to have her demand the impossible of me so consistently, and to blame me like that for how he was getting sicker every day. It made me feel worse than anything she'd ever said to me. I could not ignore a homeless person on the street without her detailing the ways in which I was responsible for his misery, absent policies and initiatives never having established a common weal, as if the hundred thousand sins of omission that were my unfulfilled destiny added up to national and individual catastrophe. It was easier to bear when she blamed me for the woes of strangers, even when they fell out of the sky or burned in their churches. I can make even little children faceless, but my father could never be anonymous to me, and for some reason, as the weeks went by in Florida, I believed her, better than ever, when she told me that every wrong thing I'd done could be redeemed in one miracle, and that if I could make my father well with one hand, then with the other I could do the same for the whole world.

"Make me dinner," my father said, so I did. It was only three in the afternoon but no matter what time of day it was, the meal was always dinner, and always it was the same thing, a chocolate milkshake with a banana and a raw egg and a little Ativan in it. When I brought it to him he took a sip and he was done. He turned his head and opened his mouth like a baby bird—this was the signal for pain medication, so I took the morphine out of my pocket and dropped in a few drops. He smacked his lips and turned back to the television, then closed his eyes. "Now I'll take a nap," he said. "Go to your room."

I made going-upstairs noises but went outside instead. It was another brilliant blue afternoon. He kept saying he wanted a storm. We mostly watched television when he could stand to have me around in the living room with him, and we always watched the weather. It was hurricane season but all we'd had was near misses. "Look at that!" he'd say, pointing at a gigantic storm swirling across the Atlantic, or he would shout "Fool!" at the hapless reporters clinging to light poles and declaiming the magnificently obvious. Hurricanes were the enemy when I was a child—they tore up trees and scattered fruit. But now he spoke the names of the female hurricanes with great fondness. "I've always liked them," he said when I asked him about it.

Our nearest neighbor was a mile away, so nobody asked what I was doing when I hung the hurricane shutters on the living room and kitchen windows, and my father asked no questions from inside. He slept so heavily now that a few times, with his arms and legs always so cold, I thought he had already died. I nozzled up the hose and propped it so it would spray on the shutters, and just at dusk I turned it on. The angel was half-ugly and half-kind because I was half-stoned. "You play tricks on him when you should be calling him out of his bed."

"It's not a trick," I said. I spent another few moments watching the sky and taking just the smallest nip of the morphine and then went in. When I came into the living room with a candle he asked what was going on. "A big storm," I said.

"Finally!" he said.

We had a party during the storm, two more dinners and Ativan and morphine all around, and the storm picked him up, so he was more alert for a while and told me stories of hurricanes past, of ruined crops and toddlers surviving miraculously when a tornado stole them from their homes and deposited them in the next county.

"I know you have secrets," he said suddenly. And then he said, "Your sister tried to drown you when you were two—do you remember?"

"No," I said, and asked him to tell me more. But then he thought I was my sister Charlotte.

"How could you hurt a little baby like that?" he asked, and I said I've done a lot of bad things.

"Tell me about it!" said the angel. I took another drop of morphine, right in front of him because his eyes were closed, but then as if he could smell it he opened his mouth, so I gave him some, too. And then I took some more, and gave him some more, and then switched to the Ativan. But still the angel was a harpy. "Put out your hand!" she said. "Another angel is coming!"

"It's all right," my father said. And then he whispered, "Your mother tried to smother him once. Just a little, with a blanket, and she told me about it right away. But she was depressed, and that's what you do when you're depressed."

"If you were a great man," the angel said, slurring now, "if you were president—and you could have been president—then I would be a national conscience!"

"Shut up," I said quietly to her, thinking I had pitched my voice so she would hear it and he would not.

"Don't tell me to shut up, sassy girl!" he said, and I gave him some more morphine. Though he hadn't asked for it he sucked at the dropper when I put it in his mouth.

"You can do it," she said, her face flashing beautiful for a moment. And she showed me, putting out a hand that was soft and white on one side and hairy and rough on the other. She held it over his chest. "All you have to do is finally stop fucking up."

"You're ruining it," I told her, and took a swig of the Ativan, just a tiny sip really, but you are only supposed to take it drop by drop and I knew why as soon as I took the swig. It was too good, and it made everything too beautiful, not just the angel, whose ugly skin flew off as if blown by a real hurricane wind, so her wings were clean again and her naked face and body were open and compassionate. Even my father's face became beautiful, still yellow and sunken but now utterly lovely, and how strange to see a beautiful face that looked so much like my own. The room shined with something that was not light, and there really was a thrilling storm blowing outside and shaking the walls. Every so often he would reach blindly for something not there in front of him, and he did this now, so I reached with him, and the angel reached, too, all three of us putting out our hands together.

"You have to be ready at any time to have the conversation," Janie Finn told me, meaning the conversation where you sorted everything out and said your goodbyes, and the dying person sorted everything out and lost all their regrets. "You talk about things and then you let go," she said, making an expansive gesture with her hands, as if she were setting free a bunch of doves or balloons. It was just the sort of thing that hospice people always say, and it's because they say things like this that I think they should all be put slowly to death, half of them ministering to the others as they expire by deadly injection, having their conversations and dwindling, half by half, until there are only two, and then one, and a little midget comes in and shoots the last one in the face.

But suddenly I thought that this must be the conversation, as we opened our mouths in turn and shared something wordless and important and lovely, and the whole room seemed like a great relief to me, and I knew it must to him, too. The angel was struggling, though, seeming to wrestle with herself. Her face was beautiful but then her body was ugly again and my bottles were almost empty. My father's mouth was open but I took the last of the morphine myself and gave him a drop of water. He opened his eyes and looked at me and said it again, "You!" and he shook his head, then closed his eyes again. But when I put my head on his chest he didn't push it away, and though one hand was reaching out blindly above him, he let me put the other on my neck. "I want a better angel, Dad," I told him. "That's all I need."

"I'll take a nap now," he said. "Batten down the hatches and go to your room." But I stayed where I was, and took a nap myself. I woke up the next morning on the couch, the fake rain still drumming at the shuttered window, with no recollection of how I got across the room. The angel was in the corner, her face ugly again, but only in that way that all weeping faces are ugly. I sat down next to my father, who must have died sometime very recently, because though his face was cold and his open eyes already had the look of spoiling grapes, his chest and his belly were warm. I put my hands on his chest, and my head on my hands, and stayed that way for a long time before I called Janie to tell her that it had happened.

THE CHANGELING

My father and I stand in the kitchen, staring at the toaster and waiting for the waffles. Since my son became ill, we have been taking turns with the meals, so he handles breakfast and I do lunch and then we both take care of dinner. We have a waffle iron, but the prospect of making the batter was somehow too much this morning, and though I believe that waffles made from scratch would carry some premium of affection, I know once-frozen waffles won't matter to Carl, and I recognize my father's exhausted posture from the latter days of my mother's illness and my divorce, and I know better than to suggest that frozen waffles will somehow work against us today. Our stretched and inverted images look back at us from within the toaster-chrome.

A spring is broken inside the toaster, so nothing jumps up like it should. The waffles rise slow and stately. Carl used to say that the toast looked like it was rising from out of a grave, and made jokes about zombie-strudel and vampire Pop-Tarts. He wasn't an entirely normal kid, even before he got sick. My father takes the waffles out, butters them up, and puts them on a plate, then puts that on a gigantic silver tray of the sort a butler would carry around, complete with a handled silver dome. "Get the syrup," he tells me, and starts upstairs.

He pauses outside the door and knocks. He always knocks; I never do. He says it's important to treat Carl with respect, and I agree, but the thing presently in his bed could care less if we are polite toward it. It asks of us a specific set of behaviors and everything else is superfluous. "Who is it?" comes the reply. The voice sounds like dozens of voices speaking at once. Sometimes I convince myself that I can hear Carl's voice in there, sounding very small and incredibly far away.

"Who else?" my father says as he opens the door.

"I was hoping for satisfaction," Carl says from the bed. He is restrained there by soft straps that we took from the hospital. They are called posies and bring to mind the image of someone tied down with flowers, but they are not so benign as that. We only tie him down at night, and only because if we didn't he would wander into high places, the tops of bookshelves or the roof or a tall tree in the yard, to shout out requests for justice and vengeance and satisfaction. Aside from the restraints, it is his same old bed, done up in baseball sheets, and his same old room, covered with pictures of historical personages and dams and bridges and other engineering marvels, except that we have had to take down every picture of an airplane, because these made him cower and cry out in fear.

"Behold!" my father says, after I've undone the straps and shifted Carl up into a position he can eat from. My father takes away the silver dome with a flourish. He can manage the flourish even when he is dispirited and tired. "Waffles!"

"We are not satisfied with waffles," Carl says, his face drawn up in a look of haughty disapproval, but despite that look and his words his mouth snaps at the fork when my father brings it close, and chews and swallows eagerly. Though his words and his expressions seem to have passed into the possession of another, Carl's appetites remain his own and have become more childish as the weeks have passed. The mouth spews complex obscenities and harsh judgments but is partial to waffles and cheesy mac and vienna sausages. "Waffles are not justice," he says with his mouth full.

"But justice isn't delicious," says my father, though he is always telling me not to talk to "It," especially when we are trying to get Carl to eat. "And justice will never be the most important meal of the day."

"We are the dead," Carl says. "Where is our blood sacrifice? What have you done for us today?"

"Every good boy loves waffles," my father says, and shovels them in. I dart in with the napkin between bites, and catch the bits and half-chewed pieces that fall out of Carl's mouth. It's always easier to keep him clean during a meal than it is to clean him up afterward. He fought like a cat the one time we tried to get him in the tub, and even a sponge bath makes him wriggly and abusive. I keep my eyes down and try to tune out the noise Carl is making, bits of song in a dozen voices, and noises that are not words. But just as we are finishing up I look too long on my son's face, and his eyes, which have been rolling every which way in his head, following the action in some waking dreamscape, suddenly lock on to mine. It is always very hard to look away when this happens.

"Do you love your son?" the voices ask me.

My father hisses at me in an unnecessary warning. I know I am being baited but can never be silent in the face of that question.

"You know I do," I say.

"Well, what a way to show it, to abandon him. Abandonment

is practiced in degrees, and you have gone beyond the pale, it's true. He is practically one of us now."

My father is shaking his head. "Breakfast is over," he says. He puts the lid on his Jeevesy platter and walks toward the door. "Come on," he adds, because I am still sitting on the bed.

"I'll be right there," I say.

"It's not going to help," he says. "It's not . . ." He doesn't finish, just shakes his head again. He looks terribly sad, and Carl is smiling quite fiendishly.

"I'll be down in a second," I say.

"Goddamn it," my father says, and shuts the door.

"Goddamn it all," says Carl. "Goddamn your faithlessness and your short memory and your tiny selfish heart and your . . . ah!" I interrupt the tirade by slamming my finger in the drawer of his nightstand. I watch his face as I do it: It opens up and becomes a child's face again, even before it becomes particularly his own face again. There is awe and delight written upon it, and then it falls into an expression of sadness and confusion and Carl starts to cry in the ordinary sobbing of a nine-year-old, without any keening choir overtones or screeching old-lady echoes. Every time this happens he acts the same way, sleepy and confused and sad.

He cries and looks around his room and recognizes me.

"Dad," he says, "what time is it? What *time* is it?" which is exactly what he said when he woke up from his operation.

I say, "Nine o'clock, pal. It's going to be a great day." And I draw him over into my lap and hold him against me while he cries. From the way my finger is already bruising I figure we have at least an hour.

*   *   *

One night he went to bed as Carl, a not entirely ordinary nine-year-old who read too much and hated sports and had a somewhat morbid imagination; the next morning he awoke as something else: a vengeful spirit, thousands of angry strangers, a changeling. I knocked on his door to wake him like always, and didn't actually go into his room until he failed to show himself downstairs with only twenty minutes left before the school bus would come. In his room I found him still in bed, a lump under the covers. This usually meant that he had been up reading until only a few hours before. My father and I always checked to make sure his light stayed off, but he kept a dozen little penlights here and there around his room, and we could never manage to take them all away.

"Pal," I said. "Are you awake?"

"We are awake," came the reply, and I didn't really notice the difference in his voice because it was muffled by the sheets and blankets.

"Well, Your Highness, the bus will be here in twenty minutes. So let's get moving." Lately he had been reading obsessively about Elizabeth I, and my father had even caught him dressed up in one of his mother's old nightgowns with a lampshade turned upside down around his neck, issuing decrees to his own reflection. I thought he was just using the royal "we."

"We do not ride in buses," he said, and then sat up, flexing straight from the waist, still covered in his blanket. Even before the blanket fell away, and he turned toward me so I could see his face, I was afraid for him. "Or in automobiles or airplanes, but we drift on the original wind that rose up as the towers fell, and we are always restless."

He stared at me with alien eyes, looking at me, not like he didn't know me, but like he knew me very well and didn't like me at all.

"Carl," I said, "knock it off. This isn't funny."

"He's gone away," he said. "Don't worry too much, we'll keep him perfectly safe."

I opened my mouth to yell at him, and stepped forward toward the bed to give him a shake, to tell him to snap out of it. Knock it the fuck off, I was about to say, though I hadn't cursed at him or around him since before his mother left. But somehow I knew he wasn't trying to be funny, and that, whatever was happening, he wasn't doing it on purpose. This was something very different from every other time he had pretended to be someone he was not, dead kings and queens, Old Yeller, Miss Piggy . . . he had a long history of transient impersonations. Someone in a book or television show caught his fancy and he decided to be them, but no matter how hard he pretended he never before managed to seem so not like himself as he did now. I didn't yell at him. I didn't even stay in the room. I went and got my father instead.

Carl sticks around for a while. Eventually he calmed, like he always does, and we had the same conversation about what was happening to him, how he was sick, how he was asleep a lot. And he said, like he always did, that he was sure he had been dreaming, though he couldn't remember even the briefest scene of the dreams, or recall if they were good dreams or bad dreams. When I had him on these visitations I always wanted to just sit with him and talk about nothing, or listen to him tell me fascinating trivia about some dead president or king, something that had passed for normal in the old days. He always got bored with me, though, and when I wouldn't let him go to school or go for a bike ride or to a friend's house or to read by himself he would get angry, and usually I would calm him by reading to him from some dull biography until he was gone again. But today I take him for a walk.

"Why do I have to sit in this stupid chair?" he asks me as I strap him into his fancy wheelchair. It was sort of a gift from the hospital. Not that we didn't pay for it, but one of the puppyish residents wrangled it for him, insisting that there wasn't any reason that he should have to stay inside all the time when he went home. It was one of the fancy chairs that cerebral palsy kids get. "I look like a retard," Carl said.

"You might fall asleep," I told him as I tightened his seatbelt. He never fell asleep outside, but he might chase somebody, shouting "Fire on Babylon!" if he could get out of the chair too easily. "That's what happens," I say. "One minute you're playing tennis and the next you're sound asleep."

"That's narcolepsy," he says. "Do I have narcolepsy?"

"Not exactly," I said. "But you sleep a lot. You're getting better, though."

"I hate tennis. When was I playing tennis?"

"It's a figure of speech," I say, and then my father comes stomping into the room. He usually hides when Carl is back, and when Carl asks after him I say he is out for a drive or buying new teeth or on a date with some lady who is a hundred and five. "Look who's back," I say to him.

"You're a fool," he says, so quietly and so close to my ear I am probably the only one who can hear him. "It's not right. It's not what they told us to do." I shrug, and turn the chair around, as if presenting him with his grandson. It's the only answer I can give him, to say, Look, I don't care what they told us in the hospital. They don't have a fucking clue what's happening, but here's Carl back, for a little while.

"Look at me, Grandpa," Carl says. "I'm a retard."

"The retard is standing behind you," my father says, then bends down and clutches him in a death hug.

"Ouch," Carl says. "I'm coming *back*." My father doesn't say anything else to either of us, just turns and goes outside behind the house, where he starts chopping wood. It's still too early in the autumn for a fire, but this is what he does when he's very upset. We already have enough to last through the whole winter.

"Where do you want to go?" I ask Carl as I maneuver the wheelchair down the jury-rigged ramp that goes from the side door off the kitchen to the driveway.

"Where haven't I been lately?" he asks cheerily, and I'm struck by how quickly he seems to recover from his time away, and how ordinary he seems. It's hard to believe that there's anything wrong.

"Everywhere," I tell him, which is true, and we make a plan to walk all the way down to the river, but we only get as far as the park before he says he wants to stop and asks if he can go on the slide. "Better not," I say. "It's high up. What if you fell asleep?"

"Then I'd just slide down," he says, and I have a hard time arguing with that, or else I am just being careless, and hoping without any evidence or precedent that he might just stay how he is. I don't even have him unstrapped from the chair when a plane flies a bit lower than usual overhead and he cowers away from it, trying to throw himself out of his chair. "Get down!" he shouts. "It's in the sky . . . it's coming!" We don't live anywhere near an airport, and I shout at the plane as it flies over, because there's no reason it should be here, or that it should fly so low, except to torture us. The mothers and nannies look away from their toddlers to watch us, and the whole playground seems to go silent as the jet noise fades away. And then Carl straightens up and says, "What was that?" and the regular playground sounds are back again.

"Just a plane," I say, and strap him back in, then push the chair over to a bench and sit down next to him. He doesn't mention the slide again. Already there is something accusatory in his eyes, though his voice is still his own. A boy across the playground is bouncing a red ball, and Carl tells me that Mars years are almost three years longer than Earth years before he falls entirely silent. I don't want to go home yet. I don't want him trapped again, in his sickroom in our sickhouse, and I don't want to be trapped there with him. The voices come back but there is nobody around my bench.

"Guilty," he says, pointing at the moms and the nannies. "Guilty, guilty, guilty." The boy with the ball kicks it our way and runs after. I kick it back but he runs up to us anyway, ignoring the ball when it shoots past him, and he stands before us, three or four years old, smiling, not saying a thing. "Not guilty," says the entity. "Yet."

In the ER they diagnosed Carl with altered mental status, after subjecting him to a gaggle of tests that were all normal. Eventually they let me understand that they didn't know what was going on, but that something was going on, unless he was faking it all, which they put forth as a distinct possibility. I thought you'd have to be a pretty committed malingerer to submit to a spinal tap. During that procedure Carl lay absolutely still, not even squeezing my hand though they didn't give him anything but a little local anesthetic around his spine. When, halfway done, the doctor asked him how he was doing, he said, "We are the dead, and what is a needle compared to a hundred-and-fifty-thousand-pound airplane? Or two? Poke away, physician. You can't hurt us like *that*."

They called in the psychiatrist, and the nature of our visit seemed to change. A police officer took a permanent seat outside our room, and everyone except a kindly clinical assistant named Rebecca treated us a little differently. I think they were afraid of Carl, of the terribly unusual things he was saying to them, and about them, and of the electric sound of his voice. I was still too afraid for him to be afraid of him.

Where the ER doctors poked and prodded and irradiated in search of an answer, the psychiatrist just talked and talked. She wanted to know everything—*everything*—that had ever happened to us. Though it was only the late afternoon, we got a resident with a middle-of-the-night quality about her—she seemed exhausted and tired and not happy to meet any of us this late in her day. She talked to all of us together, then each of us alone, first me, then my father, and then Carl. When she talked to me her little yellow pencil would flutter madly in her notebook, and she made sympathetic noises when I told her about the divorce and then about my mother's death, and she kept saying, "You've been through a lot lately," then, "He's been through a lot lately." I wasn't sure if she meant my father or Carl or even me.

Finally she talked to Carl, kicking my father and me out and shutting the door, waving the policeman down with a practiced gesture when he stood up. We paced outside, trying not to intrude on other people's emergencies, until Rebecca showed us to a little waiting room down the hall, but it was too far away from Carl, and after five minutes in there we both stood up without discussing it and walked back to stand quietly outside the room. The resident came out crying a few minutes later.

"What happened?" I asked.

"I just need to talk to my attending," she said and walked off down the hall. In the exam room Carl was lying flat on his stretcher, looking at a picture of Elmo waving benevolently from the ceiling.

"What did you say to her?" I asked him.

"What we say to everyone," the voices answered, though he didn't look at me. "You will weep, too, at our message, and harder, since we bring it specifically for you. We are here because your faithlessness called us to you, and we will stay until you remedy it with sincerity and sacrifice." He had pointed at me while he said this, though he still didn't turn his head, and for the next ten minutes he pointed at me wherever I went in the room, and when my father tried to fold Carl's arm back over his chest he couldn't move it. In ten more minutes the resident came back and said cheerfully, "We're going to keep him!" As if that were the best news in the world.

It's macaroni and cheese for lunch. I am making it from scratch, more for my own sake than Carl's. He prefers it from a box, even in his natural state, but I like the process of grating the cheese and boiling the pasta, and there is something soothing about the circular motion of stirring and stirring. Outside, my father is still chopping, but he's slowed down considerably, and though I can't see him from the window I know he's spending most of the time sitting on an upended log, with the ax head on the ground between his feet, his hands folded on top of the handle and his chin on his hands, staring out at the woods.

Noontime is always a little pensive for us. I get lost in complicating some very simple dish and my father takes a nap or plays his guitar, and the high sun always has a calming effect on the entity. Carl is quiet in his room now, unrestrained and sitting on the edge of his bed. He'll stay that way for hours if we let him.

I am thinking of Carl's mother, wondering, as always, where she is, and wondering if it would make any difference if she was around and could have been called to her son's sickbed. He hardly remembered her, and never asked about her, which they said was part of his problem in the hospital. When I think about it I usually decide that she would just make things worse if she were still around, because she had always been a deeply strange woman, and this was just the sort of illness that would have appealed to her. It's occurred to me more than once that she probably would have been jealous that Carl had gotten it instead of her.

"This dumb shit has got to stop," my father says behind me. Still stirring the mac, I turn to look at him, half-expecting him to have the ax with him to enforce his demand, but he's empty-handed. I turn back.

"He stays a little longer every time," I say. "Have you noticed?"

"You talk like he's not always there. Like it's ever anybody but him."

I shrug.

"It's the worse thing for him, to play along with it. You know it is."

"I don't know anything lately, except what works."

"What you're doing isn't working," he says. "It's not progress. It's hurting him."

"You want to help me bring this up?" When he doesn't answer I turn around to ask him again but he's gone. I listen for the sound of the ax again, but the house stays entirely silent. I stand there a little while, stirring aggressively, wondering how he can look at Carl and think that he could contain such a reserve of pathology to pull off this unwitting impersonation, this utter ruination, this scourge. I don't know what's worse, or harder, to believe, that a little boy could be fucked-up enough to harbor the sort of sadness and rage that the entity presents us with every day, or that thousands of souls could be fused by a firebomb into a restless collection of spirits that hungers for a justice it can only define in terms of punishment.

I don't know how many times I've made macaroni and cheese in the same pot, on the same burner, at the same time of day over the past few weeks, but I seem to have noticed for the first time that the side of the pot is immensely hot, and I lay my forearm against it for as long as I can stand, and then as long as I can stand again, before I take the bowl upstairs. Not knowing where my father is in the house, I never make a sound except inside my head, but I don't even have to show Carl my blistered skin before he is falling back into himself.

"Let's talk about that day again," Dr. Sandman said to Carl. I was watching them from behind a piece of one-way glass, along with the rest of the "team," two residents and a nurse practitioner and a social worker and a ridiculous medical student who only looked a couple months older than Carl. We had been there for a week and a half already, and I had gotten to know their secret-spy room quite intimately. They asked a lot of questions, and they watched Carl sitting by himself, refusing to play with the variety of toys they put in front of him, watched him reduce another resident to tears, watched him sitting there doing nothing at all. They watched me talking to him, and listened as the thing I was coming to know as the entity listed my sins, personal and paternal and civic, all the ways I had disappointed these thousands of strangers. I kept saying, "Carl, Carl, come out from in there," though I wasn't supposed to say that, I wasn't supposed to do anything that would make Carl feel uncomfortable, or like he had to do something. They were always telling me what not to do with him, and always in the friendliest way: *You might not want to raise your voice at him. You might not want to tell him that he's making you angry. You might not want to tell him he is making you sad.*

"Our birthday," Carl said, smiling.

"Is that what it was?" Dr. Sandman asked. He was a large man, three inches taller than me, with at least fifty pounds on me, and not fat. He looked more suited to hunting down bail-skipping criminals than ferreting out the secret pain of children.

"Of course. We were born in the fire even as we died from it."

"Yes, you've told me that. But what were you doing? What was happening in the house when you heard about the planes. It was a long time ago, but do you remember?" He had asked me the same question, in the same room, before I was brought to the other side of the glass. He asked if we let Carl watch the television footage of the planes crashing into the buildings and I said not we, but somebody did. His mother wanted him to see it. She thought that it was important.

"Other people forget," Carl said to Sandman. "We never will. We were doing . . . everything. You could never understand. You have always been just one, we are thousands."

"Help me understand." *So his mother went away after the . . . disaster?* he had asked me, and I said *yes*, for the first time. And he sat there tapping his pencil against his teeth for something like a full minute.

"Help you? Help *you*? We are dead, you are alive. There is an arithmetic of obligation. Why don't you help us?"

"I'm trying to help you. By talking with you." *Does he ever ask about his mother now,* Sandman had asked me. *Does he ever ask where she is?* I said that we didn't really talk about her much.

"Words are not sufficient. Words are not justice. You promised that everything would be different, that everything would be better, but everything is the same, or worse. Now we require satisfaction, and words do not satisfy us."

"Talking is the best way to feel better," Dr. Sandman said. "You've got to trust me on that one, Carl."

Then Carl wouldn't say any more, but only glared furiously around the room, and every time Sandman spoke he only mocked him by raising his hand and moving it like a gibbering mouth. You may not want to tell him to trust you, I thought. You may not want to call him Carl.

Back in his room I sat with him, waiting for my father to come and take over. We split the days, and Carl was never alone, but it was harder than having him at home is, because we were always with him. He had a roommate, a bald six-year-old who seemed more peculiar than psychotic. A loose-lipped nurse told me that he pulled out all his hair and ate it. He always called my father and me "sir," and otherwise did not speak much to us.

I fell asleep that afternoon in the chair next to Carl's bed, because he was so quiet, probably still angry from Sandman's questioning. It wasn't for long. Carl woke me again, talking, and before I was fully awake I realized there was something different about his voice. It still had that electric, many-voiced quality, but it was kind, or at least not accusatory, and not angry.

"Every promise is broken," he was saying, "but we must take up the broken promises and bind them whole again with blood."

"I like blood," said a voice behind me, and I understood that Carl was talking to the weird bald kid. "It makes me happy when I drink it."

"We are never happy," Carl said. "For those who can get happiness from drinking blood, we say let them do it, but my blood bindings are not red. Blood is sacrifice. Everything else is irrelevant, or a worse mistake."

"You are sad spirits," said the boy. "I think you must be missing your brother, like me."

"We miss everyone. We are a host but we are utterly alone. Yet it is the faithlessness of brothers that pains us, too."

"Sad spirits! I knew so many, when I was younger. Do you speak the language of grief, then?" And the kid started to make barking, sobbing noises at Carl.

"We speak every language," said Carl, and he started to bark and sob back at the bald kid. My father came through the door, thinking, I knew, that things could not possibly get any more fucked-up than this.

"Time for me to go, pal," I said and stood up too quickly. I knocked my head hard against a heavy lamp suspended over Carl's bed, and it hurt like hell. I shouted, "Fuck!" Carl's eyes went wide, at the curse, I thought, and then his sobbing barks turned to ordinary sobbing, and for the first time in a week and a half he sounded like himself. In his own voice he asked me what time it was.

My father has a lifelong habit of never staying angry at me for long, even when he's on the right side of the argument. We make spaghetti for dinner, because Carl is still back, despite the risk of a mess if he should go away again. "What did you do?" my father asked me, looking at my bruised face and hands for new marks, but my burn is covered by my sleeve.

"Nothing," I say. "Nothing at all. He's just . . . back." And then I say, though I know I shouldn't, "Maybe it's over. Maybe it's just over."

It's harder getting the medication into Carl when he's back, but he's supposed to take it at dinnertime. There are tears before he'll take it, but that doesn't make the slightest difference to my good mood, or my father's, and we rub off on him.

"It tastes like feet!" he says, but he's smiling. We eat downstairs, for once, and my father sets the table as if for a holiday, with fancy plates and candles. Carl twirls his pasta expertly and pretends that he's been in a coma for ten years.

"Do we have a lady president yet?" he asks.

"Yes," says my father. "A black lady."

"All *right*! Are people living on the moon?"

"And Mars," I say. "Terraforming is under way."

"Cool," he says. "Cancer?"

"Defeated," my father says.

"Finally," Carl says. "But who's at war?"

"Nobody," I say.

"Peace everywhere," my father says.

"And nobody is starving except the teenagers who kind of want to," I say.

"A perfect world," my father says, leaning back and laughing as he raises his wineglass to us, and I smile, too, but uneasily, because I realize all of a sudden that we are all pretending, and maybe that's not the best thing for us to be doing as a family. And as if on cue Carl's smile vanishes, and he sneers, and in the electric voice he shouts, "Liar!"

It's just a spasm, but the rest of dinner is somber. We don't play any more games, and limit our conversation. Carl tells us about the way a dynamo works.

I use up the last minutes of his presence with a quick bath; by the time he's back in bed, he's gone. "What did you do for us today?" he asks me as we strap him into his restraints for the night. "Have you made the change I asked you for?"

"Nighty night," my father says, and kisses Carl on the head. Carl turns his head and spits, not much volume but he makes a loud noise, "Ptui." My father goes to the door and waits for me, glaring, waiting for me to hurt myself again. I lean down close to Carl.

"You are breaking my heart," I say.

"Yes," say the voices. "Into two thousand, nine hundred, and ninety-eight pieces."

I wasn't the only one to leave work. Dozens of us disappeared, going home to be with our families as the world ended. I came home early that day. Carl's mother had already picked him up. His teacher had called in a panic, as if the preschools were going to be the next target.

I expected to find them doing something ordinary—making cookies, playing a board game, reading a story in the yard. I don't know why I expected his mother to manufacture a sense of peace around him, or to prepare one for me. As I said, she was a strange woman even before she became intolerably strange and selfishly crazy, before she went off on the journey that Carl and I were not allowed to accompany her on. This was the sort of thing she had been waiting for all her life, confirmation that the world outside was just as fucked-up as the one inside her.

I walked in the door and saw them standing hand in hand in front of the television, watching the replay footage of the towers falling.

"Do you see?" she said to him. "This is just what I mean. It's

kairos, breaking through time to make history. Do you feel it?"
she asked him, and she shivered all over.

"Dad!" Carl said, when he saw me. "There's people in there!"

He was three years old.

The house is old but not very big. My father will sleep through
anything short of screams of bloody murder, and I have earplugs,
but I'm afraid to put them in because I want to hear if Carl should
happen to become himself in the middle of the night. I am thinking as I lie there, listening to him mutter, that that will never happen. I press on the burn on my wrist and regret the lie I told my
father, that Carl had just gotten better, that whatever was in him
had just tired of us and gone away, without anyone having paid
some departure price. I wonder if things would be different if we
had spent that day making cookies and playing games and pretending that the world had not changed, or if it would be different if his mother had never left, if the chaos she radiated would
have been better for him than the dull peace that my father and I
have provided. I wonder if it would have helped to have asked
him every day if he missed his mother, if he thought I drove her
away, if he worried that she was dead.

The answer to those questions is always that I don't know, and
usually I drift off to sleep to the mumbling voices in an agony of
not-knowing, not knowing what I did wrong or what I am cur-
rently doing wrong or what I am going to do wrong tomorrow to
perpetuate my son's suffering and my own.

But tonight I just lie there, in unrelieved paralysis, until very
suddenly the not-knowing breaks apart into a very clear certainty,
and it's like I always just fell asleep too soon for certainty, and a

certain comfort, to come settling on me in my bed. I get up and go back to Carl's room, undo his restraints, and sit him up.

"What do you want?" I ask him.

"You know it," the voices say. "Every day we tell you. Justice. Satisfaction. Vengeance."

"What do you want?" I ask again, and this time I poke him in the chest.

"You know!"

"Tell me!"

"You said it would be different, but everything is the same. You were supposed to become your better self, and where is he now? Pay us our blood price. Bring him back!"

"Him? My son?"

"Fool! Your self!"

"I just want my son back," I say. "Just give me back my son." I push him again, harder, so he falls back against the headboard we've padded with blankets, and the voices laugh.

"Prove to us that you deserve him. Prove to us that you will be different." They laugh and laugh and laugh at me. I grab Carl by the front of his pajamas and haul him out of bed, and drag him with me, still laughing, downstairs to the kitchen, and I hold him dangling next to me while I look around frantically at the butcher knives, the oven, the microwave, the vacuum cleaner, trying to think . . . what can I do that will be enough, a final proof, enough to get him back forever. I take him through the door and down the steps, around to the back of the house.

It's a little rainy but warm. Low clouds reflect the streetlights back at us and the whole yard is bathed in a soft orange light. I push Carl down too roughly against the neat wall of wood my father has made, enough for two long winters. I kneel down beside him and take up my father's ax. Carl has stopped laughing and smiling. His gaze is fixed on me.

"Coward," he says. "Fool. Promise-breaker." But the voices are speaking very softly. I put my hand down against the top of the stack of wood, looking at the bruises and the burns, and it occurs to me that I have always kept one hand whole and untouched, and that the vast majority of my body is unbruised and untouched by Carl's ordeal.

I switch the ax to my injured hand. It's not easy, not, like one might hope, a matter of a single stroke. I don't know how many it is—three or four, I think, but it feels like I am chopping away in an eternity of effort at something much more durable than flesh and bone. I only look at my wrist for the first stroke; afterward I find my mark without looking at it. I am staring at Carl, at the thing that is in him, asking them both with every stroke, "Is it enough?" And I think I mean is it enough to prove to them I love my son, or that I deserve to have him back, that I mean it when I say I promise to take better care of him, that I promise to be a better father, to unroot whatever fault in me threw him into the company of these angry souls who died to make us all citizens of the world, and that I'll be better to them, too, and never step out of the shadow of the day they died, if that's what it means now to be good. "You *fuckers*!" I shout. "Is it enough?"

Carl's face changes: he looks proud, then curious, then he seems to be gorging on the blood and anger and pain in the air. His face gets ruddy and full and more and more pleased, and then all of a sudden it is entirely blank, and then he is wearing an opposite face. His grinning mouth contracts to an O of sorrow and distress, and he waves his arms around so it looks like he is falling through the air, like he is falling back into himself. He gives a start in his whole body and his face is changed so fundamentally

I feel sure there can't be anything foreign left in him. I am listening so hard to him cry, trying to hear a trace of the other, that I forget to breathe and forget to cry myself, and I would not be surprised if I forgot to bleed. Then I fall over next to him, my wrist jammed against my side, and I can't get the words out to tell him what time it is, or to answer when my father comes out with a flashlight to curse me to hell and ask me what I've done.

A HERO OF
CHICKAMAUGA

✳

There is not much to do, when you are dying, but lie on your side
and watch the progress of the battle. I have taken an early hit on
the first day at Chickamauga. It's an inglorious end, one for which
my father and my brothers would never settle. They are still load-
ing, shooting, advancing toward a field where Rebels sprout like
contrary weeds. "Shoot one for me, Captain!" I shouted to my father as I fell. He did not look away from his aim, but said, not
without some tenderness, "I'll shoot you a brace of 'em, my boy."

The way I have landed there are long blades of grass tickling
my lips. When I nibble on them, they have a green and sour taste.
All around me, expiring actors are crying out for their mamas, for
God to spare them. "O God O God O God," says a voice from
ahead of me. I wish they would shut up. I always thought if I died
for real, I would die quietly, because pending oblivion would
surely snatch away my voice. Sometimes the thought of death
makes me silent even as I pass through an ordinary living day. The
wind shifts and carries a burning whiff of naphthalene to my
nose—some reenactor has been storing his uniform in mothballs.
"Ain't I too young to go? Ain't I too young? Who will look after
my Frieda?" The boys cry out for their Friedas, their Birgits, their

sweet little Maueschens. We are supposed to be an all-German regiment.

"Hey, dead man," says a voice just behind me, after the cries of the wounded have quieted to moans. Someone's fallen there: I can feel a foot resting against my thigh. "You got a view? What's happening?" He sounds like a little boy.

"Much shooting," I say. He kicks me square in the ass.

"Farb!" I say accusingly. I want to clutch my ass, but the dead don't rub their hurts.

"It's a contraction of the thigh muscles," he says. "Authentic. It went on. I got documentation. Some boys flailed like puppets as they went. So tell me what's happening, or I'll do it again."

"Son of a bitch!" I say, because I'm not accustomed to being kicked by boys from my own side. "Shit-house adjutant!" He kicks me again, hard, and I tell him what's happening. The Ninth (that's us) is making steady progress across the field. The Fifty-fifth Ohio is with them, but where the rest of the brigade has got to, I have no idea. There's Colonel Kammerling bouncing stoutly across the field on his Appaloosa. He is the sort of brave or foolish colonel who carries his own messages into battle. Goddamn he's been hit! Just as he pulled up beside the captain some dirty Reb has plucked him off.

That last bit is untrue. The colonel is entirely well. Little Billy Kicking Boots can see this when he sits up with a curse. "Farb!" he says. "Kammerling didn't die at Chickamauga!" I can already tell he's the sort of stickler for historical accuracy that can be the bane of improvisation, if not fun. I turn my head to look at him, trying to be ready when he kicks me again, and see that he is not a boy after all, but a boyish-looking girl. She has tried hard to make herself mannish, but her face is pretty and gives her away. I think immediately of Joan of Arc, who was surely cursed with all sorts of medieval defects, smelliness and hairiness and bad teeth. The other dead and wounded are calling for her to lie down, and she does.

"I'll fix you," she tells me, but doesn't kick me again. She has positioned herself so she can see the battle; I am positioned so I can see only her face. A good sport, she calls out soft updates to me. I don't need them. Chickamauga was dinner-table talk at my house when I was growing up. My father would shape peas and carrots into infantry lines to illustrate the battle. "So here," he'd say, taking away a piece of carrot and eating it, "you can see how Rosecrans left a gaping hole in his line, and Longstreet was not the sort of fellow to ignore such an opportunity." And Rebel peas went rolling through the gap. A lifetime of dinners like that puts history in your head. I know Chickamauga backward and forward, and since these reenactors pride themselves on absolute fidelity, I know just what will happen on this first day of battle. I have died repulsing Cleburne's near-duck attack on the Union left. It was not a spectacular battle, not a Pickett's Charge or a Thomas's Stand, though we are in fact going to do Snodgrass Hill tomorrow. That will be the big blowout of the whole weekend.

When the battle is over, a lone bugler rides through the smoke. He pulls up amid the wounded, dying, and the dead to play taps. The dead rise, fat hairy boys who, when they are not fighting to preserve or destroy the Union, are lawyers or mechanics or the owners of pool-cleaning services. They rise, stretch limbs made stiff by death, give each other pats and hugs and ass slaps. "That was damn fine!" My brothers and my father come back to catch me up in the traditional post-battle group hug. We raise our father up on our shoulders and bounce him like a child. I find myself looking back to Joan of Arc, who ignores the men squeezing her shoulder and thumping her back. She is staring hatefully toward the enemy line. The Rebs are sauntering over from their line through the low-hanging smoke and the red sunset light, their hands stuck out before them for shaking.

My great-great-grandfather was a hero of Chickamauga. He gave his life to save a hapless drummer boy. Like him, I am a soldier in the Ninth Ohio, though I am not one of those people who think that antecedents make you a blue-blood reenactor. I have no patience with the Sons of Confederate Veterans or Grand Army of the Republic snobs. At dances the only medal I wear is my Boy Scouts Civil War Hiking Trail medal, which I earned with my own two feet.

Rebel-hating, not medals, was handed down in my family, but I'm not fanatical. The disdain was heavily diluted by the time it reached me. My great-great-grandfather ended every letter he ever wrote with "Jeff Davis drives the goat," but my father moved from Ohio to Florida. He set up a dermatology practice in Orlando. At family reunions in Ohio, I was the Rebel cousin. "You're from the South now!" said my cousin Libby, pushing away my hand when I tried to feel her up during a basement make-out session. The fact was, Orlando was not the South. And the South that my cousin, in the family tradition, was brought up to hate, was not anywhere anymore.

I don't like to be at these things. I don't like pretending. I don't like guns, or the noise they make. I don't like wool—it itches, and when I get rained on I smell like a dog. My boots fit poorly. But if I did not come out to play like this, I would risk a dishonorable discharge from my own family. It's their passion, my two older brothers', and my father's and my mother's. Clay, my little brother, hated it. We could complain to each other once, but he is not here at the reenactment celebrating the 135th anniversary of the slaughter at Chickamauga Creek. Death has delivered him from his obligations.

"I told you I'd get you!" says Joan. I blink stupidly at her, rubbing at my neck. I'd assumed, when she said she would get me, that she would do something sneaky, march behind me and spit in the tin drinking cup I've got hung on my backpack, or steal my gun and pound a cork down the barrel. But she took her revenge direct. She made a claw of her thumb and forefinger and pinched me so hard I screamed.

I'm glad for the pinch, though it hurt like hell, because I wanted to talk to her. I want to be near her in the way that I do sometimes with certain people. I try not to indulge this instinct, not to make myself a pest to strangers, even when I feel, like I did with Joan, an immediate affinity, a craving that only intimate acquaintance will satisfy. My father, who has delved too deeply into the nineteenth century for his own good, calls that immediate affinity "omniphily," and has told me before how M. Fourier (one of his heroes) wrote that such affinities should be cherished and exploited, and how when they blossomed between every man and woman on earth, they would prove to be the salvation of humankind. But I remember an affliction named Susan Greer, who bothered me with her devotion through the whole of second grade, who followed me with a jar of paste until I consented to sit with her behind a palm tree and partake of it as a lover's meal. We were married by that paste. Cross-eyed Susie, whose tongue was a little too big for her mouth, was my unwanted loving companion until she moved away to Tallahassee. I remember her and think that a body ought not to press itself on a body, because it's not such a long trip from "How do you do" to "Partake thou of my paste."

All this means I am very careful not to initiate pressingly upon people I like for no good reason. So I was happy when Joan sprang out and pinched me, and I am happier still when she asks me to dinner.

"I'm making coffee and beef stew," she says. "Want to mess with me?"

"Are you going to pinch me again?"

"Are you going to make me angry again?"

"I hope not."

"Well, that's fine, then." She takes a few steps and I follow after, but we haven't gone ten feet before she stops. "One more thing, though. I need you to tell me something. You're not from around *here*, are you?" She sweeps out her arms, as if indicating this little parcel of Georgia, but something about her expression tells me she is indicating the whole of the depraved, sore-losing South.

"No," I say.

"I mean, you're a Yankee, aren't you?"

I point at the brass infantry horn on my kepi. "Looks that way."

"No," she says, reaching toward me, so I think she's about to pinch again, but she only puts her arm flat against my chest, over my heart. No one has ever put their hand there, just like that, and it feels very pleasant. "I mean, are you a real Yankee?"

"Sure," I say. And because it seems like I ought to, I say, "Of course. Absolutely. I'm no Reb, if that's what you mean."

"That's fine, then," she says. "That's fine." As we are walking we pass near the place where my family has pitched its tents. My oldest brother is polishing our father's saddle. He looks up and sees me. I put my finger to my lips, but he shouts anyway. "Where are you going?" I don't answer.

"Who's that?" asks Joan.

"I have no idea," I say.

"Have you seen the pictures?" she asks me while we're waiting for the stew to cook. "Nobody smiles in them." She has an old stereopticon and a collection of stereographs. She puts pictures in the viewer and I put my eyes to the lenses. The pictures are fuzzy at first, but then the boys jump out at me in startling 3-D. A grim-faced Yankee sitting for a portrait: Maybe it's for his mama, or his sweetheart. His shoulders are round and small, but his neck is so thick I doubt I could get my two hands around it.

"I was a View-Master junkie when I was little," I tell her. I would flip through the pictures with such wild abandon that I tore out the advancing lever. Then I would steal Clay's and break it, too. He was pretty forgiving as a child, reacting to slights with sadness instead of anger.

Joan switches pictures, and shows me a Rebel cavalryman with immensely serious eyes. His saber is held in salute.

"What are they looking at?" she asks me. "What do you suppose?"

"The camera," I say. But really I think they were looking at the future, suddenly made quite real to them by the prospect of their death. There was something about that in Clay's diary, of which I became the secret keeper after he died. It was under his mattress, an obvious place, but, then, he was very trusting. I was cleaning up the room on the night he died, because that seemed like something bearable, something I could do. But I didn't clean. I sat on his bed, on the sheets and old unwashed blanket that absolutely reeked of him, and read. *The future is shapeless and unreal*, he wrote on the first page, *except when I am there, when I am close, and then it has the shape of death, and the reality of death. Why is that comforting?*

"I think it was more than that," she says and switches pictures again. This time the blurry image resolves itself into something gruesome: dead Rebs strewn along the fence on Hagerstown Pike. She shows me dead Rebels with their silent guns in front of the battered Dunker Church. She shows me the bodies of dead Rebels packed in a sunken road. I know all the pictures. My father showed them to us, projected on a big screen in our living room, as if recounting a vacation into the past.

"They lie as they fell," I say, rubbing my eyes and looking at her. A dreaming look passes from her face and she says, "They got what they fucking deserved."

Joan is at the dance that night, looking very smart in her dress uniform. My brothers are there, and my parents, my mother in a stylish oval hoopskirt and a purple velvet Zouave jacket and a hat piled high with fresh flowers. She kept the hat in the refrigerator at home and brought it to Chickamauga in a cooler. By day she plays a nurse because in real life she is a nurse. Some overeager ambulance types took me off the field last year and brought me to the hospital tent, where I lay on a stretcher and watched my mother exulting in all the fake blood. She saw me and came over to where I lay. I thought it was to say hello, but when she leaned her bloodstained face over me she only said, "Scream." I didn't scream. I just lay and watched, listening to all the enthusiastic shrieking the other boys were doing. It seemed to me that they were not a damned thing like the screams of men who were bleeding from the belly or getting their legs sawed off. I remembered how my father had screamed when he got the news that Clay was dead. He always claimed to have seen it coming, but I know he was screaming because he couldn't believe that his son was gone. Probably that was a pretty close approximation of the sort of scream you make when someone saws off your leg, a scream not just of pain but of disbelief.

"I hate them," Joan confesses to me as we are dancing. She tosses her head to indicate the Rebel officers. People are hissing at us, "Farb! Farb!" I don't care. I think we make a dashing couple. If I am a failure at everything else in life, I am at least a success at a polka, and Joan is no slouch. "Have you ever even thought about how they got away with it? How they got away clean. How they are still getting away with it."

"What do you mean?" I ask her, not caring what she means, because I am holding her and dancing with her, and the pressure of her against my chest is a little like when she put her hand there.

"Hundreds of years of abomination, is what I mean. I mean people owning other people and then pretending like they *never did.*"

"That was a long time ago."

"That's what they say! That's exactly what they say. But it was *yesterday.*"

I don't like kissing, Clay wrote. *All the sucking gives me an ache in the back of my head.* Joan and I pitch our dog-tent together. You need two people to make a whole tent—each private carries half of one rolled up on his back. You button them together and they make a pretty sorry sort of shelter, sure to leak in the rain, and not proof at all against the cold. She has got a wool blanket and some mattress ticking that we stuffed with hay and corn husks provided by the hosts of the battle. We strip down to our red flannel long johns and crawl between the blanket and the hay. We lie there, her belly to my back. She sings in a low voice:

> *Many are the hearts that are weary tonight,*
> *Wishing for the war to cease,*
> *Many are the hearts looking for the right*
> *To see the dawn of peace,*
> *Dying tonight,*
> *Dying tonight,*
> *Dying on the old campground.*

Then she is silent, and I think she must be sleeping, but suddenly she cries out, "Spoon!" and we flip over, so now it's my belly in her back. I am shivering, and not from the cold. She calls spoon a few more times, until one time I turn and find that she hasn't. Her face is right before mine, and she kisses me. I get an aching in my head, but I like it.

"What's the worst thing you've ever done?" she asks me later.

"I don't know," I say.

"There must be one thing."

"Not really," I say, except there is. It springs easily to mind, as if it had been waiting for someone to ask just this question. Once, during a big, hysterical, pan-family blowout, I held Clay's arms at his sides while he struggled to get away. I was trying to keep him from running out the door, because when he did that we never knew when we would see him again. But my mother took that opportunity to slap him hard across the face, while I was holding him, and I felt like I'd hit him myself, like I'd punished him for the crime of being miserable.

"Then what's the best thing you've ever done?"

"I don't know. I probably haven't done much good. How about you?"

"I know it but I haven't done it yet. I have something planned. It's something really fine."

At the regimental inspection the next morning, I am bleary-eyed and wrinkled. The Ninth Ohio has fallen in, then opened ranks so Colonel Kammerling and his aides, my father among them, can walk down the lines to check us over and see if anyone is guilty of anachronism or harboring unsafe equipment. I pull out my ramrod and drop it down my musket barrel, then undo the flap on my cartridge box. My father pulls the ramrod up an inch or two, then lets it drop. When it makes the requisite bright ringing noise, he nods gruffly. A dirty gun will give a dull thud, or no noise at all. He flips open my cartridge box, checking unnecessarily for penny wrappers or stapled cartridges—these are hazardous. They can put out someone's eye, or even do them in. But my father rolls all my cartridges because I make such a mess of them when I try to do it for myself.

"Fine cartridges, son," he says, and moves on to scold a poor farby next to me whose gun is dirty, whose buttons are sewn upside down. "You're a disgrace!" he tells him, and it sounds for a moment like he is talking to Clay.

Joan is behind me. I can hear the colonel praising her. Her musket barrel has rung so purely it has moved him practically to tears.

"It's obvious, soldier," he says, "that you care deeply for that weapon. I think it must be the best-cared-for gun in the whole Army of the Cumberland."

"I love it, sir," she says. "I love it like it was my own baby."

After drill I help my father give an informative talk for the civilian spectators, "What Was in a Typical Haversack?" I am his dodo, or translator. He is in character as great-great-grandpa, and I am there so he does not have to come out of it, to answer questions whose answers are beyond the ken of his nineteenth-century persona.

"You had your eating implements," he says, pointing at the little table upon which he'd emptied out his sack. "Knife and fork, a real big spoon, a tin plate, and a dipper."

"Wouldn't a spork have been more economical?" asks a man. He leans forward from the ring of people surrounding us and points at the big spoon. "Wouldn't a spork have been better? Why didn't you use a spork?"

My father gives a me a confused look. "Spork?"

"A combination spoon and fork," I say, hating that he is pretending not to know what a spork is. "Sir," I say to the pale, fat man, "they didn't have sporks back then. Thomas Alva Edison invented the spork in 1878, thirteen years after the war's end." My father glares at me. There are few offenses graver, in his book, than giving out misinformation at a haversack talk. But I like to remind myself how lying and pretending are different. He moves on to the food you ate with your implements.

"Hardtack, beans, desiccated vegetables, fatback, and salt pork." He has me pass around some hardtack. We always have a big hardtack bake-off before we leave for a reenactment.

"They ate this stuff?" asks Sporky.

"Yes, we did," says my father. "But we did not like it." He sings a few verses of "Hard Crackers Come Again No More." A child bites into the hardtack—one always does—and says it tastes like cardboard. My father points out some personal items, letters and a Bible and a jacknife. A lady is concerned that letters from home would get greasy if you put them in with the fatback. The fatback is being passed around, too, and she is holding it at arm's length like it's a dead rat. My father admits that greasy letters were a problem.

"How long did the war last?" asks the child who tried the hardtack.

"Four years," says my father.

"Like high school," says the fatback lady.

"Very much," I say. "Brutal and hellish, and when you were in it, it seemed like it would never, ever end."

"You had your armaments," my father says. "You could maybe put your bayonet in your haversack, if it was properly sheathed." People clamor for him to talk about his gun. Nobody ever had to ask him twice to do that.

"This is a U.S. Springfield Model 1861 rifle-musket. Named after the armory where she was manufactured, but I call her Sally." Sporky raises his hand with another question. "Yes, sir?" my father says.

"Did they hide behind those when they were shooting?" he asks, pointing at the stacks of cannonballs that spring up everywhere on the field, commemorating the fall of this or that general, and the tall obelisks commemorating the brave stand of this or that regiment.

"In fact they did," I say. "Whoever reached the monuments first enjoyed a distinct advantage."

*   *   *

My father throws me out of his talk. He gets my mother to be his dodo, which is fine with me. I go looking for Joan and find her in her tent with a one-pound can of powder open between her legs, rolling cartridges. I crawl in and sit down next to her. When I lean over for a kiss, she pushes me away.

"Don't!" she says. "You'll mess it up."

"I thought you had a full box already."

"I need a special one," she says, folding up the tail of the cartridge she is working on. She tosses it to me. It has an unfamiliar weight, and it takes me a long stupid moment to realize it's because she's put a real minié ball in there.

"What's this for?" I ask her.

"What do you think?" she says. And then she does kiss me. I sit and smooch with her, her not-blank clutched in my hand, when I should be running to my father or the colonel to report. I'm going to leave now, I tell myself. This is somebody's life in my hands. But I don't leave.

I am buddied up with Joan for the big event, the reenactment of Thomas's Stand on Snodgrass Hill. It seems strange to me, sometimes, how the historians talk. Time after time, they say, Thomas was assaulted by furious Confederate attacks, but somehow he managed to hold on. As if he did all the fighting himself. As if he died again and again and again over the course of the day. As if this was a battle between two giants—handsome, noble Thomas, and drunken, contrary Bragg—and not a thing fought by little men who come to know as they duck and kill how their lives are infinitely precious and cheap.

I have a plan to stay near Joan and steal her cartridge when she tries to use it. "Coming over!" I shout, and then fire past her

169

shoulder at the Rebs climbing the hill between the thin oaks. We are lined up in regiment, just two deep, and I am in a position to see her every move. The live cartridge is wrapped in funny papers, not ordinary newsprint. I will know it when I see it. I am ready to stop her.

Who is guilty? Clay wrote. *I am guilty. I am guilty. I look back on my life and it is all shame.* I have his journal with me at the battle. I carry it around always. At first I carried it everywhere (it's small and fits in any pocket) for fear that someone would discover it if I left it alone, and then because I got in the habit of consulting it, like some people consult their Bible. *Who is guilty?* I read that passage before we went up to the hill.

The Rebs keep charging and falling back, ululating as they come. Their peculiar cry makes them sound like reckless, hooting drunks. It was supposed to be formidable, 135 years ago. It unnerved the Union soldiers greatly, and they struggled unsuccessfully to come up with a cry of their own, an answer, a great hurrah to raise their spirits as they rushed forward to die, but contemporary accounts tell that they mostly sounded like they were about to vomit. The Rebel charges must fail. They won't take the field until Thomas makes an orderly retreat to Chattanooga.

Where does it go? That's what I want to know. That's the question I'd like to write in Clay's book. Where does it disappear to, all the pain of an anguished life, after that life has ended? My parents and my brothers, I think they believed it got sucked into Clay's coffin, in a sort of reverse Pandora's box effect. So after he died they were always sighing, as if at the sadness of everything, but really I think they were sighing with relief, because they would no longer be tortured with his torturedness.

Joan turns and smiles at me as she loads the funny-paper cartridge. I point my gun at the ground, put my hand out to touch her shoulder. "Don't," I say weakly. All around us people are conducting the ordinary business of battle, cocking, firing, charging, taking their hits and offering up their dying groans. I don't watch her do it. I take a hit and cover my eyes while she raises her rifle and picks out her Reb. I imagine her searching, looking for a nice, juicy, backward-thinking one. "Don't," I say again, but I feel a thrill inside when I hear her fire, and I imagine Clay taking a shot at the world that heaped him. *The sky is an obscene belly. It smothers me.* I see my brother stab back at the world, not consenting to be ruined and killed by it.

I uncover my eyes. Joan is standing just in front of me, looking very calm, peering through the smoke. She raises her rifle, and I think she'll shoot again, that she has more bullets, that even if I had taken away her cartridge she still would have shot somebody. But she drops her rifle, takes a hit with a moan more of pleasure than of pain, and falls down with a peaceful look on her face.

"Crybaby," she says to me.

A CHILD'S BOOK OF
SICKNESS AND DEATH

My room, 616, is always waiting for me when I get back, unless it is the dead of winter, rotavirus season, when the floor is crowded with gray-faced toddlers rocketing down the halls on fantails of liquid shit. They are only transiently ill, and not distinguished. You earn something in a lifetime of hospitalizations that the rotavirus babies, the RSV wheezers, the accidental ingestions, the rare tonsillectomy, that these sub-sub-sickees could never touch or have. The least of it is the sign that the nurses have hung on my door, silver glitter on yellow posterboard: *Chez Cindy*.

My father settles me in before he leaves. He likes to turn down the bed, to tear off the paper strap from across the toilet, and to unpack my clothes and put them in the little dresser. "You only brought halter tops and hot pants," he tells me.

"And pajamas," I say. "Halter tops make for good access. To my veins." He says he'll bring me a robe when he comes back, though he'll likely not be back. If you are the sort of child who only comes into the hospital once every ten years, then the whole world comes to visit, and your room is filled with flowers and chocolates and aluminum balloons. After the tenth or fifteenth admission, the people and the flowers stop coming. Now I get flowers only if I'm septic, but my uncle Ned makes a donation to the Short Gut Foundation of America every time I come in.

"Sorry I can't stay for the H and P," my father says. He would usually stay to answer all the questions the intern du jour will ask, but during this admission we are moving. The new house is only two miles from the old house, but is bigger, and has views. I don't care much for views. This side of Moffitt Hospital looks out over the park and beyond that to the Golden Gate. On the nights my father stays, he'll sit for an hour watching the bridge lights blinking while I watch television. Now he opens the curtains and puts his face to the glass, taking a single deep look, before turning away, kissing me goodbye, and walking out.

After he's gone, I change into a lime-green top and bright-white pants, then head down the hall. I like to peep into the other rooms as I walk. Most of the doors are open, but I see no one I know. There are some orthopedic-looking kids in traction; a couple of wheezers smoking their albuterol bongs, a tall, thin, blond girl sitting up very straight in bed and reading one of those fucking Narnia books. She has CF written all over her. She notices me looking and says hello. I walk on, past two big-headed syndromes and a nasty rash. Then I'm at the nurses' station, and the welcoming cry goes up, "Cindy! Cindy! Cindy!" Welcome back, they say, and where have you *been*, and Nancy, who always took care of me when I was little, makes a booby-squeezing motion at me and says, "My little baby is becoming a woman!"

"Hi, everybody," I say.

See the cat? The cat has feline leukemic indecisiveness. He is losing his fur, and his cheeks are hurting him terribly, and he bleeds from out of his nose and his ears. His eyes are bad. He can hardly see you. He has put his face in his litter box because sometimes that makes his cheeks feel better, but now his paws are hurting and his bladder is getting nervous and there is the feeling at the tip of his tail that comes every day at noon. It's like someone's put it in their mouth and they're chewing and chewing.

Suffer, cat, suffer!

I am an ex-twenty-six-week miracle preemie. These days you have to be a twenty-four-weeker to be a miracle preemie, but when I was born you were still pretty much dead if you emerged at twenty-six weeks. I did well except for a belly infection that took about a foot of my gut—nothing a big person would miss but it was a lot to one-kilo me. So I've got difficult bowels. I don't absorb well, and get this hideous pain, and barf like mad, and need tube feeds, and beyond that sometimes have to go on the sauce, TPN—total parenteral nutrition—where they skip my wimpy little gut and feed me through my veins. And I've never gotten a pony, despite asking for one every birthday for the last eight years.

I am waiting for my PICC—you must have central access to go back on the sauce—when a Child Life person comes rapping at my door. You can always tell when it's them because they knock so politely, and because they call out so politely, "May I come in?" I am watching the meditation channel (twenty-four hours a day of string ensembles and trippy footage of waving flowers or shaking leaves, except late, late at night, when between two and three a.m. they show a bright field of stars and play a howling theremin) when she simpers into the room. Her name is Margaret. When I was much younger I thought the Child Life people were great because they brought me toys, and took me to the playroom to sniff

Play-Doh, but time has sapped their glamour and their fun. Now they are mostly annoying, but I am never cruel to them, because I know that being mean to a Child Life specialist is like kicking a puppy.

"We are collaborating with the children," she says, "in a collaboration of color, and shapes, and words! A collaboration of poetry and prose!" I want to say, People like you wear me out, honey. If you don't go away soon I know my heart will stop beating from weariness, but I let her go on. When she asks if I will make a submission to their hospital literary magazine I say, "Sure!" I won't, though. I am working on my own project, a child's book of sickness and death, and cannot spare thoughts or words for *The Moffitteer*.

Ava, the IV nurse, comes while Margaret is paraphrasing a submission—the story of a talking IV pump written by a seven-year-old with only half a brain—and bringing herself nearly to tears at the recollection of it.

"And if he can do that with half a brain," I say, "imagine what I could do with my whole one!"

"Sweetie, you can do anything you want," she says, so kind and so encouraging. She offers to stay while I get my PICC but it would be more comforting to have my three-hundred-pound Aunt Mary sit on my face during the procedure than to have this lady at my side, so I say no thank you, and she finally leaves. "I will return for your submission," she says. It sounds much darker than she means it.

The PICC is the smoothest sailing. I get my morphine and a little Versed, and I float through the fields of the meditation channel while Ava threads the catheter into the crook of my arm. I am in the flowers but also riding the tip of the catheter, à la *Fantastic Voyage*, as it snakes up into my heart. I don't like views, but I like looking down through the cataract of blood into the first chamber. The great valve opens. I fall through and land in daisies.

I am still happy-groggy from Ava's sedatives when I think I hear the cat, moaning and suffering, calling out my name. But it's the intern calling me. I wake in a darkening room with a tickle in my arm and look at Ava's handiwork before I look at him. A slim PICC disappears into me just below the antecubital fossa, and my whole lower arm is wrapped in a white mesh glove that looks almost like lace, and would have been cool back in 1983, when I was negative two.

"Sorry to wake you," he says. "Do you have a moment to talk?" He is a tired-looking fellow. At first I think he must be fifty, but when he steps closer to the bed I can see he's just an ill-preserved younger man. He is thin, with strange hair that is not so much wild as just wrong somehow, beady eyes and big ears, and a little beard, the sort you scrawl on a face, along with devil horns, for purposes of denigration.

"Well, I'm late for cotillion," I say. He blinks at me and rubs at his throat.

"I'm Dr. Chandra," he says. I peer at his name tag: Sirius Chandra, M.D.

"You don't look like a Chandra," I say, because he is as white as me.

"I'm adopted," he says simply.

"Me, too," I say, lying. I sit up and pat the bed next to me, but he leans against the wall and takes out a notepad and pen from his pocket. He proceeds to flip the pen in the air with one hand, launching it off the tips of his fingers and catching it again with finger and thumb, but he never writes down a single thing that I say.

*   *   *

See the pony? She has dreadful hoof dismay. She gets a terrible pain every time she tries to walk, and yet she is very restless and can hardly stand to sit still. Late at night her hooves whisper to her, asking "Please, please, just make us into glue," or they strike at her as cruelly as anyone who ever hated her. She hardly knows how she feels about them anymore, her hooves, because they hurt her so much, yet they are still so very pretty—her best feature, everyone says—and biting them very hard is the only thing that makes her feel any better at all. There she is, walking over the hill, on her way to the horse fair, where she'll not get to ride on the Prairie Wind, or play in the Haunted Barn, or eat hot buttered morsels of cowboy from a stand, because wise carnival horses know better than to let in somebody with highly contagious dismay. She stands at the gate, watching the fun, and she looks like she is dancing but she is not dancing.

Suffer, pony, suffer!

"What do you know about Dr. Chandra?" I ask Nancy, who is curling my hair at the nurses' station. She has tremendous sausage curls and a variety of distinctive eyewear that she doesn't really need. I am wearing her rhinestone-encrusted granny glasses and can see Ella Thims, another short-gut girl, in all her glorious, gruesome detail where she sits in her little red wagon by the clerk's desk. Ella had some trouble finishing up her nether parts, and so was born without an anus, or vagina, or a colon, or most of her small intestine, and her kidneys are shaped like spirals. She's only two, but she is on the sauce also. I've known her all her life.

"He hasn't rotated here much. He's pretty quiet. And pretty nice. I've never had a problem with him."

"Have you ever thought someone was interesting. Someone you barely knew, just interesting, in a way?"

"Do you like him? You like him, don't you?"

"Just interesting. Like a homeless person with really great shoes. Or a dog without a collar appearing in the middle of a graveyard."

"Sweetie, you're not his type. I know that much about him." She puts her hand out, flexes it swiftly at the wrist. I look blankly at her, so she does it again, and sort of sashays in place for a moment.

"Oh."

"Welcome to San Francisco." She sighs. "Anyway, you can do better than that. He's funny-looking, and he needs to pull his pants up. Somebody should tell him that. His mother should tell him that."

"Write this down under chief complaint," I had told him. "'I am *sick* of love.'" He'd flipped his pen and looked at the floor. When we came to the social history, I said my birth mother was a nun who'd committed indiscretions with the parish deaf mute. And I told him about my book—the cat and the bunny and the peacock and the pony, each delightful creature afflicted with a uniquely horrible disease.

"Do you think anyone would buy that?" he asked.

"There's a book that's just about shit," I said. "Why not one that's just about sickness and death? Everybody poops. Everybody suffers. Everybody dies." I even read the pony page for him, and showed him the picture.

"It sounds a little scary," he said, after a long moment of pen-tossing and silence. "And you've drawn the intestines on the outside of the body."

"Clowns are scary," I told him. "And everybody loves them. And hoof dismay isn't pretty. I'm just telling it how it is."

"There," Nancy says, "you are *curled*!" She says it like, you are *healed*. Ella Thims has a mirror on her playset. I look at my hair and press the big purple button underneath the mirror. The playset honks, and Ella claps her hands. "Good luck," Nancy adds as I scoot off on my IV pole, because I've got a date tonight.

One of the bad things about not absorbing very well and being chronically malnourished your whole life long is that you turn out to be four and a half feet tall when your father is six-four, your mother is five-ten, and your sister is six feet even. But one of the good things about being four and a half feet tall is that you are light enough to ride your own IV pole, and this is a blessing when you are chained to the sauce.

When I was five I could only ride in a straight line, and only at the pokiest speeds. Over the years I mastered the trick of steering with my feet, of turning and stopping, of moderating my speed by dragging a foot, and of spinning in tight spirals or wide loops. I take only short trips during the day, but at night I cruise as far as the research building that's attached to, but not part of, the hospital. At three a.m. even the eggiest heads are at home asleep, and I can fly down the long halls with no one to see me or stop me except the occasional security guard, always too fat and too slow to catch me, even if they understand what I am.

My date is with a CF-er named Wayne. He is the best-fed CF kid I have ever laid eyes on. Usually they are blond, and thin, and pale, and look like they might cough blood on you as soon as smile at you. Wayne is tan, with dark-brown hair and blue eyes, and big, with a high, wide chest. He is pretty hairy for sixteen. I caught a glimpse of his big hairy belly as I scooted past his room. On my fourth pass (I slowed each time and looked back over my shoulder at him) he called me in. We played a karate video game. I kicked his ass, then I showed him the meditation channel.

He is here for a tune-up: Every so often the cystic fibrosis kids will get more tired than usual, or cough more, or cough differently, or a routine test of their lung function will be precipitously sucky, and they will come in for two weeks of IV antibiotics and aggressive chest physiotherapy. He is halfway through his course of tobramycin, and bored to death. We go down to the cafeteria and I watch him eat three stale doughnuts. I have some water and a sip of his tea. I'm never hungry when I'm on the sauce, and I am absorbing so poorly now that if I ate a steak tonight a whole cow would come leaping from my ass in the morning.

I do a little history on him, not certain why I am asking the questions, and less afraid as we talk that he'll catch on that I'm playing intern. He doesn't notice, and fesses up the particulars without protest or reservation as we review his systems.

"My snot is green," he says. "Green like that." He points to my green toenails. He tells me that he has twin cousins who also have CF, and when they are together at family gatherings he is required to wear a mask so as not to pass on his highly resistant mucoid strain of Pseudomonas. "That's why there's no camp for CF," he said. "Camps for diabetes, for HIV, for kidney failure, for liver failure, but no CF camp. Because we'd infect each other." He wiggles his eyebrows then, perhaps not intentionally. "Is there a camp for people like you?" he asks.

"Probably," I say, though I know that there is, and would have gone this past summer if I had not been banned the year before for organizing a game where we rolled a couple of syndromic kids down a hill into a soccer goal. Almost everybody loved it, and nobody got hurt.

Over Wayne's shoulder I see Dr. Chandra sit down two tables away. At the same time that Wayne lifts his last doughnut to his mouth, Dr. Chandra lifts a slice of pizza to his, but where Wayne nibbles like an invalid at his food, Dr. Chandra stuffs. He just pushes and pushes the pizza into his mouth. In less than a minute he's finished it. Then he gets up and shuffles past us, sucking on a bottle of water, with bits of cheese in his beard. He doesn't even notice me.

When Wayne has finished his doughnuts I take him upstairs, past the sixth floor to the seventh. "I've never been up here," he says.

"Heme-onc," I say.

"Are we going to visit someone?"

"I know a place." It's a call room. A couple of years back an intern left his code cards in my room, and there was a list of useful door combinations on one of them. Combinations change slowly in hospitals. "The intern's never here," I tell him as I open the door. "Heme-onc kids have a lot of problems at night."

Inside are a single bed, a telephone, and a poster of a kitten in distress coupled to an encouraging motto. I think of my dream cat, moaning and crying.

"I've never been in a call room before," Wayne says nervously.

"Relax," I say, pushing him toward the bed. There's barely room for both our IV poles, but after some doing we get arranged on the bed. He lies on his side at the head with his feet propped on the nightstand. I am curled up at the foot. There's dim light from a little lamp on the nightstand, enough to make out the curve of his big lips and to read the sign above the door to the hall: *Lasciate ogne speranza, voi ch'intrate.*

"Can you read that?" he asks.

"It says, 'I believe that children are our future.'"

"That's pretty. It'd be nice if we had some candles." He scoots a little closer toward me. I stretch and yawn. "Are you sleepy?"

"No."

He's quiet for a moment. He looks down at the floor, across the thin, torn bedspread. My IV starts to beep. I reprogram it. "Air in the line," I say.

"Oh." I have shifted a little closer to him in the bed while I fixed the IV. "Do you want to do something?" he asks, staring into his lap.

"Maybe," I say. I walk my hand around the bed, like a five-legged spider, in a circle, over my own arm, across my thighs, up my belly, up to the top of my head to leap off back onto the blanket. He watches, smiling less and less as it walks up the bed, up his leg, and down his pants.

See the zebra? She has atrocious pancreas oh! Her belly hurts her terribly—sometimes it's like frogs are crawling in her belly, and sometimes it's like snakes are biting her inside just below her belly button, and sometimes it's like centipedes dancing with cleats on every one of their little feet, and sometimes it's a pain she can't even describe, even though all she can do, on those days, is sit around and try to think of ways to describe the pain. She must rub her belly on very particular sorts of tree to make it feel better, though it never feels very much better. Big round scabs are growing on her tongue, and every time she sneezes another big piece of her mane falls out. Her stripes have begun to go all the wrong way, and sometimes her own poop follows her, crawling on the ground or floating in the air, and calls her cruel names.
Suffer, zebra, suffer!

Asleep in my own bed, I'm dreaming of the cat when I hear the team; the cat's moan frays and splits, and the tones unravel from each other and become their voices. I am fully awake with my eyes closed. He lifts a mangy paw, saying goodbye.

"Dr. Chandra," says a voice. I know it must belong to Dr. Snood, the GI attending. "Tell me the three classic findings on

X-ray in necrotizing enterocolitis." They are rounding outside my room, six or seven of them, the whole GI team: Dr. Snood and my intern and the fellow and the nurse practitioners and the poor little med students. Soon they'll all come in and want to poke on my belly. Dr. Snood will talk for five minutes about shit: mine, and other people's, and sometimes just the idea of shit, a platonic ideal not extant on this earth. I know he dreams of gorgeous, perfect shit the way I dream of the cat.

Chandra speaks. He answers free peritoneal air and pneumatosis in a snap but then he is silent. I can see him perfectly with my eyes still closed: his hair all ahoo; his beady eyes staring intently at his shoes; his stethoscope twisted crooked around his neck, crushing his collar. His feet turn in, so his toes are almost touching. Upstairs with Wayne I thought of him.

Dr. Snood, too supreme a fussbudget to settle for two out of three, begins to castigate him: A doctor at your level of training should know these things; children's lives are in your two hands; you couldn't diagnose your way out of a wet paper bag; your ignorance is deadly, your ignorance can *kill*. I get out of bed, propelled by rage, angry at haughty Dr. Snood, and at hapless Dr. Chandra, and angry at myself for being this angry. Clutching my IV pole like a staff, I kick open the door and scream, scaring every one of them: "Portal fucking air! Portal fucking air!" They are all silent, and some of them white-faced. I am panting, hanging now on my IV pole. I look over at Dr. Chandra. He is not panting, but his mouth has fallen open. Our eyes meet for three eternal seconds and then he looks away.

Later I take Ella Thims down to the playroom. The going is slow, because her sauce is running and my sauce is running, so it takes some coordination to push my pole and pull her wagon while keeping her own pole, which trails behind her wagon like a dinghy, from drifting too far left or right. She lies on her back with her legs in the air, grabbing and releasing her feet, and turning her head to say hello to everyone she sees. In the hall we pass nurses and med students and visitors and every species of doctor—attendings and fellows and residents and interns—but not my intern. Everyone smiles and waves at Ella, or stoops or squats to pet her or smile closer to her face. They nod at me, and don't look at all at my face. I look back at her, knowing her fate. "Enjoy it while you have it, honey," I say to her, because I know how quickly one exhausts one's cuteness in a place like this.

Our cuteness has to work very hard here. It must extend itself to cover horrors—ostomies and scars and flipper-hands and harelips and agenesis of the eyeballs—and it rises to every miserable occasion of the sick body. Ella's strange puffy face is covered, her yellow eyes are covered, her bald spot is covered, her extra fingers are covered, her ostomies are covered, and the bitter, nose-tickling odor of urine that rises from her always is covered by the tremendous faculty of cuteness generated from some organ deep within her. Watching faces, I can see how it's working for her, and how it's stopped working for me. Your organ fails, at some point—it fails for everybody, but for people like us it fails faster, having more to cover than just the natural ugliness of body and soul. One day you are more repulsive than attractive, and the goodwill of strangers is lost forever.

It's a small loss. Still, I miss it sometimes, like now, walking down the hall and remembering riding down this same hall ten years ago on my big wheel. Strangers would stop me for speeding, and cite me with a hug. I can remember their faces, earnest and open and unassuming, and I wonder now if I ever met someone like that where I could go with them, after such a blank beginning. Something in the way that Dr. Chandra looks at me has that. And the Child Life people look at you that way, too. But they have all been trained in graduate school not to notice the extra head, or the smell, or the missing nose, or to love these things, professionally.

In the playroom I turn Ella over to Margaret and go sit on the floor in a patch of sun near the door to the deck. The morning activity, for those of us old enough or coordinated enough to manage it, is the weaving of God's eyes. At home I have a trunkful of God's eyes and potholders and terra-cotta sculptures the size of your hand, such a collection of crafts that you might think I'd spent my whole life in camp. I wind and unwind the yarn, making and then unmaking, because I don't want to add anything new to the collection. I watch Ella playing at a water trough, dipping a little red bucket and pouring it over the paddles of a waterwheel. It's a new toy. There are always new toys, every time I come, and the room is kept pretty and inviting, repainted and recarpeted in less time than some people wait to get a haircut, because some new wealthy person has taken an interest in it. The whole floor is like that, except where there are pockets of plain beige hospital nastiness here and there, places that have escaped the attentions of the rich. The nicest rooms are those that once were occupied by a privileged child with a fatal syndrome.

I pass almost a whole hour like this. Boredom can be a problem for anybody here, but I am never bored watching my gaunt, yellow peers splash in water or stacking blocks or singing along with Miss Margaret. Two wholesome Down syndrome twins—Dolores and Delilah Cutty, who both have leukemia and are often in for chemo at the same time I am in for the sauce—are having a somersault race across the carpet. A boy named Arthur who has Crouzon's syndrome—the bones of his skull have fused together too early—is playing Chutes and Ladders with a girl afflicted with Panda syndrome. Every time he gets to make a move, he cackles wildly. It makes his eyes bulge out of his head. Sometimes they pop out—then you're supposed to catch them up with a piece of sterile gauze and push them back in.

Margaret comes over, after three or four glances in my direction, noticing that my hands have been idle. Child Life specialists abhor idle hands, though there was one here a few years ago, named Eldora, who encouraged meditation and tried to teach us yoga poses. She did not last long. Margaret crouches down—they are great crouchers, having learned that children like to be addressed at eye level—and, seeing my God's eye half finished and my yarn tangled and trailing, asks if I have any questions about the process.

In fact I do. How do your guts turn against you, and your insides become your enemy? How can Arthur have such a big head and not be a super-genius? How can he laugh so loud when tomorrow he'll go back to surgery again to have his face artfully broken by the clever hands of well-intentioned sadists? How can someone so unattractive, so unavailable, so shlumpy, so low-panted, so pitiable, keep rising up, a giant in my thoughts? All these questions and others run through my head, so it takes me a while to answer, but she is patient. Finally a question comes that seems safe to ask. "How do you make someone not gay?"

See the peacock? He has crispy lung surprise. He has got an aching in his chest, and every time he tries to say something nice to someone, he only coughs. His breath stinks so much it makes everyone run away, and he tries to run away from it himself, but of course no matter where he goes, he can still smell it. Sometimes he holds his breath, just to escape it, until he passes out, but he always wakes up, even when he would rather not, and there it is, like rotten chicken, or old, old crab, or hippopotamus butt. He only feels ashamed now when he spreads out his feathers, and the only thing that gives him any relief is licking a moving tire—a very difficult thing to do.

Suffer, peacock, suffer!

It's not safe to confide in people here. Even when they aren't prying—and they do pry—it's better to be silent or to lie than to confide. They'll ask when you had your first period, or your first sex, if you are happy at home, what drugs you've done, if you wish you were thinner and prettier, or that your hair was shiny. And you may tell them about your terrible cramps, or your distressing habit of having compulsive sex with homeless men and women in Golden Gate Park, or how you can't help but sniff a little bleach every morning when you wake up, or complain that you are fat and your hair always looks as if it had just been rinsed with drool. And they'll say, I'll help you with that bleach habit that has debilitated you separately but equally from your physical illness, that dreadful habit that's keeping you from becoming more perfectly who you are. Or they may offer to teach you how the homeless are to be shunned and not fellated, or promise to wash your hair with the very shampoo of the gods. But they come and go, these interns and residents and attendings, nurses and Child Life specialists and social workers and itinerant tamale-ladies—only you and the hospital and the illness are constant. The interns change every month, and if you gave yourself to each of them they'd use you up as surely as an entire high school football team would use up their dreamiest cheerleading slut, and you'd be left like her, compelled by your history to lie down under the next moron to come along.

Accidental confidences, or accidentally fabricated secrets, are no safer. Margaret misunderstands; she thinks I am fishing for validation. She is a professional validator, with skills honed by a thousand hours of role playing—she has been both the querulous young lesbian and the supportive adult. "But there's no reason to change," she tells me. "You don't have to be ashamed of who you are."

This is a lesson I learned long ago, from my mother, who really was a lesbian, after she was a nun but before she was a wife. "I did not give it up because it was inferior to anything," she told me seriously, the same morning she found me in the arms of Shelley Woo, my neighbor and one of the few girls I was ever able to lure into a sleep-over. We had not, like my mother assumed, spent the night practicing tender, heated frottage. We were hugging as innocently as two stuffed animals. "But it's all *right*," she kept saying against my protests. So I know not to argue with Margaret's assumption, either.

It makes me pensive, having become a perceived lesbian. I wander the ward thinking, "Hello, nurse!" at every one of them I see. I sit at the station, watching them come and go, spinning the big lazy susan of misfortune that holds all the charts. I can imagine sliding my hands under their stylish scrubs—not toothpaste-green like Dr. Chandra's scrubs, but hot pink or canary yellow or deep-sea blue, printed with daisies or sun faces or clouds or even embroidered with dancing hula girls—and pressing my fingers in the hollows of their ribs. I can imagine taking off Nancy's rhinestone granny glasses with my teeth, or biting so gently on the ridge of her collarbone. The charge nurse—a woman from the Philippines named Jory—sees me opening and closing my mouth silently, and asks if there is something wrong with my jaw. I shake my head. There's nothing wrong. It's only that I am trying to open wide enough for an imaginary mouthful of her soft brown boob.

If it's this easy for me to do, to imagine the new thing, then is he somewhere wondering what it would feel like to press a cheek against my scarred belly, or to gather my hair in his fists? When I was little, my pediatrician, Dr. Sawyer, used to look in my pants every year and say, "Just checking to make sure everything is *normal*." I imagine an exam, and imagine him imagining it with me. He listens with his ear on my chest and back, and when it is time to look in my pants he stares and says, "It's not just *normal*, it's *extraordinary!*"

A glowing radiance has just burst from between my legs, and is bathing him in converting rays of glory, when he comes hurrying out of the doctor's room across from the station. He drops his clipboard and apologizes to no one in particular, and glances at me as he straightens up. I want him to smile and look away, to duck his head in an aw-shucks gesture, but he just nods stiffly, then walks away. I watch him pass around the corner, then give the lazy susan a hard spin. If my own chart comes to rest before my eyes, it will mean that he loves me.

See the monkey? He has chronic kidney doom. His kidneys are always yearning toward things—other monkeys and trees and people and different varieties of fruit. He feels them stirring in him, and pressing against his flank whenever he gets near to something that he likes. When he tells a girl monkey or a boy monkey that his kidneys want to hug them, they slap him or punch him or kick him in the eye. At night his kidneys ache wildly. He is always swollen and moist-looking. He

smells like a toilet because he can only pee when he doesn't want to,
and every night he asks himself, How many pairs of crisp white slacks
can one monkey ruin?

   Suffer, monkey, suffer!

Every fourth night he is on call. He stays in the hospital from six
in the morning until six the following evening, awake all night on
account of various intern-sized crises. I see him walking in and
out of rooms, or peering at the two-foot-long flow sheets that
lean on giant clipboards on the walls by every door, or looking
solemnly at the nurses as they castigate him for slights against
their patients or their honor—an unsigned order, an incorrectly
dosed medication, the improper washing of his hands. I catch
him in the corridor in what I think is a posture of despair, sunk
down outside Wayne's door with his face in his knees, and I think
that he has heard about me and Wayne, and it's broken his heart.
But I have already dismissed Wayne days ago. We were like two
IV poles passing in the night, I told him.

   Dr. Chandra is sleeping, not despairing, not snoring but
breathing loud through his mouth. I step a little closer to him,
close enough to smell him—coffee and hair gel and something
like pickles. A flow sheet lies discarded beside him, so from where
I stand I can see how much Wayne has peed in the last twelve
hours. I stoop next to him and consider sitting down and falling
asleep myself, because I know it would constitute a sort of inti-
macy to mimic his posture and let my shoulder touch his shoulder, to close my eyes and maybe share a dream with him. But
before I can sit, Nancy comes creeping down the hall in her socks,
a barf basin half full of warm water in her hands. A phalanx of
nurses appears in the hall behind her, each of them holding a fin-

ger to her lips as Nancy kneels next to Dr. Chandra, puts the
bucket on the floor, and takes his hand away from his leg so gently I think she is going to kiss it before she puts it in the water. I
just stand there, afraid that he'll wake up as I'm walking away, and
think I'm responsible for the joke. Nancy and the nurses all disappear around the corner to the station, so it's just me and him
again in the hall. I drum my fingers against my head, trying to
think of a way to get us both out of this, and realize it's just a step
or two to the dietary cart. I take a straw and kneel down next to
him. It's a lot of volume, and I imagine, as I drink, that it's fla-
vored by his hand. When I throw it up later it seems like the best
barf I've ever done, because it is for him, and as Nancy holds my
hair back for me and asks me what possessed me to drink so much
water at once I think to him, It was for you, baby, and feel both
pathetic and exalted.

I follow him around for a couple of call nights, not saving
him again from any more mean-spirited jokes, but catching him
scratching or picking when he thinks no one is looking, and
wanting, like a fool, to be the hand that scratches or the finger
that picks, because it would be so interesting and gratifying to
touch him like that, or touch him in any way, and I wonder and
wonder what I'm doing as I creep around with increasingly practiced nonchalance, looking bored while I sit across from him, listening to him cajole the radiologist on the phone at one in the
morning, when I could be sleeping, or riding my pole, when he
is strange-looking, and cannot like me, and talks funny, and is
rumored to be an intern of small brains. But I see him stand in
the hall for five minutes, staring at an abandoned tricycle, and he
puts his palm against a window and bows his head at the blinking
lights on the bridge in a way that makes me want very much
to know what he is thinking, and I see him, from a hiding place

behind a bin full of dirty sheets, hopping up and down in a hall he thinks is empty save for him, and I am sure he is trying to fly away.

Hiding on his fourth call night in the dirty utility room while he putters with a flow sheet at the door to the room across the hall, I realize that it could be easier than this, and so when he's moved on, I go back to my room and watch the meditation channel for a little while, then practice a few moans, sounding at first too distressed, then not distressed enough, then finally getting it just right before I push the button for the nurse. Nancy is off tonight. It's Jory who comes, and finds me moaning and clutching at my belly. I get Tylenol and a touch of morphine, but am careful to moan only a little less, so Jory calls Dr. Chandra to come evaluate me.

It's romantic, in its way. The lights are low, and he puts his warm, freshly washed hands on my belly to push in every quadrant, a round of light palpation, a round of deep. He speaks very softly, asking me if it hurts more here, or here, or here. "I'm going to press in on your stomach and hold my hand there for a second, and I want you to tell me if it makes it feel better or worse when I let go." He listens to my belly, then takes me by the ankle, extending and flexing my hip.

"I don't know," I say when he asks me if that made the pain better or worse. "Do it again."

See the bunny? She has high colonic ruin, a very fancy disease. Only bunnies from the very best families get it, but when she cries bloody tears and the terrible spiders come crawling out of her bottom, she would rather be poor, and not even her fancy robot bed can comfort her, or even distract her. When her electric pillow feeds her dreams of happy bunnies playing in the snow, she only feels jealous and sad, and she bites her tongue while she sleeps, and bleeds all night while the bed dabs at her lips with cotton balls on long steel fingers. In the morning a servant drives her to the Potty Club, where she sits with other wealthy bunny girls on a row of crystal toilets. They are supposed to be her friends, but she doesn't like them at all.

Suffer, bunny, suffer!

When he visits I straighten up, carefully hiding the books that Margaret brought me, biographies of Sappho and Billie Jean King and H.D. She entered quietly into my room, closed the door, and drew the blinds before producing them from out of her pants and repeating that my secret was safe with her, though there was no need for it to be secret, and nothing to be ashamed of, and she would support me as fully in proclaiming my homosexuality as she did in the hiding of it. She has already conceived of a banner to put over my bed, a rainbow hung with stars, on the day that I put away all shame and dark feelings. I hide the books because I know all would really be lost if he saw them and assumed the assumption. I do not want to be just his young lesbian friend. I lay out refreshments, spare cookies and juices and puddings from the meal trays that come, though I get all the food I can stand from the sauce.

I don't have many dates, on the outside. Rumors of my scarred belly or my gastrostomy tube drive most boys away before anything can develop, and the only boys that pay persistent attention to me are the creepy ones looking for a freak. I have better luck in here, with boys like Wayne, but those dates are still outside the usual progressions, the talking more and more until you are convinced they actually know you, and the touching more and more until you are pregnant and wondering if this guy ever even liked you. There is nothing normal about my midnight trysts with Dr. Chandra, but there's an order about them, and a progression. I summon him and he puts his hands on me, and he orders an intervention, and he comes back to see if it worked or didn't. For three nights he stands there, watching me for a few moments, leaning on one foot and then the other, before he asks me if I need anything else. All the things I need flash through my mind, but I say, "No," and he leaves, promising to come back and check on me later, but never doing it. Then, on the fourth night, he does his little dance and asks, "What do you want to do when you grow up? I mean, when you're bigger. When you're out of school, and all that."

"Medicine," I say. "Pediatrics. What else?"

"Aren't you sick of it?" he asks. He is backing toward the door, but I have this feeling like he's stepping closer to the bed.

"Maybe. But I have to do it."

"You could do anything you want," he says, not sounding like he means it.

"What else could Tarzan become, except lord of the jungle?"

"He could have been a dancer, if he wanted. Or an ice cream man. Whatever he wanted."

"Did you ever want to do anything else, besides this?"

"Never. Not ever."

"How about now?"

"Oh," he says. "Oh, no. I don't think so. No, I don't think so." He startles when his pager vibrates. He looks down at it. "I've got to go. Just tell Jory if the pain comes back again."

"Come over here for a second," I say. "I've got to tell you something."

"Later," he says.

"No, now. It'll just take a second." I expect him to leave, but he walks over and stands near the bed.

"What?"

"Would you like some juice?" I ask him, though what I really meant to do was to accuse him, ever so sweetly, of being the same as me, of knowing the same indescribable thing about this place and about the world. "Or a cookie?"

"No thanks," he says. As he passes through the door I call out for him to wait, and to come back. "What?" he says again, and I think I am just about to know how to say it when the code bell begins to chime. It sounds like an ice cream truck, but it means someone on the floor is trying to die. He jumps in the air like he's been goosed, then takes a step one way in the hall, stops, starts the other way, then goes back, so it looks like he's trying to decide whether to run toward the emergency or away from it.

I get up and follow him down the hall, just in time to see him run into Ella Thims's room. From the back of the crowd at the door I can see him standing at the head of the bed, looking depressed and indecisive, a bag mask held up in his hand. He asks someone to page the senior resident, then puts the mask over Ella's face. She's bleeding from her nose and mouth, and from her ostomy sites. The blood shoots around inside the mask when he squeezes the bag, and he can't seem to get a tight seal over Ella's chin. The mask keeps slipping while the nurses ask him what he wants to do.

"Well," he says. "Um. How about some oxygen?" Nancy finishes getting Ella hooked up to the monitor and points out that she's in a bad rhythm. "Let's get her some fluid," he says. Nancy asks if he wouldn't like to shock her, instead. "Well," he says. "Maybe!" Then I get pushed aside by the PICU team, called from the other side of the hospital by the chiming of the ice cream bell. The attending asks Dr. Chandra what's going on, and he turns even redder, and says something I can't hear, because I am being pushed farther and farther from the door as more people squeeze past me to cluster around the bed, ring after ring of saviors and spectators. Pushed back to the nursing station, I am standing in front of Jory, who is sitting by the telephone, reading a magazine.

"Hey, honey," she says, not looking at me. "Are you doing okay?"

See the cat? He has died. Feline leukemic indecisiveness is always terminal. Now he just lies there. You can pick him up. Go ahead. Bring him home and put him under your pillow, and pray to your parents or your stuffed plush Jesus to bring him back, and say to him, "Come back, come back." He will be smellier in the morning, but no more alive. Maybe he is in a better place, maybe his illness could not follow him where he went, or maybe everything is the same, the same pain in a different place. Maybe there is nothing at all, where he is. I don't know, and neither do you.

Goodbye, cat, goodbye!

Ella Thims died in the PICU, killed, it was discovered, by too much potassium in her sauce. It put her heart in that bad rhythm they couldn't get her out of, though they worked over her till dawn. She'd been in it for at least a while before she was discovered, so it was already too late when they put her on the bypass machine. It made her dead alive—her blood was moving in her, but by mid-morning of the next day she was rotting inside. Dr. Chandra, it was determined, was the chief architect of the fuck-up, assisted by a newly graduated nurse who meticulously verified the poisonous contents of the solution and delivered them without comment. Was there any deadlier combination, people asked each other all morning, than an idiot intern and a clueless nurse?

I spend the morning on my IV pole, riding the big circle around the ward. It's strange, to be out here in the daylight, and in the busy morning crowd—less busy today, and a little hushed because of the death. I go slower than usual, riding like my grandma would, stepping and pushing leisurely with my left foot, and stopping often to let a team go by. They pass like a family of ducks, the attending followed by the fellow, resident, and students, all in a row, with the lollygagging nutritionist bringing up the rear. Pulmonary, Renal, Neurosurgery, even the Hypoglycemia team are about in the halls, but I don't see the GI team anywhere.

The rest of the night I lie awake in bed, waiting for them to come round on me. I can see it already: everybody getting a turn to kick Dr. Chandra outside my door, or Dr. Snood standing casually with his foot on Dr. Chandra's neck as the team discussed my latest ins and outs. Or maybe he wouldn't even be there. Maybe they send you home early when you kill somebody. Or maybe he would just run and hide somewhere. Not sleeping, I still dreamed about him, huddled in a linen closet, sucking on the corner of a blanket, or sprawled on the bathroom floor, knocking his head softly against the toilet, or kneeling naked in the medication room, shooting up with Benadryl and morphine. I went to him in every place, and put my hands on him with great tenderness, never saying a thing, just nodding at him, like I knew how horrible everything was. A couple of rumors float around in the late morning—he's jumped from the bridge; he's thrown himself under a trolley; Ella's parents, finally come to visit, have killed him; he's retired back home to Virginia in disgrace. I add and subtract details—he took off his clothes and folded them neatly on the sidewalk before he jumped; the trolley was full of German choirboys;

Ella's father choked while her mother stabbed; his feet hang over the end of his childhood bed.

I don't stop even to get my meds—Nancy trots beside me and pushes them on the fly. Just after that, around one o'clock, I understand that I am following after something, and that I had better speed up if I am going to catch it. It seems to me, who should really know better, that all the late, new sadness of the past twenty-four hours ought to count for something, ought to do something, ought to change something, inside of me, or outside in the world. But I don't know what it is that might change, and I expect that nothing will change—children have died here before, and hapless idiots have come and gone, and always the next day the sick still come to languish and be poked, and they will lie in bed hoping not for healing, a thing which the wise have all long given up on, but for something to make them feel better, just for a little while, and sometimes they get this thing, and often they don't. I think of my animals and hear them all, not just the cat but the whole bloated menagerie, crying and crying, *make it stop.*

Faster and faster and faster—not even a grieving short-gut girl can be forgiven for speed like this. People are thinking, *She loved that little girl,* but I am thinking, *I will never see him again.* Still, I almost forget I am chasing something and not just flying along for the exhilaration it brings. Nurses and students and even the proudest attendings try to leap out of the way but only arrange themselves into a slalom course. It's my skill, not theirs, that keeps them from being struck. Nancy tries to stand in my way, to stop me, but she wimps away to the side long before I get anywhere near her. Doctors and visiting parents and a few other kids, and finally a couple of security guards, one almost fat enough to block the entire hall, try to arrest me, but they all fail, and I can hardly even hear what they are shouting. I am concentrating on the window. It's off the course of the circle, at the end of a hundred-foot hall that runs past the playroom and the PICU. It's a portrait frame of the near tower of the bridge, which looks very orange today, against the bright blue sky. It is part of the answer when I understand that I am running the circle to rev up for a run down to the window that right now seems like the only way out of this place. The fat guard and Nancy and a parent have made themselves into a roadblock just beyond the turn into the hall. They are stretched like a Red Rover line from one wall to the other, and two of them close their eyes, but don't break, as I come near them. I make the fastest turn of my life and head away down the hall.

It's Miss Margaret who stops me. She steps out of the playroom with a crate of blocks in her arms, sees me, looks down the hall toward the window, and shrieks, "Motherfucker!" I withstand the uncharacteristic obscenity, though it makes me stumble, but the blocks she casts in my path form an obstacle I cannot pass. There are twenty of them or more. As I try to avoid them I am reading the letters, thinking they'll spell out the name of the thing I am chasing, but I am too slow to read any of them except the farthest one, an R, and the red Q that catches under my wheel. I fall off the pole as it goes flying forward, skidding toward the window after I come to a stop on my belly outside the PICU, my central line coming out in a pull as swift and clean as a tooth pulled out with a string and a door. The end of the catheter sails in an arc through the air, scattering drops of blood against the ceiling, and I think how neat it would look if my heart had come out, still attached to the tip, and what a distinct, once-in-a-lifetime noise it would have made when it hit the floor.

WHY ANTICHRIST?

✳

My father warned me that sadness cleaves to sadness, and that depressed people go around in hangdog packs. Common disaster is the worst reason for a friendship. In picking your friends, he said, you should consider what great things you can do together. You are assembling a team, he told me, not a teatime cozy of crybabies, and he made me promise never to become part of any orphans' or bereaved sons' club, because sitting around in a circle of pity getting your worst qualities praised and reinforced was no way to move ahead with a great life. That is the way *down*, he said, making a down-roller-coaster motion with his hand, but you shall go *up*.

So I knew what it was all about, when Cindy Hutchinson started paying nice attention to me after her father died. He was the richest man in town and was doubling his money at the World Trade Center when the planes hit. Cindy became a tragic celebrity, and suddenly everybody remembered that my father had died when we were all in tenth grade, and the teachers all looked at me in the silences that fell during the frequent breaks they provided for us to talk about our feelings, as if I were somehow more grown-up than everybody else because my life had sucked harder and earlier than most. Or like I must have learned something back then, and if I would only share, it would make it easier for them all to bear up in these days. But I just stared at my desk, because I didn't know anything like that.

I caught Cindy looking at me in class or at lunch, and a couple of times she came to games and I would feel an itching on the back of my neck in the middle of a play and look up to see her there. But she didn't actually talk to me until the middle of October, and I never tried to talk to her, though like everyone else I felt bad about her dad. She was always surrounded by friends or admirers and seemed like she was getting enough sympathy to last anybody a lifetime, so I stayed away.

One afternoon after school while I was walking down to the lacrosse field I saw her with her friends, playing around on the statues outside the library. She ran after me when she saw me, but she didn't catch up till I was passing the gym. "Hey!" she said, and I stopped and turned around.

"Hey," I said, and then she just stood there, pulling at her skirt and touching the pencil that was stuck in her hair and looking at the divers falling past the windows in the gym. "Yeah," I said, because I didn't know what to say to her. "See you later."

"I know how you feel," she said suddenly, spitting the words out all at once and stringing them together in a swift mumble, but I'd heard the phrase so many times before that I think I'd understand it if somebody said it to me in Chinese.

"No you don't," I said, and walked away. Her hand was only touching my bag and she just let it drop away.

"I'm having a party tonight!" she called out after me. "You should come!"

"I don't really go to parties," I said, which was true. I didn't like to drink, and didn't like watching people get drunk, and the people I wanted to make out with were never the people who wanted to make out with me, and if I wanted to make some drunk girl cry then I could stay home and do that with my mother.

But I did go, and maybe that was the first sign, that weird pressure I felt all through practice and at home while I made dinner and while my mom watched me eat, not touching what was on her plate except to push up the potatoes in heaps, and to take strings of chicken off the bone to dangle for the dog. I was thinking of Cindy and her party all afternoon, and in the shower after practice I stood with my eyes closed under the water like I always do and felt like I was spinning in place, my bare feet turning on the soap-slicked tile, and when I opened my eyes I found I had turned to face south, down toward the river and her house. I almost never feel like I have to do something, but when I do, it usually turns out to be the right thing—I'll pass the ball to someone who looks like they're covered or pick an answer on a test that I think is wrong but feel is right, and it always works out.

"I'm going to a party," I told my mother.

"Good for you, honey," she said. "You don't get out enough. Did we show you this?" She turned down to the dog. He is part poodle but mostly mutt and the fancy haircut my mother gets for him every month always looks like borrowed finery to me. "Channel up!" she shouted at him, and he ran toward the television and turned it off with a bump of his nose. "Well, we're working on it," she said. "But go, go! You have a good time! Don't worry about these." She indicated the dishes with a sweep of her hand. "Puppy and I will take care of everything." But she went to her room not very much longer after that, the dog trailing after her, and closed her door. So I cleaned up myself before I went down the hill to Cindy's house.

We live in the same big neighborhood, one of those places on the Severn where people pay a lot of money for big woods and the feeling that they are miles away from their neighbors. On the curving roads it would be two miles to Cindy's house, but cutting down the hill through the woods it wasn't even one. She lived on Beach Road, right on the river, on a little house-sized peninsula. The drive down to the house was full of cars, but the woods covered the light and the noise of the party until I came around a bend in the drive and saw the place, every window bright. She was sitting alone on her front porch with a glass of wine in either hand, one red and one white, taking sips off each one while I watched her. I don't know why I stood watching like that but it wasn't long before she looked up at me. "I knew you'd come," she said.

"I feel like shit," Cindy said, "but I want everybody else to have a good time." That was the point of the party—the next best thing to feeling happy herself was seeing other people happy. So she floated from group to group in her house, exhorting them to drink more or laugh more or sing more or join her for a game of strip poker upstairs in her big attic bedroom. "Come on," she said to me, when I hesitated to accept a drink. "It's for charity."

I followed her upstairs and sat between her and Paul Ricker at the poker game. Paul has big eyes and a very open face, and was in his underwear within twenty minutes. Most everybody had at least taken off their shirt, but I was only barefoot, and Cindy was still fully clothed. She was in and out of the game, running off to dance downstairs, or to bring more players upstairs, or to replenish the drinks, mixing vodka and gin and ginger ale and grapefruit juice in a big bowl in the middle of her bedroom floor and then dipping out servings with a ladle.

"Hey," Paul said. "Stick on stick! Body on body!" We were on the lacrosse team together, and he liked to imitate our coach.

"Right," I said, trying not to look at his hairy belly. I had seen it before in the showers but it was different here, in a darkened room full of drunk kids, at least a fourth of whom had given up on the game to make out in front of everyone. Even drunk-droopy, his eyes were huge, and they seemed to shine in the dark. He scooted over so our legs were touching, and I moved. He put his hand out and rubbed between my shoulder blades, circles around and around.

"Did I ever tell you," he asked, "that you have a nice back?"

"No," I said, and moved away again.

"Dude," he said. "I'm kidding!"

"I know," I said. He smiled, and seemed all eyes and teeth.

"You know," he said. "I know. We both know!" And then he leaned into and started kissing my neck. He had hardly attached himself to me before Cindy pulled him off.

"We have a winner!" she said, and announced that Paul was the drunkest person at the party. Everyone applauded, and Paul bowed, then turned around and pulled down his underwear to show us all his ass.

"You may address me," he said, "as Mr. Winterbottom!"

"Mr. Winterbottom!" somebody called out. "Tell us a story!"

"Once upon a time," Paul said, shaking his ass back and forth with every word, "there was a boy named Paul."

"New game!" Cindy said, pushing Paul aside, so he fell next to her bed and nearly missed splitting his head on her night table. He rolled on the carpet and laughed hysterically. "Everybody!" Cindy was shouting over the music. "Everybody come upstairs!" Only three or four people came up, but it seemed to be enough for her. She distributed the candles that were burning on her dresser and windowsill to the people on the floor, and drew us all into a circle. The she reached under her bed and drew out a Ouija board. "This is a game," she said, "called Talk to My Dad."

Paul laughed for a moment, but even drunk as he was he noticed that everyone else had become totally quiet.

"Cindy," said a girl on the other side of the room. It was too dark to see who. "That's . . . that's just . . ."

"It's okay!" Cindy said. "It's not what you think. It's not really him. I know that. Of course I know. I'm not crazy. It's just some fucked-up spirit that pretends to be him. They can't fool me." She put the board down in the middle of the circle we'd made and started drawing people into it, pulling at their shirts if they were wearing one, or giving people hugs and then pulling on their arms, saying all the while, "Come on, come on." Soon she had us gathered close around the board. "Hands on," she said, guiding fingers to the planchette, until at least a dozen people were touching it. I just held a candle. "Quiet now," Cindy said, though no one was talking. She had closed her door but we could all still hear the music from downstairs. "Quiet and still. All the smart people, empty out your heads. All the drunk people, get serious for a second." This made Paul laugh again.

"Serious!" Cindy said. After a few moments of heavy-breathing silence, she started to hum in a low tone, as if she were setting a tone for herself, because when she called out for her dad, she pitched her voice lower than mine. "Papa," she said. "Father. We are calling for you. Come back across the river and speak to us. We are ignorant and wish to learn the secrets of the dead."

"You're ignorant," said Paul. "I'm not ignorant. I'm just fine." He snorted but didn't take his finger away from the planchette, and Cindy ignored him.

"Papa! Are you there?" The planchette moved right away, swinging in three quick arcs to spell, *Yes.*

"How have you been?" she asked, still in that deep, goofy voice.

As well as can be expected, the board answered. *Given the circumstances.* Malcolm Walker wrote down the letters as they came and then read the words out loud.

"Well," Cindy said. "It's not exactly all parades and puppy shows up here, either."

"Up?" said Paul. Cindy held up a finger to her lips.

"Will you answer our questions?" she asked.

Of course, as always. I am your servant.

"That must be nice," said Sonia Chu. "I wish I could order my dad around."

"Careful what you wish for," said Cindy. "Questions? Questions?"

"Are any of our teachers gay?" asked Malcolm.

Mrs. Lambert is a lesbian, was the reply. Sonia said we hardly needed a spirit to tell us that.

"Are the terrorists there in hell?" asked Paul, "Are they roasting on a spit?"

Hell is a heaven to the innocent eye and the unspoiled imagination.

"What kind of answer is that?" Paul asked.

Answers are questions. Questions are answers.

"Who in this room is going to die?" Cindy asked. "Give us a name!"

"Cindy!" said Sonia. "Gross!"

All to die, but one. All to suffer, but one. "Now this is getting creepy," said Malcolm.

"It's supposed to be creepy," said Paul.

"But who will die first?" Cindy asked.

What matters time when time is soon to end?

"He's never very straightforward," Cindy said. "You just have to be patient."

"But I don't want to know," said Sonia.

"Sure you do," said Cindy. "Come on, it's just a game."

It is not a game. It is the end of time. My suffering is great but yours will be greater.

"Was it horrible?" asked Arthur. "There in the tower. It must have been horrible. Did you see it coming? Did you see the plane?"

It was coming all my life but a greater disaster is coming for you.

"I think he's on their side," said Paul. Cindy told him to shut up.

"Who will die?" Cindy asked again.

All but one.

Cindy sighed exasperatedly. "Sometimes you just have to humor them," she said, "to get your answer. Fine. Who is it? Who is going to live forever?"

The Great One. Lucifer's son. Antichrist.

"The Antichrist is at this party?" asked Paul. "I'm going to kick his ass!"

He is among you. He has always been among you, sleeping and dreaming but even now he wakes.

"Who?" Cindy asked. "Stop teasing. Tell us!" And instead of letters this time the planchette swooped toward the person it wanted to name, the fingers drawing along the hands, the hands drawing along the bodies, so all twelve of the players fell forward, faces to the carpet. The planchette flew off the board and flowed over the carpet as if on wheels, stopping at the uttermost reach of their arms and pointing squarely at me. I turned to look behind me, expecting for some reason to see Cindy's mom, back early from her trip out of town with Cindy's sister, standing in the door. But the door was closed and there was nobody there.

* * *

"Crazy party," Paul Ricker said to me the next day. We were in the locker room after practice.

"Yeah," I said. "It was all pretty weird."

"I don't remember anything that happened after nine, but I heard about the Ouija thing. Don't worry about it. One of those things told my sister that she was Jesus."

"You don't remember anything?"

"Well, a couple flashes here and there. I remember singing a lot. And a little bit of the poker game. And looking for my pants. That's about it. Except . . ." He leaned down so his mouth was close to my ear. "I think I screwed somebody. Don't remember any of it—dammit!—but I woke up the next morning with this feeling, and when I felt down there it was just like after . . . you know. How's that for fucked-up?"

"That's definitely fucked-up," I said.

"I have a list of candidates, but how do you figure something like that out? You can't just walk up and say, 'Hey, Cindy, did we screw last night?' Except I'm sure it wasn't her. Anyway, I'll figure it out." He left his practice uniform in a pile at his feet and walked off to take a shower.

"Good luck with that," I said, and waited until he was done with his shower before I took mine.

Cindy found me again while I was waiting for the bus. There was barely enough light to read by but I was sitting in the grass with my history book and for once I could pay attention to what I was reading, so I didn't notice when she came up, and only saw her when she sat down next to me.

"Hey," she said. When I didn't look up she pushed my shoulder. "Hey!"

"What?" I said.

"What?" she said, imitating my voice but making me sound

like a retard. "Thanks for coming to my party last night. Too bad you ruined it by being the Antichrist."

"Whatever," I said. After the Ouija game I had left, though Cindy asked me to stay, and made a big joke of the whole thing by taking the planchette and pointing it at people, and saying things like "You're Ronald Reagan" and "You're the pope" and "You're a double-penised huffalump!" But I felt like it had been a mistake to come. I went home and felt that way for the rest of the night. "I usually don't go to parties. Something stupid always happens to me at parties."

"Not that it's bad. I wouldn't mind meeting the Antichrist. I have a lot of questions for him, because he's somebody in the know. Right?"

"I don't know."

"Well, think about it. He'd know more than us, right?"

"I guess."

"I used to be into all that shit, back in junior high. Black candles and secret piercings and praying in your fireplace and being, like, Satan is my master! I had black hair back then and hung out with Susie Freep. Did you ever know her? She goes to Trinity now."

"No," I said, still trying to read.

"Good thing. She was a bad influence. My mom practically had to send me to a deprogramming camp to get me away from her. She was like our high priestess or something. She gave it up, though. Now she's in Young Life. How about that?"

"Yeah," I said. Then she was quiet for a moment, but it was too dark to read. The sky was still bright pale blue, but shadows had come over the grass and I couldn't make out letters anymore. Cindy leaned over and put her head on my shoulder. "It's going to be a beautiful evening," she said.

"I like the fall," I said, not moving.

"It's my favorite season," she said. "Still, even with September and shit. Hey, my mom and my sister are going to be gone until Friday. You should come over and watch a movie or something." She was quiet a little while longer, and I was wondering where the bus could be, when she said, "Last night I dreamed I was having sex with my father."

"Everybody has that dream," I said, which is true, if a therapist saying so makes a thing true. Cindy took her head off my shoulder and when I turned to look at her she threw water in my face.

"Jesus," I said. "What was that for?"

"Does it burn?" she asked. "Does it hurt you?" And even though the water was in a regular squirt bottle I knew it was holy water.

"Jesus Fucking Christ," I said, grabbing it away from her and taking a long swig of it. It was very warm, and I thought as I drank it that she must have been keeping it close to her body all day. I threw the bottle down. "How's that?" I asked. "Now will you lay off? Now will you just leave me alone? I don't have any answers for you. I don't know shit." And I picked up my bag and my stick and walked off.

"It was just a joke!" she called out. "Come on. I'll give you a ride!" But I kept walking all the way home.

I was mad all through dinner, so I barely talked at all when my mother asked me questions about the party. She said she was sorry if it wasn't very fun, and told me I shouldn't judge all parties by one party, and that to give up on all on account of the one would be like giving up on people just because my father was a boor and a cheat. Then she told me stories about parties she had gone to in high school, and about the prom, when she'd nearly died in a boating accident, except that the natural buoyancy of her dress saved her. I had heard the stories before. I hardly ate anything before my stomach started to hurt. I kept thinking it was being so mad that gave me the stomachache.

I was nauseated later, but didn't throw up until close to midnight, just after I fell asleep. I woke up to it—a horrible burning stab in my belly, and then a feeling of fullness, and then I was throwing up right in my bed. When I turned on my light I saw that it was bright blood that had come up. It covered my sheets and my pillow, so I changed them, thinking that was all that was going to happen, and even feeling a little better, but then the burning came again, and though I made it to the toilet this time, I had barely finished throwing up before I had to sit down and shoot black blood out of my ass. I sat there for a little while, shaking and cold, before I got dressed and knocked on my mother's door.

"Mom," I said, "I need to go to the hospital." I knocked again, and called out again. The dog barked, but there wasn't any other answer. So I drove myself.

"I hate social workers," Cindy said. She came to visit me in the hospital, though I didn't want any visitors. She showed up with my homework and a bunch of homemade cards, and I had thought that the art teacher had made everybody draw a card for me, like we used to do in grade school when a kid got sick or their dog died, but when she gave them to me I saw that she had made them all. "One of them kept coming to our house. This Red Cross lady. I don't even know how she found us, but she kept showing up and my mom kept letting her in, and they would sit around having tea, and then she would talk to each of us in private. Like my mother didn't already have a five-hundred-dollar-an-hour therapist before my dad died. 'It's hard to lose your father,' she told me, 'but it's even harder when it's a national tragedy and not just a personal one.' I told her that was very wise, but I said it like, *wise*, you know? Like you could tell by the tone of my voice how I thought she was clueless. But she thought I was complimenting her and she told me I was very mature for my age. So when she came again, when we were alone, I leaned over to her, and guess what I said?"

I was staring out the window at the perfect fall day. I wanted to be at practice.

"Guess what I said?"

"I don't know," I said. The hospital social worker had just finished talking to me when Cindy came in, asking me again about why my mother couldn't bring me to the hospital. When I said again that she'd been sick, she asked again with what, and I said she should talk to my mother about that. She's better about lying in that way than I am—she can make up a whole story in the time it takes to tell it. I knew I would screw things up by talking too much so I just stared at the lady and told her my stomach was starting to hurt again, so she left.

"I said, 'I'm not a fucking disaster area.' And she said, 'You must be very angry. I understand your anger.' I *hate* social workers."

"Somebody has to do the social work," I said.

"But I bet it really knocked her for a loop when you told her you were the Antichrist. There's a rehab job none of them could resist."

"We didn't talk about that."

"He is the son of the Devil but I think that with the right role models he could be a very productive member of society."

"Very funny," I said. She got out of her chair and sat down next to me on the bed, and took my hand. I didn't pull away, and she didn't say anything. We just sat like that for a while. A nurse came in to put some medication in my IV. They were treating me for an ulcer in my duodenum, the part of the small intestine that comes right after the stomach. The doctor kept asking me if I was worried about something, because this is the kind of ulcer you get from worrying very intensely.

"Do you think people are forgetting already?" she asked, after the nurse was gone. "About my dad, I mean."

"It's hardly been two months," I said.

"Long enough," she said. "People usually forget about shit like this in a couple days. I mean, imagine if it hadn't been . . . how it was. If he just died drunk driving or something. Nobody would have remembered in a week. I almost liked it, before, how people kept saying that nothing was ever going to be the same. Because it wasn't—not for me. And I wanted it to not be for anybody else, either."

"It never gets back to normal," I said.

"Not for me," she said. "But I mean for them. You know, I liked it, when they kept playing the footage over and over again. My mom kept turning off the television but I kept it on in my room. And I kept saying, 'Yes, do it again. Show us every fucking morning so nobody ever forgets what they did to my dad.' But now I have to watch it on my tape."

"That sounds like a bad idea," I said. "I get sad just looking at my dad's picture." She turned and looked at me then, and brought my hand up to her heart.

"You know, we are exactly alike, me and you. Exactly alike."

"No, we're not," I said, taking my hand away. "My stomach hurts. I'm going to take a nap."

"Okay," she said. "Hey, I almost forgot." She rummaged in her suitcase-sized duffel bag and brought out a present.

"You already gave me the cards," I said.

"Just open it." It was another Ouija board, just the regular kind, not fancy like hers. "You're not supposed to play with it alone. It'll make you crazy or possessed if you do."

"I don't need one of these," I said, and she leaned close.

"You don't have to pretend with me," she said. "You don't have to put up an act. I know you want to talk to your dad."

"Jesus Christ," I said, and dropped it on the floor.

"You're going to be all over it when I'm gone."

"Jesus! Will you knock that off!"

"You keep saying Jesus like that and you're going to get gonorrhea or something," she said. "It's not good for you to say Jesus all the time." I pushed the nurse button, to ask them to kick her out, but she left by herself. "What do you want me to bring you tomorrow?" At first I said nothing, but then I said my lacrosse stick and a ball. Then she was gone, and I reached down and slid the game underneath the bed. When the nurse came in I told her I didn't need her, but she stayed for a minute, refilling the water pitcher and straightening the blankets.

"Your girlfriend is pretty," she said.

"Yeah," I said, not knowing why I didn't say she wasn't my girlfriend. I turned over and thought about lacrosse plays, because that usually helps me sleep, and I think I slept for a couple of minutes, because I had a dream that Paul and I were facing off together in front of a huge crowd. Which made no sense because we play on the same team and Paul's a goalie. When I opened my eyes I was staring at a whole window full of blue sky.

I flipped through the cards. They said things like *Hope the bleeding in your stomach stops soon* and *You are going to live!* One was a stick-figure lacrosse player saying *Your team needs you back.* Only one of them said *Get well soon, Antichrist!* I threw that one away.

*   *   *

It'll just be another day, my father said, meaning the day he would die. And he said not to mark it, or make it special, or keep it like some black holiday. Parents come and go, he said, that's how it's supposed to be, even though he was only forty-two. He made me promise never to use his death as an excuse for not trying at something, and not to be one of those people who give up on life because God demonstrates early to them that it ends. Cindy said it was like he wanted me to get over his death before he even died. And she said that for her every day was the day. She didn't have to wait for the one-month or six-month or one-year anniversaries. She marked the time every morning, and every morning when she woke the two planes flew into her head and the towers fell down all over again.

I don't know when we became friends, or even when she stopped being annoying to me, or when I started to look forward to sitting with her after practice, waiting for the bus. She helped me change the note from the doctor to say I could play again in a week instead of a month. We would lie on our backs, staring straight up at the sky, not even looking at each other when we talked. And sometimes the bus would come and go in that time, and she would give me a ride home.

She had become less popular, either because people were forgetting about what had happened, like she said they would, or because they just didn't like having her bring it up all the time, or talk about it like it had just happened that morning. It made it easier to be around her when she stopped always drawing a crowd wherever she went. It didn't bother me when Paul Ricker made fun of me for having a crazy girlfriend, even though I didn't think of her as a girlfriend.

She left the Antichrist thing alone, mostly. Every once in a while she would say something like, "When you come into your kingdom you will have to do something about him," meaning our obnoxious English teacher or the headmaster or one of the people who were starting to make fun of her. Or she would say very casually that she had reached one of the terrorists with her board and he had saluted her as an FOA. If she made me mad with it, then she would laugh and hit my shoulder and say that she was kidding. She admitted that the ulcer had just been a coincidence with the holy water, and by late November I thought she had given up on it, and given up on trying to prove that it was true.

But we went out driving one night, the same day of the first big snow. After I made dinner for my mother I walked down to Cindy's house and found her making a ramp for her sister to jump off on their skis. There was a little mound over their septic tank that you could go down and build up speed. The ramp was too close to the house, though, and I told her so.

"It's fine," she said. But when her sister jumped off of it she skied right into the garage.

"I told you," I said. Her sister had gone crying into the house, threatening to tell their mother that Cindy did it on purpose.

"Let's get out of here," she said. We went out like we always did, driving up and down the hills in our town, then out to Generals Highway. I slouched back in my seat and put my feet on the dashboard, not thinking of anything while Cindy talked. She stopped and picked up a pizza to go with the beer she'd stolen out of her fridge, and we took it to a place we'd been before, a development under construction about ten miles up the river from where we lived. When we arrived it was dark, and the backhoes were giant shadows among the trees. "Home at last," Cindy said, pulling the car into a driveway that ran up to an empty foundation.

Right away she climbed into the backseat. Usually we talked for a while, both of us lying back in the seats with our eyes closed, not always about our fathers or the attacks or even school or lacrosse, and then it would get cold and she would say it would be warmer in the back where we could sit up against each other.

"Don't you want any pizza?" I asked her.

"Not just yet." She patted the seat next to her, and I went back.

We never did much. It would have disappointed Paul and his lurid imagination. He always asked about very particular things, acts and insertions I had barely ever imagined, until I blushed enough to make him shut up. Cindy and I would kiss, and hold each other, and I would usually take off my shirt because she liked to put her cheek right against my chest, and sometimes when I held her like that is when we would talk most about our fathers, usually just a story about something they had done when we were kids, something bad or something good—it didn't matter. And then we would kiss again, and I knew that she wanted me to do more than I could. It was only fear that kept me from going as far as she would let me. I think I wanted to, but I felt sure that something horrible would happen if I did. "Maybe something terrible *should* happen," she said when I told her this.

It all seemed so usual already, and so familiar. The way the leather car seat felt against the skin of my back, and the way the whole car seemed to glow when the moon shined through the fogged-up windows, and the way she pulled on my hair to tilt back my head so she could get at the space under my chin. It was all fine. I never minded when she muttered things I could only half understand, or spoke sentences where I would only catch a single word, like "falling" or "sky" or "open." But that night she had opened up my pants with one hand, though she didn't reach in, and she was pushing her hips into me so forcefully I thought we would break through the undercarriage and fall onto the snow, when she put her mouth right in my ear and said, "I want you to put your fist through the whole world like you did through those two towers."

I sat up and pushed her away. "What?"

"Nothing," she said. "I didn't say anything." And she tried to kiss me again, but I pushed her away.

"I should go home," I said, and put on my shirt.

"Whatever," she said, watching me as I climbed into the front seat. I sat there for a little while, with the pizza in my lap again, staring straight ahead while she asked me to come back again. Finally she heaved a big sigh, then got out of the car and walked around to the driver's seat.

"How could you say something like that?" I asked her, when we were about halfway home.

"Don't judge me," she said. "What do you know?"

"That's fucking horrible. You of all people should know how horrible that is."

"Fuck off," she said. "What do you know? You can't even be hurt. And don't tell me I'm horrible when you're the son of the fucking Devil."

"You're crazy," I said.

"Totally," she said. "Who would have thought the Antichrist would be such a loser?" I had nothing to say to that, and I thought about asking her to stop the car so I could walk home, but it was snowing again.

"You missed my turn," I told her when she drove by Severna Forest Road.

"You can walk from my house," she said. And she sped up as she got closer to her house, taking the sharp turns on Beach Road at thirty miles an hour in the ice and snow. When I told her to slow down she didn't say anything, but just before we got to her house she turned and looked at me and smiled, and then she reached over and with a practiced motion undid my seat belt from its clasp. Before I could ask what she was doing she floored the accelerator and aimed the car at the garage, running straight at the ramp she'd built earlier.

She let out a scream when we flew off the ramp. It might have been a word, but I couldn't tell what. I had barely got my seat belt in my hand when we went through the garage door and hit the wall on the other side. Her car was a Volvo—the safest thing her father could buy her. But she must have disabled the airbag on my side. I went straight through the windshield.

If I passed out, it was just for a moment. The lights were on in the garage, so when I sat up where I'd fallen across the hood I could see how I was covered in pizza, not blood. When I stood up I was very stiff, and when I touched my nose it was sore. Cindy was cursing and disentangling herself from her airbag. Her door wouldn't open; she had to come through mine. I was just standing there, looking around at the shelves full of paint and old trophies and gardening tools.

"I told you!" Cindy shouted, pounding me on the chest, either attacking me or congratulating me, I couldn't tell which. "I fucking told you!" Behind her a door opened and I saw her sister's face appear, hovering just to the left of the jamb.

"Boy, are you going to get it," she said.

*   *   *

Cindy had another party. I don't know how she convinced her mother to leave her home alone again when she went out of town. It had only been two weeks since she wrecked the car, though she was able to explain that by saying that the car skidded on some ice. I had stopped talking to her. When she sent me notes, I sent them back unread, and after practice I would walk home right away, instead of waiting for the bus.

Nobody went to the party this time. I took the trip down to her house but stayed in the woods, watching. Every once in a while I would see her face at the window. She would stare for a long time at her empty yard, and then disappear. It made me sad to think of Cindy sitting alone in her big house, feeling like everyone had forgotten her father and what had happened just a couple of months ago, her worst suspicions about people validated. But I couldn't imagine going up to the door, and not just because I was afraid of what she might do next to prove who she thought I was.

"How was the party?" my mother asked when I got back home. She was sitting at the kitchen table with the dog, who liked to lie on his belly on the table with his head on his crossed paws. While my mother drank they would sit that way for hours, staring into each other's eyes until it was time to watch television or go for a walk or go to bed.

"I left early," I said.

"Bad time?"

"Just a little boring."

"Well, that's a shame. How about a little drink?" she asked, both offering one and asking for one. I took her glass and got her some new ice and poured her some more vodka and got some water for myself. When I sat down, the dog turned around, never rising but turning himself by making swimming motions with his paws, so he rotated clockwise until he faced me. My mother batted at his thumping tail. "I'm having a bad night, too," she said. "Puppy and I have been talking." I put out my hand to the dog, expecting him to shy away from it, or to growl at me, but he rubbed his face against my palm. "I have been asking him, 'Where is it written that a woman has got to suffer all her life? Where is it written that your father should die and your mother should die and your brother should die and your sister should die and your husband should die?'"

"He's just a dog," I said.

"I am not asking him to get an answer," she said, drawing herself up and looking down her long nose at me. "The table may as well answer me, or the carpet, or the sky. Haven't you been listening to a word I've said?"

"Did you ever worship the devil?"

"What? What sort of question is that? Why would you ask such a thing?"

"I don't know." The dog turned back to her, as if he were offended by the question, too.

"If you don't want to talk," she said. "If you're *sick* of me, then just say so." She stood up and snapped her fingers. The dog jumped off the table and ran to their room, and she followed him there without saying anything else and slammed the door. I stayed a little while at the table, drinking my water, then poured myself some of her vodka, and I sat in her chair, drinking and thinking about things, but I knew even as I tried it that it would not be my way, and that it wouldn't help me any, to sit there like she did. I went to my room.

I had thrown out the Ouija board five times already, and five times I had gone and gotten it out of the garbage again, and set it in my lap to talk to the mind or the spirit that said it was my father's. That night I sat for a long while talking to it. It said, *You are not a creature, but were born out of my mind and my desire, and the perfect part of you fills you more day by day. One day soon there will be nothing human left. Today a pinprick makes you bleed, a prayer makes you sick to your stomach. Tomorrow you will walk naked on battlefields, and crush houses under your heel. Raise your hand then, and an eagle will perch on your fist. Shout an insult at the sun, it will tremble in the sky. Again and again you have felt it, just for a second you know your power, and you are amazed until the necessary lie wraps you up again, and you forget, and the great astounding truth seems just an idle daydream. One day soon the very opposite will be true, and you will wake upon a mountain of skulls from a daydream of being sullen and ordinary, and wonder, Was I ever that way?* I put it away for five minutes and then got it out again and listened again while it spoke to me, letter by letter: *Again and again you ask me, over and over I answer. You have always known why. You have always felt it, the wrongness in you going out in great circles to corrupt the whole world. I say corrupt; I mean perfect. So how can you ask me why, when the very problem you lament is its own answer and solution? Beloved son, when will you stop sorrowing after the very thing you should celebrate?*

For two hours I listened, message after message. Like always, when I was finally done I felt as ashamed as if I had been masturbating. I got into bed but only turned from side to side, thinking in turn about Cindy and Paul and my father. When the moon rose high enough to shine in my window, it made the room too bright, even with the shades drawn.

I went under my bed, something I used to do when I was small, especially if my parents were fighting or there was something else going on that was frightening me. Back then every other kid I knew was scared of the space beneath their bed, but for me it was always the one place where I never felt afraid, and the darker it was, the better I felt. I pulled my blanket so it hung down almost all the way to the ground, blocking out all the light, and then I closed my eyes and hugged my knees. Why Antichrist? I asked, this time not necessarily of anything or anybody. But I wanted to know. Why that? Why did that have to be the answer to the problem in me?

"I haven't seen your crazy girlfriend around lately," Paul said to me after the last practice of the season.

"She's not my girlfriend," I said. "She never was."

"Well, that girl who is your friend," he said. "Where is she?"

"I don't know," I said. "At home, I guess."

"You should leave her alone, anyway. Let her decompress. Let her de-crazy, you know?"

"I guess. Hey, you know on Thursday when you were running with a Trinity defenseman toward the goal and the guy was trying to check you but he could only get your glove and he was trying so hard to check you he didn't notice that Malcolm had set himself up as a pick?"

"Yeah," he said, not turning around from his locker.

"And he bounced off of Malcolm and you got that sidearm shot between the legs of the goalie?"

"Uh-huh."

"That was a great play."

"Thanks, man," he said, and he turned around and smiled. "You're not so bad yourself." We were alone in the locker room because he took forever in the shower and I had hung around talking to him the whole time. He turned back to keep packing up his bag, and there was something in the way that he was smiling that made it seem like the only thing in the world I could do was walk over and put my arms around him. It seemed as inevitable as flying through the windshield when Cindy's car hit the wall of her garage; just like that it was something nobody could have stopped. And just for a second, when I stood there with one arm across his chest and another across his belly, and I could feel him relaxing against me, it seemed like everything was right everywhere, and a whole other set of days was opening up in front of me, that had nothing to do with Cindy or her Ouija board or being the son of the Devil. I thought for sure he was going to put his hand on my hand, and say my name, and I had closed my eyes to wait for it. But he knocked me back with his elbow, then turned around and pushed me. "What the fuck?" he said. "What was that? What's your problem?" I just looked up at him, rubbing my chest where he'd pushed me, because I didn't have an answer for him.

I walked home after practice, and went right to my room, and didn't come out even when my mother knocked on my door and asked what was for dinner. I kept picking up the board and putting it down again, and sat with my back against the wall, staring at the space under my bed, but I didn't crawl under there, because I was afraid I might not come out again if I did. I listened to my mother making herself something to eat, and talking to the dog, and watching the television. It was after midnight by the time she went to bed. After I heard her door close I left my room and left the house. I walked down the hill, cutting through the woods, to Cindy's house.

There was a light in her window, flickering blue and red and orange, like she was watching television. I threw a couple of crab apples lightly against the glass.

"There you are," she said. "You want to come up and watch a movie?" I said I did. She came downstairs and let me in, and led me by the hand through her darkened house, past her mom's bedroom and her sister's bedroom, careful not even to step on the light that seeped from underneath their doors.

"The party was last week," she said, when we were in her room.

"I know," I said.

"Well, better late." She sat me down on her bed, turned off her television, and then fiddled with her computer. "You want some popcorn?"

"No, thanks."

"Good. It wouldn't be appropriate. I got this for my birthday." She held up a digital projector, turning it from side to side. "It's better than just the screen. I'd do it downstairs if my mom and the little rodent weren't at home. You can make the picture really big in the living room. And you can do this thing where, when one of them jumps, then you jump, too, from off of the stairs. Except you land on the couch, right? Not that you would need to. Here we go."

She pressed a button and a whole section of her wall became a harsh digital-blue rectangle, and then a softer-blue rectangle of sky, and then the camera swung down to show a man talking silently at a café table, sipping at his coffee and waving his hand to punctuate his silent exclamations. The towers were clearly visible behind him.

"I always watch it from the beginning," she said. "Hope you don't mind."

"It's fine," I said, and I took her hand. She pulled it away.

"Hey, pay attention. This is your education, not mine. I've been educated."

"Do you watch it every night?" She shrugged.

"That's Antonin," she said, pointing at the man. "That's his name. I found that out." The plane flew in behind him, and the explosion seemed to blossom into the whole room. Cindy startled and took my hand back. "Here we go," she said. We sat and watched, Cindy biting her lips and squeezing my hand. "Now," she said, standing up just before the second plane hit. "That one never surprises me. Are you feeling anything? Are you remembering anything?"

"Like what?"

"You know. Memories. Reasons. Your father."

"No," I said. "Come here."

"You can't see their faces," she said. "Even on the living room wall. When they jump you can't see their faces. I thought if I could project it against the side of the house, then maybe. Maybe if you saw a face, then you would know who you are."

"I know who I am," I said. "I know what I want."

"You're the same as always," she said, shaking her head. "Wait a minute. Take off your shirt. Just your shirt. I didn't say your pants. Anyway." She picked up the projector and turned it away from the wall so it shined on me, and, stepping closer while she focused it, she made a rectangle just the size of my chest. I closed my eyes and tried to feel the heat from the fire. "How about now?"

"No," I said.

"Goddamn." She faced the projector into the mirror, but when I tried to look at it, it was too bright. Then she took off her own shirt, and stood where the images would shine on her. "See?" she said. Now people were jumping, and I saw them fall from her face, disappearing in the black space above her shoulder to rush past her ribs. "Do you see? When you do it this way, then you can almost feel what they were feeling. Isn't it horrible? Doesn't it make you remember why you did it?" I walked over and did something that seemed so much the opposite of what I had done with Paul. I held her from the front, and there was nothing tender in it, and it made me feel like everything was wrong, and going to be wrong.

The projector shined above her bed. When she lay down the light passed over her, but I could feel the towers on my back when I was on her, and when she sat on top of me I could see them reaching up her body, and then suddenly reaching down as the first one fell. We rolled on her bed, and I felt like the projector was wrapping us in light, even as darkness reached in between to enfold us, too, uncoiling from out of the mirror and from the window and from under the bed. It filled up my head, so all I saw was light flashing in the boundless dark. Cindy went away, and the whole world went away, and even the sadness I'd felt, not just since my father died but every day of my life—that went away, too. I heard a voice that said, "There you are. There you are."

"There," Cindy was saying, when I opened my eyes. "There you are. It's hard. It's really hard, being the son of the Devil, but you'll get used to it. People get used to anything." I stayed where I was, pressing my face into her shoulder, crying, not just because I was sad but because I finally knew who I was, and believed it, grateful and happy for the ruin I had just done, for the ruin I had brought and the ruin I would bring, every catastrophe more beloved to me than the next, thinking that even though I wasn't looking at them on the wall I could see the buildings in my mind—*O father, let them burn their heat is as perfect as my glee*— lit up like birthday candles to celebrate the first day of my life.

ACKNOWLEDGMENTS

Many thanks to the editors whose careful attention greatly improved these individual stories: Cressida Leyshon, Eli Horowitz, Tom Chiarella, Tyler Cabot, Michael Ray, Don Lee, Lois Rosenthal, Lee Montgomery, and Ben George; and especially to Eric Chinski, Eric Simonoff, and Stephanie Paulsell, whose generous investment of time and effort improved the collection as a whole.